TRULY, MADLY, DEADLY

Also by Hannah Jayne

truly, madly, deadly

HANNAH JAYNE

sourcebooks
fire

Published by Sourcebooks Fire, an imprint of Sourcebooks
P.O. Box 4410, Naperville, Illinois 60567-4410
(630) 961-3900
sourcebooks.com

Library of Congress Cataloging-in-Publication data is on file with the publisher.

Printed and bound in the United States of America.
VP 10 9 8 7 6 5 4 3 2 1

CONTENT WARNING

This book contains depictions of
partner violence, drunk driving, suicide,
and predatory sexual harassment.

*To my mother, who probably doesn't know
that the fact that she went after her dream
gave me the courage to go after my own.*

ONE

"Thank you for coming."

The words rose and fell on the soft pile carpet, and Sawyer wondered whether she should brush the small ball of fuzz from Kevin's earlobe. It stuck there, stark and white against the dark navy blue of his suit.

"I couldn't have gotten through today without you," Mrs. Anderson said, squeezing Sawyer's ice-cold hand.

Sawyer knew she should say something comforting, something warm and thoughtful, but all she could focus on was that little bit of fuzz on Kevin's left ear.

"They said it was immediate," someone whispered. "They said he was drunk."

Sawyer had heard those words tumble over and over in her mind every minute for the past forty-eight hours. *It*

was immediate, Kevin was drunk, he didn't stand a chance.
She wasn't crying—couldn't anymore—as she stared down
at Kevin. His eyes were closed, his lips slightly parted, and
his hands were gently crossed against his chest. Sawyer
couldn't help but think from somewhere dark, somewhere
deep inside of her, that at least he couldn't hurt her
anymore.

"You must be devastated."

Sawyer felt Mr. Hanson, her Spanish teacher, lay a gentle
hand on her shoulder. She shrunk away, the smell of lilies
suddenly overwhelmingly cloying. "I'll be right back."

She took the stairs two at a time, her black ballet flats
falling soundlessly on the carpet. She paused on the top floor
landing when she saw the girl at the end of the hall.

The girl blinked at Sawyer.

She was tall and thin—unfortunately so—with a boyish
body that was all edges and angles. Her long brown hair was
looped in a herringbone braid that fell over one shoulder, and
baby hairs stood up in a static-y halo around her head, shot
out from the loose weave of the braid. The girl's eyes looked
like they may have been velvety brown and deeply alive once,
but they were sunken and flat now. Her full lips were barely
pink and pulled down at the edges. This girl wore her mourning black like a second skin.

Sawyer swallowed; the girl swallowed.

Sawyer paused for a full beat before tugging self-
consciously at her braid, then averted her eyes from the mirror

that reflected a girl she scarcely recognized. She continued down the hall, moving quickly.

She knew from nights lying to her parents and sneaking, shoeless, past his parents' room that Kevin's door was the last one on the left. She slipped in there on a sigh, clicking the door shut softly behind her. A curl-edged painting was taped to the back of Kevin's door and Sawyer, stunned, fingered it softly. It was a beach scene she had painted the first day Kevin spoke to her. They were in art class, and she was lost in her own brushstrokes, squinting, leaning close to make the crush of the waves as realistic as possible.

"You're really good," he had said, his chin jutting toward the scene. Sawyer could still feel the overwhelming heat in her cheeks as her index finger followed the curl of foam on the forever-still water.

She heard a soft breath in the yellowing light that filtered through the blinds and cracked across the painting. "The recruiter came to see him, you know."

Mr. Anderson said it without turning around. Kevin's father was perched on the end of his son's bed; his head was bowed and his back was toward her, but Sawyer could see that his fingers were working the silky fabric of Kevin's number twenty-one Hawthorne Hornets football jersey while an army of gold plated football trophies looked on.

"He talked about marrying you." Mr. Anderson looked over his shoulder then, his watery blue eyes finding Sawyer, a reminiscing half smile on his chapped lips. "He said that he'd get into Cal and you'd get into the Art Institute and that would be it."

Sawyer tried to smile, tried to remember the moments when she and Kevin would sprawl in the grass, her hand finding his as they talked about a future that was far off and pristine, that sloughed off divorce and jealousy and high school pressures and rivalries. She remembered telling Kevin that she wanted to go to the Art Institute, remembered the far-off look in his eyes when a smile snaked across his lips.

"What?" she said, barely able to keep the grin from her lips.

Kevin shook his head and squeezed Sawyer's hand gently. "How perfect is that? I'll go to Cal, be the dashing football star, and you'll be across the bay at the Art Institute painting portraits of your beloved."

"Portraits of John Lennon? I think I'd get tired of that."

Kevin tugged at her arm—gently, softly—and Sawyer slipped into his lap, loving the feeling of his arms wrapped around her. She felt so safe, so warm, and when his lips nuzzled her ear, she felt the spark move low in her belly.

Now the memory caught in her throat. *That was when things were good*, she told herself.

Mr. Anderson sucked in a sharp breath that brought Sawyer back to the present; she looked up just in time to see Kevin's father double over himself, heavy hands hugging his sides. There was no sound except the ragged tear of his breath as he cried.

Sawyer felt her bottom lip quiver, and when she pinched

her eyes shut, she saw Kevin, cheeks pink and alive, lips pressed up into that half smile he shared with his father. In her mind's eye, that grin turned into a snarl. She heard the sickening smack of skin against skin in her head. She reeled, feeling the sting again.

"He loved you so much."

Sawyer felt Kevin's warm breath, heard the deep rumble of his voice as he told her he loved her for the first time. She remembered the shiver that zinged from the top of her head to the base of her spine, amazed, delighted, enraptured. Kevin—Kevin Anderson, the most popular boy in school— loved *her*. She was everything in that moment when Kevin's fingertips brushed against the small of her back, when his lips pressed up against hers. Her life—her family—had splintered. Her mother had moved across the country, her father loved another woman, but Kevin Anderson wanted Sawyer. He wanted Sawyer Dodd, and that made her feel *real*. She wanted to hold on to that moment, was desperate to hold on to that moment and nothing else—not when he got angry, not when she made him mad, not the tear-racked apologies that followed.

Sawyer nodded, the tears slipping over her cheeks. "I loved him too."

The mood at school on Monday was somber, and Sawyer was tired of people averting their stares when she walked by.

Third-period choir was her favorite escape, and when she slipped into the band room, she couldn't help but grin when Chloe Coulter, seated on the piano with long legs kicking, caught her eye.

"Sawyer!" Chloe vaulted off the piano, her blond ponytail flailing behind her. She tackled Sawyer in an enthusiastic hug, not caring as students shoved past them.

"How are you?" Chloe's eyes were a bright, clear blue, and today they were wide and sympathetic, framed by too-dark black lashes and heavy brows. "Are you okay?"

Sawyer nodded slowly, and her best friend squeezed her hand, then blew out a sigh. "Did you just get back in town?"

Chloe waved a pink late pass. "Yeah." Her eyes searched Sawyer. "I'm so sorry, Sawyer. I wish I could have been there. Was it awful? It was awful, wasn't it? I should have been there with you. God, I suck."

Sawyer swallowed hard. "It was your grandmother's ninetieth birthday. No one expected you to come back."

"But I would have," Chloe said, blond ponytail bobbing.

"I can't believe he's gone," Maggie Gaines said, her ski-jump nose a heady red. She was flanked on either side by stricken onlookers who offered condolences and Kleenex as Maggie murmured to them in a voice just loud enough to be overheard. When she caught Sawyer staring, Maggie's glossy eyes went immediately hard and sharp.

"Look at her," Chloe spat. "Kevin was your boyfriend,

but Maggie needs to be the inconsolable center of attention. That should be you."

Sawyer shrunk back into her baggy sweatshirt. "Let her have her moment," she mumbled. "They dated for a while too."

Chloe snorted. "Like a hundred years ago."

Mr. Rose kicked open the side door and shoved a costume rack into the choir room. The student chatter died down and kids leaned forward, eyes glued to the new choir uniforms.

"Ladies and gentlemen," Mr. Rose started, "I know you've all been waiting with bated breath to see what you're wearing for this year's regionals."

The group groaned as a well-tuned whole.

The Hawthorne High Honeybee choir was known for only two things: being four-time back-to-back national champions and having the ugliest uniforms known to man. Sawyer's freshman year featured an army-green taffeta number with balloon sleeves and lace inlays for the girls, and equally unattractive green velvet blazers for the guys. Sophomore year the budget was cut, and the Honeybee choir showed up looking like an exceptionally well-tuned army of white-vested waiters. At the end of last year, the school had taken "pity" on the choir and offered up some leftover graduation gowns onto which the costume department had stitched fighting hornets and musical notes. That was what the group was expecting when Mr. Rose began his excited introduction.

"So, without further ado..." Mr. Rose pulled the black sheet off the costume bar and a collective "ah" sailed through the classroom. Maggie stopped sniffing into her Kleenex, Chloe gasped, and Sawyer sat up straighter.

"OMG!"

"They're gorgeous!"

With one hand, Mr. Rose held up a simple black satin sheath dress, its waist cinched with a thick red satin sash. In the other hand, he offered a black blazer with a red tie. The Honeybees cheered.

Mr. Rose, apple cheeks pushed up into a full-face smile, beamed. "The school board heard your fashion protests and decided—finally—that the Singing Honeybees should look like *five*-time regional champions!"

Once the students had dropped back into some semblance of order, Mr. Rose handed out the plastic-wrapped garments. When he got to Sawyer, he paused, giving her the sympathetic smile she was so quickly growing tired of seeing. He rested a soft hand on her shoulder, cocked his head. "Are you doing okay, Sawyer?"

Sawyer took her dress and offered him a small smile. "Yeah, I am. Thanks Mr. Rose."

"You know, I'd like for the Honeybees to add a small tribute number to Kevin in our set list. He was such a big part of the Hornet community."

Sawyer felt a lump growing in her throat and she nodded. "That sounds nice. Kevin would have liked that."

"I'd like to feature you in a solo for that number." Mr. Rose's eyes were kind, his puffy gray eyebrows high, expectant. "Would that be okay with you?"

Sawyer nodded mutely, dread, excitement, sadness, and anxiety welling up inside her all at once. "Thank you, Mr. Rose," she finally managed.

Mr. Rose passed Sawyer and Chloe, continuing his costume distribution to the other Honeybees. Chloe leaned in, excitement evident on her face.

"A solo?" she asked breathlessly. "Oh my God, that's awesome! It just sucks that—" Chloe avoided Sawyer's eyes, looked at her own hands folded in her lap. "It just sucks that Kevin couldn't be here to hear you."

Sawyer tried to form a response or a cohesive sentence, but nothing came out.

Mr. Rose took his spot behind the piano, and the Honeybees did their warm-ups. At the last note, he beckoned to Sawyer. She made her way to the front of the class, feeling the heat of all eyes on her. When she turned, it was just Maggie, her eyes narrowed, challenging. Sawyer offered a small noncombative smile that Maggie ignored.

We used to be friends, Sawyer heard herself plead silently.

Maggie's hate rolled off her in waves.

When the bell rang, Sawyer and Chloe gathered up their backpacks and new uniforms and headed toward the door. Maggie, arms crossed in front of her chest, stopped Sawyer dead in her tracks.

"A solo?" she said. Her eyes raked over Sawyer, the distaste evident.

"Can you move, please? I need to get to my locker before fourth." She was too tired to deal with one of Maggie's jealous rages.

But Maggie remained in Sawyer's way.

"Do you think I'm going to fall for you and your stupid little 'woe is me' act? Doubtful. You don't deserve this solo, and you didn't deserve Kevin. A real girlfriend wouldn't be able to pull herself together, let alone do a solo."

Sawyer wanted to fight back, but she was exhausted and emotionless. Maybe Maggie was right—she didn't deserve to be Kevin's girlfriend—didn't deserve to be at the blunt end of his anger, a small voice inside her head nagged. Sawyer shook it off and shoved Maggie aside with more force than she meant.

"Lay off, Maggie."

"Get over yourself," Sawyer heard Chloe growl. "Sawyer doesn't need to play the chick who can't get herself together— you do it too well. It's just too bad you've been doing it ever since Kevin dumped you. When was that exactly? Nine, ten months ago now? Little long to be carrying a flame, don't you think?" Chloe flicked a lock of Maggie's long hair, then wrinkled her nose. "It's probably time to drag your obsessively depressed ass into the shower. It'll make us all feel better."

Chloe shoved past Maggie and linked arms with Sawyer, steering her down the hall.

"You didn't have to do that," Sawyer said, hiking her backpack over one shoulder. "I can handle Maggie."

Chloe's blue eyes went wide and baby-doll innocent. "Oh, honey. I didn't do it for you." She blinked, a wry smile spreading across her passion-pink lips. "I did it for me."

"*Hola, señoras.*" Mr. Hanson was the school's sole Spanish teacher, but at barely thirty years old, he looked more like a student than a faculty member. He edged his way between Sawyer and Chloe and grinned, while a hallway full of girls drooled. "*Perdon, perdon.* Ah, Sawyer! *Has estudiado para la prueba?*" he said, looking expectantly at her.

Sawyer felt the redness bloom in her cheeks and shifted her weight. "Um, *sí, señor.*"

"*Bueno!*" A wide smile spread across Mr. Hanson's face, his eyes crinkling with the effort.

"Ohmigod, what did he just say to you?"

Sawyer shrugged. "Honestly, I have no idea. My stock answers are *sí*, *no*, or the often-used 'how do you say menstrual cramps in Spanish'?"

Chloe wrinkled her nose. "Ew."

"They never ask you to translate that sombrero thing if they think you've got cramps."

Chloe watched the back of Mr. Hanson's head as he disappeared into Principal Chappie's office. "Screw French. I'm transferring into Spanish."

"You were bound to waste it on some French Canadian anyway."

"Don't you love him?"

Sawyer glanced over her shoulder, caught the last of Mr. Hanson's dark hair as he disappeared into the office. "Don't you think he's a little overeager?"

"Please. Half my teachers don't even know my first name. Hanson's like, fresh out of teacher school, or whatever, and still hopeful. He still believes in us." Chloe batted her eyelashes sweetly.

"Whatever."

"Besides, I heard he gave Libby a ride home the other day."

Sawyer unzipped her backpack. "And I'm sure she thanked him appropriately."

Chloe crossed her arms in front of her chest, bored now. "Are we still on for tomorrow night?"

"You mean our convocation?"

"Ooh, *convocation*. SAT word?"

Sawyer laughed. "My ticket out of suburban hell. Let me call you about tomorrow, though. Dad and wife number two are finding out the sex-slash-species of the Spawn. I'm sure they'll want to do something educational and emotionally satisfying out of their *Blended Families/Blended Lives* book."

"Ah, another evening rubbing placenta on each other and worshipping the moon?"

Sawyer sighed. "Are you sure you don't want me to come over and watch your parents' passive aggression as they avoid each other while showing their extreme disappointment in your choices?"

Chloe folded a stick of gum into her mouth and chewed thoughtfully. "Hell no. Wednesday is fried chicken and mac-and-cheese-as-vegetable night at the double-wide. That dysfunction is all mine. And they're not my parents—Lois and Dean are my guardians."

Sawyer cocked her head, her arms crossed in front of her chest. "Not Mom and Stepdud anymore?"

"Hopefully not. Haven't seen Dean in over a week. And I'm using the guardian thing so hopefully Lois will finally cave in and admit that I'm adopted."

Sawyer grinned. "Except that you are the spitting image of your mother."

"Sawyer Dodd, that is a horrible thing to say."

"Of course. A thousand apologies. I take it back."

"Better." Chloe blew Sawyer an air kiss. "I'll be waiting by the phone with greasy fingers for your call."

"I'll have the ambulance on standby," Sawyer called over her shoulder.

She grinned, watching her best friend skip down the hall. For the first time in what seemed like forever, things felt normal and light again.

"Excuse me." Logan Haas smiled shyly at Sawyer and she stepped aside, letting him get into the locker under hers. Logan bore the unlucky high school triumvirate of being slight, short, and nearsighted, but Sawyer liked him.

"Hey, sorry," she said.

Logan stacked his books, slammed his locker shut, gave

Sawyer an awkward salute, and headed down the hall, eyes glued to his shoes. Sawyer spun her combination lock and yanked the door open, her lips forming a little *o* of surprise when she did so. Among her neatly stacked binders and books was a short, fat envelope in a pale mint green. Her name was printed on it in a handwriting font. She took the envelope and looked over both shoulders; no one milled about, red-faced or smiling, indicating that they had slipped the note in her locker.

She tore the envelope open and pulled out a matching mint green folded card, a tiny plain oak leaf embossed on the bottom. When she opened it, a clipped newspaper article slipped out. Sawyer didn't have to read the headline to know what it said: "Local High School Student Killed In Car Wreck." She swallowed down a cry and read the note on the card.

It said, simply:

You're welcome.

TWO

Heat, like a live wire, raced down Sawyer's spine. The note was signed, "an admirer," and that word, *admirer*, clawed at her. Her fingers started to shake, and she flicked the note back into her locker and slammed the door shut, pressing her forehead against the cool metal.

It's nothing, she told herself. *Someone probably sent flowers—everyone sent flowers.* Each hour after Kevin's death was reported a new bouquet seemed to show up—gaudy, pitiful, with drooping spider mums and cheap, glittered ribbons in the Hawthorne High School colors. Each bouquet reminded Sawyer of Kevin—especially when they died.

She suddenly hated flowers.

"I'm sure that's what it is," Sawyer mumbled.

"Tick tock, Ms. Dodd." Principal Chappie tapped his

mammoth wristwatch as he strode by, giving students his principal snarl and ticktock warning.

Sawyer hiked her backpack onto her shoulder and stepped away from her locker, but that meager line—*You're welcome*—was like an invisible string pulling her back. She spun her combination lock and reached for the note, her fingers hovering tentatively over it as though it would burn her. Finally, she snatched it up and tucked the note into her bag, heading toward her AP biology class.

Chloe appeared in the hallway halfway to Sawyer's class and fell in step with her. She leaned in. "You look awful," she whispered.

Sawyer swallowed heavily and licked her lips. "There was something in my locker."

"Like a dead mouse?" Chloe shuddered.

"Ahem," Mr. Rhodes said from inside his classroom. "As soon as Ms. Dodd is through with her conversation, we will begin our class."

Sawyer looked from Mr. Rhodes to Chloe. "Gotta go."

Chloe peeled off into her own class as Sawyer beelined through the open door and pulled it shut behind her, whispering apologies as she did.

"Nice of you to join us, Sawyer. Take your seat."

"Sorry." She ducked into her desk at the back of the room and pulled out her biology book, working to rein in her mind as it shot off in multiple directions. As the day wore on, Sawyer tried to put the note out of her mind, but each time the bell rang, her heart would start to punch against her ribs. She purposely avoided her locker—which was easy to do, since her speech class didn't require a book and she was planning to buy her lunch anyway—but she couldn't avoid it at the end of the day. She sat in her last class, doing her best to avoid the clock. But each time another minute ticked off, a hot coil of dread burned through her. When the bell finally rang, she took her time gathering her things.

Chloe poked her head through the doorway from the hall, glaring at Sawyer.

"Oh my God, Sawyer, the glaciers are melting," she moaned. "Come on already!"

Sawyer slung her last book into her backpack and hitched it over her shoulder. She followed Chloe into the crowded hallway, and as they approached the junior hall, icy fingers of anxiety—or fear—pricked at Sawyer. She tried to shake the feeling off, to remind herself of her well-constructed flower theory, but the note—and its message—hung heavily in the back of her mind.

"Hey, are you okay?" Chloe asked.

Sawyer shook her head, shrugged.

"Didn't you say you got something?"

Sawyer sucked in a stomach-quivering breath, her eyes focused on her locker. *Would there be another note?* She fumbled with the lock and tugged it open, letting out a whoosh of air when she saw that her locker was just as she had left it: her neat stack of books, two tubes of Chapstick, a picture of her and Kevin—and no note.

"Earth to Sawyer?"

"Sorry, Chloe. I'm just—I'm just tired, I guess. I'm not sleeping very well."

"I thought your doctor gave you some sleeping pills or something."

Sawyer nodded, swapping the books in her locker for the ones in her backpack. "He did, but if I take one of those I'm dead to the world."

"Sounds like heaven."

Sawyer rolled her eyes. "Heaven with the teensiest bit of hallucinations tossed in."

Chloe bounced on the balls of her feet. "Oh, insurance-sponsored hallucinogens? Sign me up!"

"And then I run like molasses the next morning."

"You dropped something." Chloe bent down and plucked the mint-green envelope from the linoleum. "What's this?"

Sawyer swallowed. "It's nothing." She snatched the envelope back while Chloe cocked an eyebrow.

"Grabby."

Sawyer bit her lip, then forced a nonchalant smile. "Call me later?"

"Will do."

Sawyer felt like she was sleepwalking all through track practice—and Coach Carter told her the same. She was glad when he finally let the team leave after their timed trials.

"You okay, S?" Coach Carter asked as students trickled off the field.

"Yeah, I'm sorry, Coach, I was just—" Sawyer bit her bottom lip, suddenly certain that Coach Carter could see right through her, would know that she was lying. "Distracted."

Coach nodded. "That's not like you." He broke into a friendly grin and trotted backward. "You're going to bring it next time though, right?"

Sawyer smiled back, for once glad that Coach Carter cared about nothing more than her performance on the track.

"Sure," she mumbled, forcing herself to smile.

Sawyer skipped changing in the locker room and went directly for her car in the school parking lot. She threw her backpack—note safely tucked in the front pocket—on the passenger seat. She drove a brand-new midnight blue Honda Accord with all the extras. Though she was thankful, she wasn't as wowed by the thing as her friends had been. Where they saw shiny new wheels and imminent freedom, Sawyer saw her parents' last unified attempt at appeasement—or apology—while her mother moved two thousand miles away to run a corporate office and her father and wife number two moved Sawyer to the outer regions of hell. Her parents had presented the car as a reliable necessity for Sawyer. Her father's new subdivision and her new, just-like-every-other-house-in-the-tract home were thirty-three miles away from Chloe, Hawthorne High, and every other bit of civilization in Sawyer's life.

She sunk her key in the ignition, plastic Fighting Hornet key chain dangling, but didn't start the car. Instead, she bit her lip and listened to her heartbeat speed up, grimacing as hot needles pricked at her spine. She unzipped her pack and pulled out the note, studying the envelope as if some new, revealing clue would suddenly appear. There was nothing. On a sharp breath she plucked the card from its envelope and opened it, reading the handwriting font once again:

You're welcome.

She said the words out loud, and they seemed to fill up the whole car, to squeeze the air out of the cab. Sawyer chewed her bottom lip, glancing from the newspaper article back to the note. *I'm welcome for what?*

She heard the football coach's whistle blow in the distance, signaling the end of their practice. Football players, muddied and sweaty, began to trickle into the parking lot, their hoots, howls, and general chatter muffled by the Accord's rolled-up windows. The team girlfriends hung back with the cheerleaders, who walked into the lot in bunches, talking animatedly, ponytails bobbing. A group of band members lugged their instruments, and from behind them Sawyer watched as a group of varsity football players ambled by, all wearing matching shirts—hornet green, the words "We Will Never Forget You" printed above a bright white number twenty-one and the last name Anderson.

Kevin.

Sawyer looked from the jerseys to the note in her hand.

Her breath hitched and her fingers—and the note—began to tremble.

Someone knew.

———————————

A navy blue sedan was blocking Sawyer's driveway when she came home from track practice. Sawyer parked behind it and stepped out of her car, the dusk already setting, already pushing the estates into a hazy darkness. She blinked when she saw the spark of a cigarette from the side of the house. Sawyer guessed the owner of the sedan was checking out the bones of the houses nearby; it wasn't unusual for potential buyers to check out the Dodd family's "model home."

"Hey, Dad," Sawyer started, "it looks like someone's looking at the—" She paused, looking at the three heads that swung to look at her.

Her stomach rolled over on itself as she felt all eyes fixate on her, studying her with a look she was starting to recognize—and loathe—sympathy mixed with curiosity, with just the tiniest hint of frustration.

Sawyer's dark eyes washed from her stepmother to her father. "What's going on?"

Andrew Dodd blinked at his wife and cleared his throat. They were perched on the new ecru couch, pillows undisturbed, but their faces were drawn. A man sat on the couch directly across from them, a small leather notepad balanced on his knee.

"Is this your daughter?" the man asked.

"Yes," Andrew Dodd said, jumping up and going to her. "This is Sawyer." He put his hand on the small of Sawyer's back and ushered her into the living room. "Sawyer, this is Detective Frank Biggs."

Frank Biggs looked exactly like you'd expect a man named Frank Biggs to look—like a mustached fireplug in a short-sleeved, button-down shirt; a stained blue tie; and khakis that could use an iron or a dumpster.

Sawyer shook his hand and he smiled, breathing out a whoosh of overly minted, Nicorette-smelling air. "Nice to meet you."

"Dad, what is this about?"

"Detective Biggs just wants to ask you a few questions about Kevin." Andrew cleared his throat a second time, avoiding Sawyer's gaze. "About what happened to Kevin."

"Just a few routine follow-up questions," Biggs said, flipping a black ballpoint pen over his hairy knuckles.

Sawyer nodded. "Okay. But I told the other officer everything I knew."

Biggs nodded and flipped open his notebook. "So did you see Kevin the night of the accident, Sawyer?"

He pronounced her name *Saw-yah* and fixed her with his flat, brown eyes.

"Yes. I saw him before"—a sob lodged in her throat—"before the accident."

"Were you in the car with him at any time?"

Andrew let out a hissing sigh. "Is this really necessary? She already said that she had been on a date with Kevin and then walked back to her car."

Sawyer turned to her father. "It's okay, Dad."

"So you were in Kevin's car. Up until when?"

"I don't know; nine o'clock, maybe?"

"And that was on the hillside."

"Yeah."

"So you weren't in the car with Kevin as he went down the hill."

Sawyer shook her head. "No. No, he'd been drinking. I walked down myself. Can I ask why you're asking me this? The other officer—I mean, he asked me about pretty much everything."

Detective Biggs looked up from his notebook. "We found a shoe stuck in the mud near the accident site."

"A shoe?"

Biggs nodded and produced a color photograph of a shoe lined up next to a ruler. "It's a ladies' size seven and a half. What size shoe do you wear?"

Sawyer cocked an eyebrow. "Seven and a half."

Tara cleared her throat from her spot on the couch. "I wear a seven and a half, as well, Detective. It's a pretty common size for women."

The detective regarded her with a small bob of his head. "We're not making any accusations here, Mrs. Dodd. Just trying to establish some facts." He turned back to Sawyer and pressed the photograph toward her. "Do you recognize this shoe?"

Sawyer took the picture. "I have those shoes. But so does pretty much every girl at Hawthorne."

"May I see them, please?"

She was taken aback. "My shoes?"

"Just what exactly are you getting at, Detective Biggs?" Andrew asked.

"We're working on a theory—just a theory—that there may have been someone else in the car with Kevin that night."

Sawyer's breath hitched. "What?"

"The passenger seat was moved back—just enough for someone to have slipped out the door."

"But the car—everyone said it was smashed. Wouldn't a passenger have been killed? Or at least hurt pretty severely? And why would someone not say something? Why wouldn't they say they were in the car?"

Detective Biggs held up his meaty hands. "Right now it's just a theory. Like I said, we're just trying to establish the facts, figure out as best we can exactly what happened that night. The seat being in that position could just be a coincidence. And the shoe stuck in the mud—well, it could have been left in the car prior and gotten kicked out on impact, or it could have even just been there on the side of the road. You kids spend a lot of time up there on Hicks. There's always a lot of junk left behind."

Sawyer felt strangely ashamed, like the detective had stumbled on her generation's dirty little secret.

"May I see the shoes, Sawyer?"

Sawyer nodded mutely and climbed the stairs, her mind tumbling over the idea that someone could have been in the car with Kevin. *If someone had been there*, she mused, *why would that person let him drive if they knew he'd been drinking?*

She picked through the detritus on her closet floor, shoving past prom shoes and track sneakers. The pair in question—a fairly nondescript pair of mall-issued metallic flats—wasn't there. Sawyer flopped back onto her butt on the floor, frowning. She did a cursory check under the bed before half-heartedly picking through a bulging cardboard box labeled "Sawyer."

Twenty minutes later she stepped down the stairs and shrugged. "I can't find them." Sawyer gestured toward the photo Detective Biggs laid on the coffee table. "But those can't be mine." She licked her lips, forcing the words past her teeth as the images of that night flashed in her mind. "I wasn't wearing them that night."

Detective Biggs sucked on his teeth and seemed to consider Sawyer's statement. Everything in her went on synapse-snapping high alert and suddenly, without knowing why, Sawyer felt guilty. When the detective broke the silence what seemed like eons later, Sawyer finally breathed.

Biggs thrust out a hand to Sawyer's father and stepmom.

"Sorry to have bothered you, Mr. and Mrs. Dodd." He nodded at Sawyer. "You have a very smart daughter there."

Sawyer watched her father and Tara shake Biggs's hand, frustration prickling her spine when no one corrected Biggs, no one reminded him that Tara wasn't her mother. When the detective offered his hand to Sawyer, she shook it woodenly, saying nothing. Once the door closed and he was gone, Sawyer blinked.

"I'm going to go take a shower."

"Don't you want to eat something first?" Tara asked.

Sawyer shook her head, feeling the deadweight of... something...sitting in the pit of her stomach. "No, I'm not very hungry."

She turned her back on Tara's and her father's expectant stares and pulled her backpack over her shoulder. Once she got to her room, she shut the door, dumped the pack, and stashed the note where no one would find it. Then she turned on the shower as hot as she could get it, as if the water could wash away the last year of her life.

Sawyer was in her pajamas, hair wrapped in a towel turban, and stretched out on her bed when there was a knock on her door frame. She looked up from her Spanish homework and blinked at her father.

"Hey," he said softly.

"Hey."

He walked in, sitting on the edge of Sawyer's bed, one hand fanned out on her bedspread. "She's trying, you know."

Sawyer didn't say anything. She kept her pencil moving even though she had ceased conjugating verbs and was now doodling circles on her notebook paper. "I know."

"It's not easy for her."

Sawyer looked up, betrayal flashing in her eyes. "It's not easy for me, either."

"I know. And Tara understands that. But this is all new to her. New husband, new house. New teenage daughter. It's a lot to take in. She just wants to make this work. She wants us all to be a family. Can you give her a break?"

Sawyer felt the tears stinging behind her eyes. She gritted her teeth, digging deep into her molars until her jaw hurt. "It's a little new for me, too. Remember? When she was getting a new husband, I was getting a new stepmom. And a new house." She swallowed hard, trying to wash down the thick lump in her throat. *And losing my real mom*, she wanted to say.

Andrew rubbed his palm over his mouth and sighed. "But you're strong, sweetheart. Tara's not like you. She needs a little more help."

Sawyer caught on that word, *strong*. When her parents' marriage fell apart, people started calling her *strong* just because she didn't start cutting herself or bring a gun to school. But she wasn't strong. She was weak and small and afraid, and she felt safe when Kevin opened his arms to her, tucked her forehead under his chin. She remembered the rhythmic rise and fall of his chest, the first time they had had sex, the first time in so long that she didn't have to be strong. Back then, Kevin protected her.

"Sawyer?"

The lines of her binder paper blurred in front of her, but she refused to cry. She sniffed instead and nodded. "Sure, Dad. I'll try."

Sawyer flopped down in her bed at half past eleven, her body heavy with exhaustion. But sleep wouldn't come. The words of the note hung heavy on her periphery, like if she just read a little more into them, gave them a little more thought, they would reveal her mysterious admirer. At close to 1:00 a.m., Sawyer finally kicked off her covers, frustrated, and retrieved the note from her underwear drawer where she had stashed it. She read it, turned it over and over again in her hands, but nothing was shaken loose, no memory or insight. She was smashing the letter back between a pair of boy shorts and a sequined thong Chloe had given her as a gag gift when light flooded the room. It came in a smooth, blue-white arc, pouring over her open bathroom door, her computer desk, her bulletin board, until it shifted over Sawyer. She was paralyzed under the bright light. When it had washed over her, plunging her back into blackness, her eyes burned and the adrenaline rushed through her, working her already aching muscles.

"Oh God." Sawyer grabbed at her chest, feeling the

spastic thud of her heart under her hand. "Now I'm scared of light."

She felt the giggle twitter through her as she crawled back into her bed, sinking into her pooled covers. When the arc of light came one more time, she talked herself out of her nerves, out of the niggling feeling in the back of her mind that something was wrong.

"Headlights, freakazoid," Sawyer said out loud, keeping her voice throaty and low. "Nothing weird about—" She sat bolt upright and kicked out of bed, falling to her knees on the carpet. She pressed her palms against the windowsill and sunk down so only her eyes and the top of her head were showing.

She swept the street.

"Who the hell is driving out here now?" she mumbled in the darkness. She had no neighbors, no guests, and civilization—anything other than cows and model homes— was at least a twenty-minute drive from her housing tract.

Sawyer poked her head up another half-inch and craned her neck, trying to see down the connecting streets. But it was dead silent outside. There was no wind rattling what remained of the leaves this autumn, no neighbors with lights still on or TVs blaring. Sawyer hated the empty housing development. During the day, the houses looked cheery and welcoming, like some apron-wearing mom was in the model kitchen baking cookies, her perfect kids ready to spill out of the front door at any moment. But in the dark, the same houses seemed to boast their emptiness, and the windows that looked like they hid the perfect American families by day were gaping, menacing, and black at night. There was no sound and no movement—until Sawyer caught a beady red eye out of the corner of her eye. It was the taillight of a car—the other must have been broken—and it sailed down the street, a leisurely coast. Had it been daylight, a lone car on the street wouldn't have piqued Sawyer's interest—people were always cruising through, pretending they were heading to their new homes, she guessed. But tonight was an unusually dark night, starless, and without streetlights, there was nothing to see—unless you knew what you were looking for.

Sawyer shuddered and pulled her curtains closed. She slipped slowly back into bed, pulling the covers to her chin, her eyes wide, focused on the ceiling. She willed them to shut but then her mind kept spinning. She rolled over onto her side. Her eyes—suddenly very used to the darkness—flicked over her nightstand, the stack of books lying there, and settled on the prescription bottle shoved behind this week's US magazine. Sawyer sighed and rolled over, clamping her eyes shut.

And then she rolled back.

"No, I hate that stuff," she muttered. "It makes me feel freaking crazy." She flopped back hard against her pillow and pulled another one over her face.

As her parents leveled their "news"—divorce, split homes, a move for Dad to the outer regions of housing tract hell, the "chance of a lifetime" for Mom that moved her across country, they doted on Sawyer and looked at her with troubled expressions. And when a new car and promises of a "good, new start" didn't make her smile—or sleep at night—it was Dr. Johnson, one hour a week of "and how does that make you feel?" and finally, the Trazodone.

After tossing and turning for another twenty minutes, Sawyer was in the bathroom, filling up a glass of cold water and popping a dose of the medication.

"Just so I can get some sleep," she mumbled to her sallow, sunken-eyed reflection. Then she crawled into bed and fell into a restless, heavy slumber.

THREE

Chloe fell into step with Sawyer as they walked down the junior hall the following morning. "So I didn't hear from you last night."

Sawyer worked the straps on her backpack, her eyes on her shoes. "Sorry. I got busy."

"Were your dad and Tara howling at the moon or something equally metaphysically odd?"

Sawyer thought about the lone shoe, about Detective Biggs perched on the edge of her couch. "Did a detective come to your house?"

Chloe stopped cold, spinning to face Sawyer. "Huh?"

"Never mind."

"A detective? No. Never. But the DEA came out to bust my neighbor's pharmaceutical business once." She wagged her head. "Leave it to the Feds. Always trying to take down the small businessman. Hey." She reached out and pinched Sawyer hard on the arm.

"Hey! Ow!"

"You're zoning out on me."

"I know, DEA."

"It was funny. You didn't laugh."

Sawyer forced a smile as big as she could muster. "I've just got a lot on my mind."

"So unload." The final bell rang and Chloe shrugged, her hand on the door to her English class. "Later."

———————

It was dark by the time Sawyer made the turnoff to Blackwood Hills Estates. The days were getting shorter, and though Sawyer usually liked the crisp, cozy days of fall, the impending darkness now felt like sheets of doom across the empty housing development. Her father kept promising that the streetlights that now reached out like cold, stiff hands toward the sky would be lit soon. *Soon*, Sawyer figured, probably meant when another family moved into the housing tract.

Now Sawyer's headlights made only dim slits in the blackness, obscured even more by the bales of fog rolling over the brand new blacktop. That was the thing about living in a town that billed itself as "oceanside adjacent." No real ocean views but all the ocean fog and the occasional brackish scent of filthy bay water.

Sawyer zipped through the blackened streets, sighing as she passed empty house after empty house. The Dodd house was the first to be populated, though it sat at the very back of the housing tract. It rested on a gentle slope, and once the rest of the neighborhood was full, the house would have an excellent view of twinkling lights before the miles of cypress trees beyond. The brochures called Blackwood Hills a "forested oasis." Sawyer called it an annoyingly long distance from civilization and creepy in the dark.

The porch light glimmered at the front door of the Dodd house, and Sawyer picked her way through rocky dirt and a maze of landscape flags and spray-painted future walkways. She sunk her key into the lock, kicked open the front door, and dropped her backpack on the marble foyer floor.

"I'm home." Her voice echoed in the empty house, ricocheting off the sixteen-foot ceilings and through the new drywall. "Dad? Tara?" Sawyer expected a massive spray of pink or blue balloons or—God forbid—one of each, but there was nothing save for the boxed remains of her old life butting up against her parents' wedding gifts and cheery stuff for the baby. She toed a floppy giraffe and stepped over the boxes, flipping on the lights in the kitchen.

"Hello?"

Sawyer sucked in a sharp breath, hearing the racing double-thump of her heart when she saw the note on the kitchen table, propped up against a bottle of sparkling cider. She clawed at her chest and laughed a weird, maniacal giggle when she recognized her father's precise writing on the note.

"It's a girl!" she read out loud. "Just think of all the things you can teach your new baby sister. Tara and I have gone out to celebrate. There's pizza in the freezer. Love, your always proud, Papa. Papa?" Sawyer snorted, flicked the note, and eyed the cider.

"Brilliant." Sawyer flicked on her cell phone and walked to each corner of the professional-grade kitchen, eyes glued to her cell screen. She balanced on one foot near the bay window and then hopped up on the granite countertop, looking for a cell-phone signal. She let out something halfway between a groan and a growl and snatched the landline phone from the wall.

"What kind of place doesn't have cell service?" Chloe said the second Sawyer picked up.

"Hell and Blackwood Hills Estates. Scratch that. I think Hell's gone fiber-optic now."

"So, convo—wait, what did you call it?"

"Convocation." Sawyer smiled. "Aren't you supposed to be the smart one?"

"No, I'm the scrappy bootstrap one who will win a scholarship for her writing prowess, making everyone in the trailer park titter."

Sawyer jutted out one hip. "Titter?"

"It's a TP thing. You tract home chicks wouldn't understand. So, are we hanging out or not?"

Sawyer's lower lip pushed out. "Doubtful. I've got sparkling apple cider and an apparent baby sister."

"Cider?" Chloe sputtered into the phone.

"And a baby sister on the way."

"And they expect you to toast the mutant spawn with sparkling cider?"

"I don't think she'll be a mutant. Tara's gorgeous." Sawyer looked around the eco-green kitchen. "And so very environmentally correct."

"Whatever," Chloe said, rattling cellophane on her end of the phone. "You know what goes well with sparkling cider?"

"What's that?" Sawyer asked, pouring herself a mammoth bowl of cereal and rearranging herself on the glazed granite countertop.

"Beer."

Sawyer wrinkled her nose, crunching her cereal. "That sounds gross."

"You want me to head over? If I leave now I can be there by next Tuesday."

Sawyer frowned. "No, thanks. I'm not feeling company-worthy right now. Can we convocate next week?"

"Wow, convocate?"

"I think I just made it up. Anyway, I think I'm just going to eat my celebratory pizza chaser after my cereal, take a bath, and resign myself to failing Spanish."

"*Que bueno*. Have a great night in the graveyard of American dreams."

"Try not to let your Airstream rust."

Sawyer set her bowl in the sink and changed into her pajama pants, turning on every light in the house as she went. Though a new build, the Dodd house still settled and creaked in ways that made the hair on the back of Sawyer's neck stand up. She turned on the television and cranked the volume, letting the canned laughter and faux family's voices fill her empty house.

The rest of the week passed uneventfully with no new notes and Sawyer burying herself under a mountain of college applications and midterm prep. So when the door of her Spanish class opened the following Friday afternoon, Sawyer was knee-deep in Spanish verb conjugation hell and didn't look up.

"Flower-grams!"

Sawyer's heart ached, remembering last year's onslaught of fundraising carnations. She and Kevin had just started dating and he had showered her—a dozen per class—in pink and white beribboned flowers, each bearing a special message: *I love you, You're beautiful.* Those flowers were pressed in a cardboard box marked "Sawyer's Room" now, right next to the note she thought was her favorite—a fuzzy bunny rabbit drawn on binder paper with the words *I'll never hurt you* printed across it. Sawyer swallowed back a lump, hid her moist eyes behind her book.

Maggie was the head of the flower fundraising forum, and she marched into the classroom now, beaming in a waft of carnation-scented air, her minions flanking her, arms laden with blooms.

"Mr. Hanson, members of the junior class. As you know, our flower-gram program not only raises school and personal spirit—"

"I think I feel my lunch being raised," someone muttered.

Maggie shot daggers. "As I was saying, these flower-grams raise spirit and cash for our junior prom. So, if you're one of the few who don't receive a flower today, there are still three more days to get yours." Maggie donned a dazzling, pageant-worthy grin and narrowed her eyes at Sawyer. "Or consider sending one to yourself. No one but you and I will know, and it's for a good cause."

Sawyer rolled her eyes and went back to the verb *to play*.

"Now, without further ado, your flower-grams."

Maggie cleared her throat and started reading off names as her minions zigzagged through the classroom, depositing single stems, sentiment cards tied with ribbons and fluttering like leaves.

Maggie paused, seeming to choke on the next name. "Sawyer Dodd." She said it with a curled lip, no attempt to mask the disdain in her voice. "Two flowers."

Maggie's minion deposited two flowers on Sawyer's desk without making eye contact. Sawyer lowered her Spanish book. It seemed as though the room dropped into a curious—and accusatory—silence. If Sawyer's boyfriend was dead, their stares seemed to say, who was sending her flowers?

Sawyer unfurled the first note with trembling fingers. Would her admirer reveal himself—clear up the mystery message?

To Tom Sawyer —
Goin' up river.
All my love, Huck Finn.

Sawyer felt her blood start to pump again and she grinned. Chloe was Sawyer's Huck Finn—and Sawyer had painted more than a few fences for her—and although the "up river" joke wasn't original or new, it never failed to bring a smile to her lips.

Confident now, Sawyer reached for the second note and smoothed it against her desktop.

Her smile dropped.

Dear Sawyer—
    You've got a great smile, but I don't get to see it enough. Maybe I could change that if you'd let me take you out.

                                        —Cooper

Sawyer swung her head to the right, her glance just catching

Cooper Grey's flushed cheek as he picked up a pen, started doodling, and focused hard on his notebook.

Cooper was new to Hawthorne High—a transplant from Kentucky or Kansas with a soft, sexy drawl, a well-muscled body, and a shy smile that Sawyer had often seen from the corner of her eye. He and Sawyer sat next to each other but never really spoke.

Sawyer swallowed hard and reached for Cooper's arm just as the bell rang. The aisle flooded with students pushing their way out the door.

"Hey, hey, hey," Mr. Hanson shouted, flapping his hands like broken moths. "Tests. Come pick them up on the way out."

Sawyer was deliberately slow putting her things away. Though Cooper seemed sweet, dating was the last thing on her mind. She wanted to let him down easily, privately, but once she turned around, the classroom had emptied, and he was gone.

Sawyer hiked her backpack over her shoulder and was stopped at the head of the class by Mr. Hanson, what she supposed was her Spanish test tubed in his hands. He thumped it against his palm once, then held it out to her.

"Your test." It was almost a question, and Sawyer was suddenly unsure whether or not she wanted to reach for it. Mr. Hanson was handsome, with dark hair that backed away from his forehead and eyebrows that rose expectantly. Sawyer wasn't sure why, but the raised eyebrows paired with Mr. Hanson's narrowed, leather-brown eyes unnerved her. She steadied her backpack and felt her eyes dart to the back of the classroom to the door, to the rows of abandoned desks behind her. Finally, they flitted over the page in Mr. Hanson's hand.

"This is mine?"

"You know, Sawyer, I'm worried about you." Mr. Hanson handed her her test, and she swallowed hard.

"Forty-seven percent?"

He offered her a sympathetic smile, set his hand on her shoulder, and squeezed gently. The motion sent something warm through Sawyer, and she wondered if she could slip away without seeming rude.

But then she thought of Dr. Johnson.

Dr. Johnson was her father's go-to shrink for all things teenage trauma–related. Getting a divorce? Drop your kid at the shrink. Kid's boyfriend dies? Shrink. Grades dropping, kid not coping, possibly cutting? Shrink, shrink, shrink.

"I'm sorry about this." She shook the test. "I'll try harder. I know I'll do better next time. But maybe I can do some extra credit or something? I really do want to boost my grade."

"Extra credit?" Mr. Hanson's eyebrows went up. "I suppose we could work something out."

"Thank you. I just—I just really need to end up with at least a B in this class."

Mr. Hanson moved his hand to her upper arm, his thumb rubbing a small circle on her bare skin. His touch sent a cold, electric shock through her—Sawyer thought of a wet, serpentine eel darting through rocks—and her skin prickled with gooseflesh.

"Ooh," Mr. Hanson said, rubbing both of Sawyer's arms now. "You're freezing."

"No," Sawyer said, stumbling backward. "I'm okay." She swung her backpack from one shoulder, putting it between herself and Mr. Hanson. He took a step closer anyway.

"I should get going."

"You know, Sawyer, your grade is dropping like a stone. That's not like you."

"I know, I—"

"I know you've had a really rough month."

Sawyer nodded, a rush of tears forming behind her lashes. She was angry; she was terrified; she wasn't even sure at what. But she would not cry, she told herself. She had already spent too many embarrassing hours bursting into tears at inopportune moments. She gritted her teeth and clenched her fists, nails digging half-moons into her palms.

"I'm not trying to be the bad guy. I know you're probably really sad and confused."

Mr. Hanson's eyes were dark, an intense shade of brown. When he moved to touch Sawyer's cheek, she tried to dodge him—in her mind, at least. Her body was rigid, her feet rooted to the floor.

"Probably even a little lonely." Mr. Hanson smiled softly. "That's normal. I lost someone, too, so I understand." He slipped the test from her stony fingers. "But a college might not be as understanding. They're strangers. Those people won't know what a smart, talented girl you are."

Sawyer's spine stiffened. "Mr. Hanson, I—"

"I want to help you." He laid the test aside on his desk, peeled the backpack from Sawyer's stiff fingers, and set that aside too.

"I think I can probably get my grade up if I just work a little harder." She took a microstep backward. "I'll do that. I mean, I know I can…if I just…work harder."

Mr. Hanson's hand fell from her elbow, his fingertips trailing just slightly over the bare skin of her forearm, giving her goose bumps. Mr. Hanson smiled. "You don't need to be afraid of me. I help out a lot of my students."

"Oh." Sawyer's mind was working, ticking. *Everyone loves Mr. Hanson*, Sawyer's mind reasoned, *he's just being friendly. Stop being such a freak.* She forced a laugh that was too loud, sounded tinny and too high-pitched in the empty room.

"Would you like me to help you? It'll only take a minute." Mr. Hanson picked up the teacher's guide to Sawyer's Spanish textbook and she immediately relaxed, suddenly feeling embarrassed.

See? He's a teacher. Stop. Being. A. Freak.

Sawyer nodded slowly, trying to force some nonchalance into her stance, into her voice. She shifted her weight. "Sure. Thanks."

Mr. Hanson pulled out his desk chair for Sawyer and ushered her into it. She sat primly, and he slid her test paper in front of her. He leaned close, one hand on her shoulder, the other caging her at his desk. "You see right here?" He pointed, and Sawyer nodded quickly.

"It should have been *nosotros*," she answered slowly.

"Right." He squeezed her shoulder. "See, that was probably just carelessness. Now, what about this one?" He pointed to something lower on the page and Sawyer bent to examine it, his fingers trailing down her spine and resting on her lower back. He began to make small circles with his thumb and Sawyer swallowed heavily, her heart beginning to thud. Every muscle in her body screamed that something was terribly wrong, but when she turned to look at Mr. Hanson, his face was open, his smile kind.

He's helping me, Sawyer said to herself, swallowing hard. *That's all it is.*

"I know you can get this. You're a smart girl." Mr. Hanson winked. "Not just a pretty face."

Sawyer glanced at the clock and pushed away from the desk, standing. "I really should get going. Um, thank you. Uh, for helping me."

"That's all I want to do for you, Sawyer. Help." He opened his arms for a hug, and the stupidity that Sawyer felt crashed over her in a tremendous wave.

She stepped into his embrace and felt his arms wrap around her, a quick, innocent squeeze.

See? Innocent. Stop being such a jumpy stupid freak.

But his hands locked behind her, and his lips found her ear. His breath was hot and moist. "I'm always here to help," he whispered.

He hugged her just a little bit tighter, and Sawyer stumbled forward, off balance. She pressed her face into the collar of his Lacoste polo shirt. She tried to right herself, to push herself apart from Mr. Hanson, but he was still mid-hug.

Suddenly, all Sawyer wanted was to get away. It was illogical and rude, she thought, but she felt stifled and trapped and uncomfortable. Six minutes or six seconds could have passed—Sawyer couldn't be sure—but Mr. Hanson's scent, smoke and musky cologne and sweat, choked her, and she gritted her teeth, biting her lip hard in the process. She tasted the blood in her mouth just as she felt Mr. Hanson's fingers slip from the small of her back, trailing to the waistband of her jeans, then resting on her back pockets.

He doesn't know, he doesn't know, he doesn't know, she screamed in her head. *He doesn't know that he's touching me.*

A hundred thoughts zipped through her mind. *Step back casually. Don't mention it. Don't embarrass him.*

She tried to back away, her whole body stiffening, but he didn't let her go. Finally she ground her palms against his chest, pressing against him.

"Mr. Hanson, I have to go. I have to go right now."

"What are you talking about? You came to me." His breath was raspy, muffled by her hair, and Sawyer paused, anxiety welling up inside her. *She had come to him. He only wants to help.* Her head started to spin. *He is trying to help…right?*

He pressed against her once more, his belt buckle digging into her, and something inside of her snapped. Terror—and anger—shot through her.

"No!" She grabbed fistfuls of his shirt and brought her knee up, hard and fast, catching him off guard and between the legs. Mr. Hanson groaned and doubled over, grabbing her ponytail. Sawyer stumbled backward, wincing at the dried-leaf sound of strands of her hair breaking as Mr. Hanson pulled against her. She pushed away again, hand clawed, nails raking over his cheeks, leaving an angry red wake puckering his skin.

"Jesus, Sawyer!"

"Stay away from me! I have pepper spray!" She held her backpack in front of her like a shield, blindly digging through the front pocket while keeping her eyes fixed on Mr. Hanson. He pressed his palms forward and chuckled, the sound shooting ice water through her veins.

"I don't know what you're thinking. I was just trying to offer you some homework help." He crossed the room in three long strides and pulled open the door. "I'm sorry if you misunderstood."

Sawyer shook her head, willing herself not to cry. "No, I didn't misunderstand. You—you—"

Mr. Hanson crossed his arms in front of his chest and leaned one hip against his desk. There was a hint of a smile on his lips—Sawyer couldn't tell if it was kind or sly—and one eyebrow was quirked. She could feel the cheek-reddening heat in her face, and a strand of hair was pulled out of her mussed ponytail, flopping in front of her eyes. But Mr. Hanson looked fresh and at ease. Sawyer stumbled back, her mind tumbling.

"You—you did."

She tried to force what happened to the forefront of her mind, but already it was slipping behind the haze of self-doubt.

Kevin always said she overreacted. He said she was oversensitive, that she always took things the wrong way. Maybe this was one of those times?

Sawyer snuck a glance at Mr. Hanson through the filter of her chestnut–colored hair.

"I appreciate you coming in for homework help, Sawyer, but you should get going now. The building is almost empty." He cocked his, head pressing his lips to into a thin smile. "You never know what's lurking out there after dark."

Sawyer glanced down the deserted hall and back at Mr. Hanson. His smile took on a sinister edge, the glint in his eyes unmistakably challenging. She tore down the hallway, the heels of her boots slapping the linoleum, the sharp sound bouncing off the walls and echoing in her ears. She didn't breathe until she burst through the double doors onto the campus lawn. She took one look at the darkening sky, then doubled over, hands on knees, tears and snot rolling over her cheeks and dripping from her chin.

"Sawyer?" Logan's voice was kind and tentative. "Are you okay?"

She straightened up quickly, used the heel of her hand to swipe at her eyes and chin. She sniffed, forced a small smile, and masked a hiccup.

"Logan, hi." She saw the polite concern in his cocker-spaniel eyes and opened her mouth, but she stopped herself when Mr. Hanson's icy glare and challenging smile flashed in her mind. She felt like he was all around her, like his breath was still bathing her neck. Her skin burned where his fingers had been. "I'm okay, thanks. It's just that—"

"I know," he said softly.

Sawyer's stomach seized. "You do?"

"Kevin."

"Kevin?" Sawyer paused for a beat and then pumped her head. "Right, Kevin." She shirked off the guilt that pricked at the back of her neck for using Kevin—what happened to Kevin—to cover. She dug in her pack for her car keys. "I should get going. I didn't have track. My parents are probably wondering where I am." She knew she was babbling, but it felt somehow comfortable to talk about normal things.

The hard crack of the double doors opening behind her stopped her, made her heart drop to her already weak knees.

"Sawyer Dodd. Just the young lady I was looking for." Mr. Hanson's voice—light, unaffected—oozed through Sawyer like a searing poison, and everything inside her tightened, went on high alert. She didn't turn to face him. She heard Logan rattle around in his bag, heard him pull out something cellophane, and everything dropped into slow motion, the tiniest, most inconsequential sounds—cellophane tearing, Logan chewing—became suddenly deafening.

"Oh, hello there, Logan."

Sawyer didn't have to look at him to know that Mr. Hanson was smiling at her. She could feel his stare, his breath coating every inch of her.

"Hey, Mr. Hanson. Want one?" Logan asked, offering up his pack of peanut butter crackers.

"No, thanks. I'm allergic to peanuts, remember? And actually, I was looking for Sawyer. She forgot her Spanish test. She must have been in some hurry to get away today."

"Sorry." Sawyer's voice sounded robotic, automatic, and she felt herself turn slowly, but she kept her eyes fixed on Mr. Hanson's scuffed leather topsiders. "I was in a hurry."

Mr. Hanson held out the test to her, and she pinched it between forefinger and thumb. He didn't relinquish it to her until she met his eyes. They were flat, serpentine.

"Why don't you come to my classroom and we can talk?"

A jolt of anger shot through her. "No." It was short-lived, and Sawyer felt her knees begin to shake. A bead of sweat rolled between her breasts and she heard Logan crunch another cracker, chew it loudly.

"I promised Logan I would drive him home, and I've already made him late." She crumpled the test in her left hand, locked Logan's wrist with her right. Logan stood quickly, eyes wide with surprise, the half package of peanut butter crackers rolling off his lap. "Sorry, Logan. I'll take you home now. My car's in the lot."

Sawyer hurried down the steps, dragging Logan behind her. Finally, he shook her hand from his and paused. "I didn't ask you to drive me home. I can take the bus. It'll be here at 3:50."

Sawyer looked over his shoulder and saw Mr. Hanson still standing in front of the double doors, a suspicious smile on his face.

"That's almost an hour away. You'll be waiting here alone. I can drive you. It's no big deal."

"I have to go to work. I work at Cassini's Market." Logan looked skeptical. "It's pretty far out of the way."

"You're in luck. I'm going pretty far out of the way. Besides, I could use the company."

Logan paused, considering. "Okay, I guess."

"This one's mine." Sawyer sunk her key into the lock, her back toward Mr. Hanson. She didn't want to turn and look. She told herself she wouldn't turn and look. She threw her backpack into the car, buckled her belt, and glanced, surreptitiously, out of the corner of her eye as she turned the key. Mr. Hanson was no longer standing on the steps, watching her.

Somehow, that didn't make Sawyer feel any better.

"Nice car. I normally only like classics, but this is pretty cool." Logan's voice snapped through Sawyer's brain, and she turned the key and hit the gas, shoving him hard against his seat.

"Sorry," she mumbled.

"I don't blame you for being in a rush to get out of here." His smile was wide and slightly goofy.

Sawyer smiled, suddenly feeling comfortable as she pulled out of the lot, leaving Hawthorne High in her rearview mirror.

"Do you always wait almost an hour to catch the bus?"

Logan stared silently out the window for so long that Sawyer wasn't sure he had heard her. "No," he said finally. "Only when I miss the 2:47."

"Stuck in class or something?"

"Something like that."

Sawyer chewed on her bottom lip. "Can I ask you something, Logan?"

He shrugged, narrow shoulders hugging his ears. "I guess."

"How come you're wearing your gym clothes? I could have sworn I saw you in jeans earlier."

She saw a muscle in Logan's jaw tremble, then stop. "I..." He drifted off, sucked in a sharp breath, and then started again. "I was wearing jeans. They're wet."

Sawyer's eyebrows went up, and Logan turned around in his seat, eyes wide. "No. No, no, not like that. I didn't pee myself or anything. I—I sort of fell in the fountain."

"The school fountain? How do you 'sort of' fall in that fountain? There's a three-foot wall around it."

Logan pinned her with a glare. "Ask the football team."

They were silent until Sawyer's car nosed out of town and onto the highway.

"So, you work at the market?"

Logan nodded, a pink triangle of tongue darting across his lower lip. "My brother got me the job last year."

"Oh, does he work there too?"

"He did through high school. He's a cop now."

"Did he go to Hawthorne? I don't think I remember him."

Logan turned to look at Sawyer full in the face. "Stephen Haas?"

Sawyer's mouth formed a tiny o of surprise. "Stephen's your brother?" She shook the look off her face.

"You don't have to hide your amazement. Nobody puts two and two together. We're not exactly"—Logan looked down at his thin legs, shook his narrow, balsa wood arms—"similar. Anyway, he's a cop now. You can exit here." Logan tugged on his bottom lip. "Um, Sawyer? Why did you want to take me home today?" He gave a small chuckle, somewhere between self-effacing and hopeful. "I mean, I know you don't like me like that. We're not exactly friends."

Sawyer turned to see Logan, head bent, eyes studying his hands in his lap.

"We could be. I was just trying to be friendly." But the twinge in Sawyer's voice wasn't convincing even to herself.

"No one's friendly in high school."

Sawyer grinned and flipped on her blinker. "Up on the left, right?"

"Right, left." He laughed, paused. "What about Mr. Hanson?"

Sawyer's stomach did an eleven-story drop, and she swallowed bitter saliva. "What do you mean?"

"He can be kind of a jerk, huh?"

Sawyer's eyes went wide, and she felt that now-all-too-familiar prickle of heat climbing her neck.

"He threatened to fail me just because he didn't like my accent."

Sawyer wished her accent was the only thing Mr. Hanson was interested in. "This is your stop, right?"

Logan glanced up as Sawyer pulled the Accord to a stop in the Cassini Market parking lot.

"Oh, right." Logan hiked up his backpack and looked Sawyer over hard, as if trying to be certain that she was really there, that she had indeed offered to drive him—and driven him—to work. "Thanks a lot, Sawyer. I'll see you at school tomorrow."

Sawyer pressed her lips together and gave him a finger wave before pushing her car into gear and veering off toward the new stretch of highway that led to Blackwood Hills Estates. The sun was bleeding over the horizon, casting long shadows over her car as she finally pulled into the housing development. What remained of the setting sun lit the windows of the finished models, giving them a homey glow and lived-in appearance that seemed to counter the howl of the wind kicking up, the snap of the *New Homes This Way!* flags.

Andrew Dodd was standing at the granite counter, chopping celery into precise little C's, when Sawyer walked in. He fixed Sawyer with a grin.

"Well, there's the big sister!"

Sawyer licked her lips and tried to smile, tried to force the memory of Mr. Hanson into the deep recesses of her brain.

She was making too much of it.

It didn't mean anything.

She would have to face him tomorrow.

Sawyer's stomach lurched at the last thought, and her father's smile slipped from his face. "Something wrong, muffin?"

Sawyer shook her head and cleared her throat. "No, no. It was just—just a long day today." She snagged a piece of celery and nibbled it slowly. "So where is our little incubator, anyway?"

Andrew jutted his chin toward the French doors, where Tara, pregnant, pink-cheeked, and hands full of fresh-cut herbs, was walking in. Sawyer's stepmom had clear, ice-blue eyes rimmed with ultra-long doe lashes and a pixie-like nose that turned up at the rounded end. Her shoulder-length hair stood in a perfectly tousled golden halo that made Sawyer reach up and self-consciously smooth the knotted rope of her own hair, mousy, thin, a "before" picture brown.

"Hey, Tara."

Tara's lips broke into a face-brightening smile. "Sawyer! I'm so glad you're home!" She crossed the kitchen with a waddling stride and dropped the herbs on Andrew's cutting board. "Your dad and I want your input on girl names." She rubbed her bulbous belly, still smiling. "My students have already been giving me their ideas." Tara was a professor of environmental biology at Crescent City College.

"But their name list basically reads like the cast of one of those housewives shows," Andrew broke in. "Is David really a girl's name nowadays?"

Tara's grin was still wide, unaffected. "Can you believe we're going to have another girl in the house?"

A rush of something tore through Sawyer—annoyance, jealousy—she wasn't sure what. She wanted to turn and run, to slam her brand-new bedroom door and pull her covers up over her head. She knew she'd be comforted by the familiar industrial laundry soap smell; Sawyer did her own laundry with the same brand her mother had left behind, refusing to use Tara's ultra-organic, made-from-sunshine-and-hippies crap. The clean chemical smell comforted and soothed her; curled up in her blankets with her eyes squeezed tightly shut, Sawyer could almost believe that her mother hadn't left.

"I can't wait to buy all those sweet little pink things." Tara beamed.

Sawyer swallowed hard, trying to bite back the bitter taste of the words caught in her throat. She looked at Tara's earnest face and her father's lovestruck, adoring one; pressed her lips together into a flat but convincing smile; and nodded her head. "Sure. That would be fun."

"Dinner will be ready in thirty," Andrew said.

"You know, I'm not really that hungry."

Tara's face fell. "Isn't today your long run day? You really need to eat, Sawyer."

"Track practice was canceled because of the rain." She

pointed a thumb over her shoulder. "I think I'm just going to hop in the bath. I'll come down and grab something later, okay?"

Tara opened her mouth to answer but closed it promptly. She nodded, a pasted smile that Sawyer had flashed all too often crossing her face.

FOUR

Sawyer did her best to scrub the memory of Mr. Hanson's touch from her skin. She was pink and raw and strawberry scented, but somehow the imprint of his touch, the cloying scent of his musky aftershave, still clung to her and made her shudder.

She slipped into her bathrobe and was elbow deep in a box marked "bathroom," rifling through half-filled bottles of lotions and body splashes when she heard the first *plink!* Sawyer straightened immediately, her hands slipping from the lotion bottles. There was a beat of deafening silence before another *plink!* rattled her bedroom window. Sawyer pulled the window up, then ducked before being pelted with another handful of pebbles.

"Chloe? What are you doing?"

Chloe stood in the driveway, hands on hips, illuminated by the headlights from her mother's car. "Finally!"

"Why didn't you call me instead of throwing"—Sawyer picked a pink blob from the windowsill—"jelly beans at my window?"

Chloe's exasperated sigh was loud enough to reach Sawyer's second-story perch. "Because I was trying to be romantic."

"Aw!"

"And your choice of habitat lacks essentials, like cell service." She wagged her phone.

"Sorry. I'll be right down."

Sawyer pulled open the front door, pinching the collar of her robe against the late-autumn chill. "What are you doing here?"

Chloe grinned. "Rescuing you. Put some clothes on. We're going out."

Sawyer began to shake her head. "No, no, I'm in for the night. My dad and stepmom are already in bed."

"All the better. There's a party at Evan Rutger's house and you're going."

"Definitely not in the party mood."

Chloe cocked her head, hands on hips. "Didn't your shrink say that you needed to get back into doing regular, teenager-y things? What's more teenager-y than red party cups?"

"Somehow I don't think Dr. Johnson was referencing

underage drinking when he said I should engage in common teen activities."

"You don't *think* that's what he meant. You don't know for sure. Come on," Chloe snapped Sawyer on the butt. "Upstairs. Get dressed."

"Fine," Sawyer said. "One hour."

"Whatever. Just be my date so I don't look like a loner."

———————

Cars, red party cups, and the errant student littered Evan Rutger's family's well-manicured lawn.

"Where are Evan's parents?" Sawyer asked as Chloe nudged her car in between two others.

"Don't know. I just heard they were gone."

"Word travels fast around here."

"You bet. Ready to party?"

Sawyer sighed. "Not really. Hey, Chloe—"

Chloe paused, her blue eyes catching the streetlight. "What?"

Sawyer thought about Mr. Hanson, thought about his hands trailing over her bare skin. A shiver rippled over her skin. "Never mind." She linked arms with her best friend. "Let's go get our party on."

The din inside the Rutger house was deafening—a thudding bass combined with shrieking laughter and the general cacophony of students shouting over one another, over the cranked-up stereo. A couple sped between Chloe and

Sawyer—she was screaming and laughing; he was yanking at the bottom of her skirt. Someone shoved a cup into Sawyer's hand and beer sloshed out of it, the cold liquid washing over Sawyer's wrist and soaking the bottom of her jeans.

"Oh, I'm sorry." Cooper's eyes were wide and fixed on Sawyer's dripping wrist.

Suddenly, Sawyer was happy to be there, happy to be a part of the throbbing mass of students swaying in the packed living room. She sucked some beer from her wrist and grinned at Cooper. "All better."

"Well you're a good sport, aren't you?"

Sawyer sipped at her beer; once the icy liquid passed her lips, she tipped the cup and gulped the whole thing down.

"Rough day?" Cooper asked.

Sawyer held up her cup. "You don't know the half of it. Do you know where this came from?"

Cooper took Sawyer's empty cup in one hand and slid his other hand into hers. His touch sent something electric up Sawyer's arm, and a warmth started low in her belly. She liked it.

Cooper and Sawyer looped through the crowd, coming to a stop at the edge of the kitchen, where a throng of students clogged the doorway. "Should be just a sec," Cooper said over his shoulder. He didn't let go of Sawyer's hand, and she wasn't sure she wanted him to.

"Here you go." Cooper handed her a full cup.

"And I thought you didn't want to party!" Chloe appeared

in front of Sawyer, clinking her plastic cup. She had one arm slung around the neck of a guy Sawyer recognized from her Spanish class.

"Hey, Ryan," she said quickly. And then, to Chloe, "How much have you had? We've only been here like five minutes."

Chloe cocked her head, a lock of blond hair falling across her collarbone. "I've had enough to make him interesting." She grinned, nuzzling the ear of the guy who was all but holding her up, sipping from his own red party cup. "Hey," she untangled herself and leaned into Sawyer, grabbing both her wrists. "We should dance."

Sawyer swayed with Chloe. "You're so drunk."

Chloe giggled. "I'm not; it's just more fun this way. What's going on with you and Cooper?"

Sawyer looked over her shoulder to where Cooper was leaning in the doorway, a slight grin on his face as he eyed her. "I don't know. Nothing. He's really nice, though."

"I think he loves you."

"Shut up." Even as she protested, a delighted spark raced through her. "You think?"

Chloe held Sawyer at arm's length. "You *are* interested!"

Sawyer felt herself flush. "I'm not ready to date. But it's nice to have someone interested. Hey, song's over."

"Next time let me lead. Boyfriend's watching you." Chloe spun Sawyer and gave her a playful spank on the rump. "Go get 'em, tiger."

"You're quite the dancer," Cooper said with a grin. He

looped an arm around Sawyer's waist and pulled her close to him, just as a couple of partygoers bumped into her on their way to the kitchen. "Do you want to go somewhere we can talk? Or at least not get mashed into?"

Sawyer looked over her shoulder at the crowd of students oblivious to her and Cooper. She glanced at the backyard behind him, pale white icicle lights dancing over the rippling water in the pool, the patio area relatively empty. "Yeah, okay. Let's go out there."

Cooper laced his fingers with Sawyer's and led her through the sliding glass door out to the Rutger's backyard. A few students hung back in the shadows, making out or smoking.

"Wow." Maggie turned out of the shadows, her scowl apparent in the dim light. Her eyes raked over Sawyer, flicked over her hand linked with Cooper's. "Didn't take you long to bounce back."

Sawyer swallowed heavily, shame welling up.

"We're just friends," Cooper said, his drawl light and sweet. He squeezed Sawyer's hand and held it up. "The place is packed. I just didn't want to lose her."

The titillating warmth from Cooper's hand shot through Sawyer, quashing the shame she felt at connecting with another boy.

"Whatever," Maggie said with a violent flick of her hair. "Kevin deserved so much better." She huffed past Sawyer, digging a bony elbow into her rib cage as she did.

"Well, that girl is just a regular breath of vile air."

Sawyer smiled thinly. "We used to be friends."

Cooper looked toward Maggie and then to Sawyer, incredulous. He wagged his head. "No, I don't believe someone like you could be friends with someone like Maggie."

Sawyer's skin prickled. "Someone like me?"

Cooper looked down at his hands. "You know, nice. Sweet. Cute."

Sawyer looked away, her smile marred by shadows.

"And this Kevin guy was your boyfriend?"

Sawyer blinked at Cooper. "You don't know?"

"Know what?"

"Kevin Anderson. He was my boyfriend."

"The name sounds familiar but..." Cooper shook his head, a blank expression flicking through his hazel eyes.

"He died." Sawyer forced the words out, feeling her whole body stiffen with the memory as she did.

"Anderson..." Cooper's eyes went up as he thought. "Wasn't he the kid in the drunk-driving accident?"

Sawyer felt heat at the back of her neck, felt her palms start to itch with sweat. "Yeah."

"Oh." Cooper's eyes were wide. "I'm really sorry. I didn't know. Are you okay?"

Sawyer felt as if she had been struck dumb. She had been asked the question so many times, day after day since the accident—"Are you okay?" "Are you okay?"—but hearing the same string of words come out of Cooper's mouth, with his eyes so sympathetic and so wonderfully real, dug at her heart.

"It's hard," she heard herself murmur. "It's been hard."

Cooper led Sawyer to an ivy-covered arch at the side of the house, and she sunk down onto a cement bench. He let go of her hand. "I didn't mean to bring it up."

Sawyer shook her head, feeling her dark hair circle her cheeks. "No, it's fine. I'm sorry." She realized she was crying and wiped her tears on her sleeve. "Not exactly the best partygoer, am I?"

Cooper sat down next to Sawyer, his shoulder and thigh touching hers. She waited for the searing heat of guilt, for her body to involuntarily cringe as their skin brushed. Since Kevin's death she had been overcome with shame, with guilt, with the inane sense that at any moment she was going to be accused of doing something wrong, something awful— something for which she would have to atone. Toward the end, she was always on edge, studying Kevin's eyes, watching the twist of his mouth. His anger was unpredictable, his emotion erratic, and without knowing it, Sawyer had come to base her every movement on what *might* happen. So when her body didn't react, when she was overcome with comfort as Cooper's skin touched hers, it was overwhelming and she pulled away anyway, rubbing her palms against her thighs as though she were chilled.

Cooper seemed not to mind. "I think you make a pretty nice date," he said, his eyes on his lap.

Sawyer smiled.

"If you ever want to talk about it, I kind of know how it

feels." Cooper clasped his hands and kicked at the dirt with one sneakered foot. "We moved here because my dad's family is here." Sawyer watched a muscle flick along Cooper's strong jawline. "My mom died twelve weeks ago."

"Oh my God."

"Cancer. It happened really fast."

"I can't imagine... But I know. One minute they're there—"

"And the next they're gone."

When Cooper turned his face toward Sawyer, his eyes were glossy, the golden flecks catching in what remained of the backyard twinkle lights. Sawyer felt herself drawn to him, a powerful force between them, and before she could consider the implication, the ramifications, she was kissing him. Her lips were pressed hard against his, and she tasted the bitter remnants of beer and then the sweet taste of Cooper as he opened his mouth, their tongues finding each other. Memories crashed over Sawyer like so many waves, breaking like shards of glass at her feet. She felt ashamed, alive, and free as Cooper's arms slipped around her waist, pulling her close to him. His touch was soft but strong, and Sawyer loved the way he held her, making her feel safe and wanted at the same time. Cooper's fingers found her hair and tangled themselves in it; she pressed her palms against his strong back, feeling the muscles tense underneath his thin T-shirt. Her heart thumped against his, and she kissed him harder, desperate to pull him closer, to pull him into her, to block out the memories of Kevin, of the note, of everything.

A shriek cut through the night, cut through the heat, and Cooper and Sawyer were thrown apart.

"What was that?" Cooper panted.

The shriek sounded again—high pitched, anguished.

"It's a girl."

"It's Chloe." Sawyer was on her feet, the delicious beat of her heart speeding up to a painful, nervous patter. "Where is she?"

Sawyer was pawing through people in the backyard now, Cooper close behind her. "Chloe!" But her voice was lost in the din, swallowed by the beat of the pulsing bass.

"I think she's in here," Cooper said, grabbing Sawyer's hand and leading her toward the house.

"Oh my God." Sawyer stopped cold in the doorway, dropping Cooper's hand and bracing herself against the door frame. "Chloe."

The party dropped off into a shocked silence as everyone turned to gape at Chloe.

Ryan was standing at her side again, but this time he appeared to be holding her up. Chloe's head was bent, her hands pressed to her face. Sawyer could see the blood as it oozed through her best friend's fingers. She felt herself vaulting across the room.

"What happened?"

Chloe was crying, her small shoulders quaking with the effort. "Someone, someone—"

"Someone attacked her," Ryan finished.

"Oh my God, Chloe! Are you okay? Who was it?"

"I'm okay." Chloe nodded, pulling her hands away from her face. There was a severe gash over her left eye. The blood had already started to congeal over the jagged, puckering skin. Sawyer rushed forward, throwing her arms around her in a quick embrace.

"Who did this to you?"

Chloe wagged her head. "I don't know. I went out to my car to get a sweatshirt, and someone was out there with the hood open."

"The hood of the car?" Cooper asked.

Ryan nodded. "It was still popped when I got out there. I heard her screaming and came running."

"I told the guy to knock it off, you know, leave my car alone, and when he heard me, he turned around and swung." Chloe's trembling fingers gingerly touched the blood over her eye. "I don't even know what he hit me with."

"And you didn't see who it was?"

Chloe shook her head. "No. He hit me and took off running, I guess. I barely even remember that. I felt it, then I know I was falling, and then Ryan was standing over me."

Cooper looked over Ryan's shoulder out the open door. "You think he's still out there?"

"Let's go, man."

Sawyer reached for Cooper but caught only the tail of his shirt as it sailed past her.

"If he's still out there, they could get hurt," Chloe said, enormous tears rollicking over her cheeks.

Sawyer nodded and took the washcloth someone handed her. She pressed it against Chloe's forehead and guided Chloe to the couch. "I'm going to go see." She tucked her hand in her pocket, protectively cupping her cell phone. *If I don't see the guys this millisecond,* she reasoned, *I'm calling 911.*

But Cooper and Ryan were standing on the sidewalk, their angry faces illuminated by a slice of yellow streetlight.

"Did you see anyone?"

Cooper shook his head. "There's no one around here."

"We found this, though." Ryan held a tire iron and Sawyer's stomach lurched when she saw the black-red blood staining the metal.

Chloe's blood.

"What was he doing out here? Breaking into Chloe's car?" Sawyer scanned the makeshift parking lot in front of the Rutgers' house. Cars were scattered everywhere, each one a better make or newer model than Chloe's mother's old, primer-colored Dodge.

"He didn't want to steal anything," Cooper said, pointing to the car. "You don't get into the cab by going under the hood."

"Well, what would someone be doing under the hood? Messing up the engine? Trying to pull some kind of prank?"

Ryan put his hands on his hips. "A prank is locking someone's keys in their car or putting shaving cream on the windshield."

"Sugar in the gas tank," Cooper suggested before bending over the exposed engine, scanning. "Hey, Ryan, do you know anything about cars?"

Ryan shrugged but looked anyway. "I know that you shouldn't keep tools under the hood."

Sawyer rushed in and looked where Ryan was pointing, squinting. She reached for the tool and held it up to the light. "What is it?"

Cooper took it out of her hand, eyeing both Sawyer and Ryan. "It's a tube cutter."

"What do you use a tube cutter for?" Sawyer wanted to know. "And why would you stash it in someone's car?"

Ryan shook his head slowly, his eyes wide and focused on the tube cutter in Cooper's hand. "You wouldn't stash it in someone's car," he said. "But you might drop it there if you were surprised in the middle."

Sawyer swallowed. "In the middle of what?"

"Of cutting Chloe's brakes."

Sawyer's stomach folded in on itself. "How could...? Someone...Chloe could have died! If she didn't have brakes, she could have died!" The realization crashed like a cold wave over her and Sawyer was stunned, her breath tightening in her chest.

Ryan swiped a finger across his cell phone and pushed it under the open hood. The blue light from the screen washed over the engine, and he pointed. "Right there."

Cooper let out a low whistle as he fingered the even cut along a thin metallic tube. "He cut clean through."

The tears were rolling down Sawyer's face now, hot tracks burning down her cheeks. "Why would someone do that?"

But she didn't need to hear an answer because she already knew it: Sawyer's secret admirer was after her best friend too.

Sawyer's head felt all at once light and impossibly heavy, and suddenly she felt the cold concrete slap against her back, her head lolling. Her nostrils stung with the smell of dirt and grass, the damp coldness pricking at her head and neck. She blinked when a bright light pierced her eyelid.

"Cooper?" Her lips felt puffy, and her head throbbed. "What happened?"

"You passed out." He helped Sawyer up, and Ryan shoved the penlight he was holding into his back pocket.

"We need to call the police," Sawyer said.

Cooper shook his head as he led Sawyer into the Rutgers' living room. It had cleared out considerably. Only a few scattered students remained, wide-eyed and quietly clutching their red party cups. Chloe sat alone on the love seat, her eyes red rimmed, her cheeks a deep pink. She pulled her knees up against her chest and hugged them.

"Chloe doesn't want us to."

Chloe looked up at Sawyer, fresh tear tracks glossy on her cheeks. "My parents don't know I'm here. They'll kill me."

Sawyer sucked in a sigh. "Chloe, this is really dangerous. Someone attacked you, and"—she choked on a sob—"they cut your brake lines. They could have killed you. They—they wanted to hurt you—bad. You have to tell the police."

Chloe shook her head. "No. I can't."

"I'm going to take her home," Ryan said softly.

"I'll go with you," Sawyer said.

"Yeah, I drove Sawyer over here."

"No problem," Cooper said, "I can take Sawyer home."

Sawyer looked from Cooper to Chloe. "I think I should go home with her. Chloe, your parents probably aren't even home. You shouldn't be alone."

"Then how are you going to get home from her house?" Ryan wanted to know. "Here, I'll take Chloe and hang out with her until her parents come back."

Sawyer opened her mouth to protest, but Ryan held up his hands. "No argument. You had a hard night too."

Cooper nodded. "You passed out. You probably should lay down or get an ice pack or something."

Chloe held out her ice pack. "Room for one more."

"Chloe." Sawyer sat down next to her, gingerly touching the dried blood over Chloe's eye. "Let me at least go with you."

Chloe leaned in, dropped her voice to a low whisper. "Sawyer, everyone's looking at me. I'm embarrassed. I don't care who's at the house. I just want to go home."

"But your car—"

"It was probably a stupid prank," Chloe said, her eyes defiant, "and I caught the guy by surprise."

"A prank?"

"We're going to get going," Ryan said, pulling Chloe from the couch.

"I'll call you later," Chloe said, shielding the cut above her eye with her sleeve.

A prank.

The word burned on Sawyer's tongue. The sliced brake line, Chloe's black-red blood—both burned into her mind's eye. If this was a prank, then someone at Hawthorne High had a really bad sense of humor.

FIVE

Sawyer watched Ryan as he gingerly settled Chloe into his car. Chloe gave a slight wave when he pulled away from the curb, and the gash on her eye caught the light from the streetlamp. Sawyer shivered and hugged her arms.

"Here," Cooper said, pulling off his zippered hoodie and settling it over her shoulders. "Better?"

Sawyer nodded. The sweater would have helped if the chill hadn't been bone deep.

"Can we get going now?"

Cooper nodded. "Yeah, of course." He dug in his pocket for his keys and Sawyer touched his wrist gently, her fingers cold on his warm skin. "Are you okay to drive?"

He smiled. "Only had half a beer and that was"—he squinted at the clock—"over an hour ago."

"Didn't seem that long ago."

"Well, there was the thing with Chloe, and before that—"
Cooper bit his bottom lip in a way that shot fire crackers
through Sawyer's system. "The thing with us."

Heat—and guilt—pulsed through Sawyer. She had been
making out with a guy—a guy who was *not* Kevin—while
someone was trying to murder her best friend.

What kind of girl are *you?* Her insides roiled.

"Ready?"

Sawyer nodded, and when Cooper rested his arm across
her shoulders, she slid out of the half embrace. She hoped to
make it seem as nonchalant or as innocent as possible, but the
hurt look in Cooper's eyes was unmistakable.

They drove in awkward silence until Cooper's car hit the
freeway.

"I'm really sorry about your friend."

"Chloe," Sawyer offered.

"Chloe. Have you guys known each other long?"

Sawyer smiled, remembering. "Remember when I said I
was friends with Maggie?"

"I remember, but I still don't believe it." Cooper grinned
in the darkened car, but his eyes sparkled sweetly. Sawyer
punched down the warmth that rose inside of her.

"It was the three of us. Best friends. We were five—
Maggie didn't know how to be evil yet."

"Ah, there's the missing piece."

Sawyer started to feel more comfortable, letting her

shoulders sag forward as she sunk into the car seat. "We met at dance class. Nothing special, but we used to do everything together. Everything. The three of us."

"So when was the huge falling-out?"

Sawyer frowned. "I don't really know what started it. We were in junior high, and Maggie started to get popular. Chloe ended up having to quit dance class, and Maggie just kept nagging at her to tell everyone why. It was like she wanted to prove to everyone how cool she was by throwing Chloe—our best friend—to the wolves."

Cooper flipped on his blinker when Sawyer showed him where to exit. "So what was Chloe's big secret? Or is that still privileged information?"

Sawyer smiled at Cooper; she couldn't help herself. "Chloe's parents—I think it was still her parents, maybe a stepdad already—just couldn't afford it."

Cooper furrowed his brow. "That's it? Not like every time she danced a puppy died?"

"No!" Sawyer laughed.

"Parents not being able to afford dance lessons doesn't seem all that tragic."

"Well, when you're eleven, whatever makes you not the same as all the other girls *is* tragic. I told Chloe I didn't care, but she was so terrified someone would find out. They moved into this crappy trailer park, sold their car. Maggie found out from her gossipy mom or something, and she pounced. Chloe's new status went viral overnight. People made fun of her, called her 'trailer trash' or 'ghetto girl.'" Sawyer shook her head, remembering. "She was crushed."

"But you stood by your friend."

"Of course." Sawyer smiled faintly. "She's my best friend."

"So that was, what? Five, six years ago?"

Sawyer nodded. "Something like that."

"And you haven't spoken to Maggie since?"

Sawyer gritted her teeth. "Nothing nice."

Sawyer remembered the day the news broke that she and Kevin had begun dating. Maggie was Kevin's ex-girlfriend; they had been apart for a little over two months, but from Maggie's bulldog expression, one would think Kevin had walked out on the one for the other. "I don't think Maggie's really the making-up type, regardless."

Cooper nodded. "You're pretty tough, Sawyer Dodd."

Sawyer turned in her seat. "Why would you say that?"

"Standing up to a bully? Even at eleven years old, that's pretty brave."

In her mind, an image flashed of Sawyer cowering in a corner while Kevin stood over her, spitting mad. Humiliation washed over her, and she looked away. "I'm not that brave."

"Chloe's lucky to have a friend like you."

"It's not like that. She's got my back, too. When I told her my parents were splitting, she came over every day with vanilla ice cream and a two-liter of root beer."

Cooper guided the car through the gates of Blackwood.

"Vanilla ice cream and root beer? No chocolate? No marsh-mallows? Sounds kind of dull."

"Not when you tunnel down the center of the carton and fill the void with root beer. It's the ultimate root beer float."

"I see," Cooper said with a grin. "So vanilla ice cream and root beer, that's what made you a tough girl then?"

Sawyer feigned anger. "What do you mean, 'then'? Cooper Grey, I'll take you down right here."

"I kind of wish you would." The comment was sugges-tive and raced like lightning through the car, hanging heavy in the air. The thrilling zing rushed through Sawyer, and as quickly as it came, it was gone, replaced by that same sense of shame, of betrayal. She saw Kevin's narrowed eyes, saw the blood seeping from Chloe's wound.

"This is my street," she said quickly.

Cooper slowed. "Which one is your house?"

"You know, don't worry about it. You can just drop me here. It's right there." She waved in the vicinity of her house, hunkering in the darkness.

"What?"

Sawyer clicked open the door, and Cooper slammed on the brakes. "I'm just going to get out here." She gathered her purse and hopped out of the car. "Thank you so much, Cooper, um, it was fun—well, not *fun* fun, but—you know. Thanks." She snapped the door shut before Cooper could say anything and gave him a curt finger wave before turning on her heel and heading toward the bank of dark houses. She hated the way they seemed to leer at her, these gaping skeletons, but all at once the air in the car had gone from barely noticeable to so heavy it pushed all the air out of Sawyer's lungs. She ran to her house and disappeared through the front door without waiting to see Cooper leave.

Sawyer couldn't remember when—or if—she fell asleep, but she was staring at the ceiling by the time the sun started to tinge the ink-black night a pinky yellow. It had been too quiet to sleep; with every breath she took, Sawyer imagined the deathly silence filling her lungs, soaking through her body. When the first finger of light broke its way into her room, she kicked off the covers and wrestled her way into a sports bra and track pants, pulling on a long-sleeve shirt and running socks. She kicked through the mess of discarded clothing and random junk on her bedroom floor until she found one sneaker; she was on the floor, flat on her chest, reaching under her bed, when the palm of her hand landed on the crumbs of something cold. She withdrew her hand and wrinkled her nose at the beads of dried mud that had embedded themselves in her palm. She brushed the mud off on her T-shirt and gave the bed a good heft with her hip, moving it a few inches. Her one errant shoe was there, flopped on its side, wedged between some books she was planning to shelve when she got around to getting shelves and a single metallic flat. Sawyer snatched up her sneaker and brushed off the dirt, trying to remember the last time she trail ran; the muck that usually clung to her shoes was red track dust. She slid the sneaker on and glanced back to the heap of books and the single shoe, the littering of dried mud. She edged the bed back in place and told herself she'd vacuum later.

The cold was overwhelming and bone deep when Sawyer stepped onto the porch. Her breath came out in puffed white clouds, and her muscles seized up as her lungs sucked in the icy air. She launched herself anyway, hands fisted, legs pumping. It didn't take long for the warmth of motion to surge through her body. She zipped past three half-built houses, studs exposed like spindly skeletons as the warm air surged through her lungs, broke through her muscles.

Sawyer was a distance runner, not a speed runner, but she left her house quickly, clearing her street and her block in record time. As she ran she could feel the memory of Kevin, of the note, of Chloe and the oozing red gash pulling her back, doing its best to weigh on her, but she pushed harder, faster, her fists punching at the air in front of her, her heart metering out a quick, hot rhythm with her footfalls as they rang out hollow in the empty street. As she ran, something nagged at her periphery—something she was missing. She was deep in thought, trying to grab the missing piece, when she heard the footsteps behind her. They were quick, keeping easy pace with her, their echo cracking against the empty streets, bouncing off the model homes. Sawyer slowed and the footsteps mirrored her rhythm.

She stopped.

Suddenly the silence was too deep, too thick. It sunk into Sawyer's chest, enveloping her so that she felt claustrophobic. Her fingers clawed at the zipper of her windbreaker, then pulled at the collar of her shirt. The street was deathly silent now.

Had she imagined the footsteps?

A branch broke behind her, and Sawyer sucked in a breath and held it, afraid to turn around—afraid not to. Her eyes searched the horizon in front of her and the breath seeped out of her body little by little as she saw each cookie-cutter house in front of her, each as perfect and as empty as the last.

She took off like a shot.

She dug into the air with her fingers and pumped her legs until her thighs screamed, wet heat breaking across the muscles. She squinted as the wind smacked at her face, turned the tears she didn't know were falling into painful blasts of cold. She was making headway, had reached the looped street that returned to her house as the footsteps became more pronounced, more frantic. Her feet ached and her left calf seized, the pain shooting through her like needles in her bloodstream. She tried to will it away, tried to command her brain to make her legs move more, faster, harder, but her knee collapsed over her cramped calf and Sawyer felt herself falling, the whole thing in achingly slow motion. She noticed every detail on this block's more finished houses as she went down—the unobtrusive almond-colored paint, the chocolate-brown trim, the shadow under one of the eaves. And she knew she was being watched.

Her shoulder hit the pavement first, sliding enough to accommodate her upper arm, her splayed palms, her belly, and her chin. She felt her skin make contact with the frozen ground, felt it tear and burn as she slid in the gravel. The smack had sucked the wind out of her so when she tried to scream, nothing came out except a low, offensive moan. She searched wildly for her assailant, for the shadow under the eave—but there was nothing there. Again the silence was everywhere, until a crumpled paper bag caught on the breeze and flitted across the sidewalk, coming to rest on a would-be porch.

Sawyer rolled onto her back and worked to pull air into her folded lungs. When she could breathe and her heartbeat dipped back to a normal thump, she pushed herself up, wincing as the gravel dug itself deeper into her ruined palms. She looked around her, her fear still palpable in the early-morning light, still aching in her exhausted muscles.

The street was deserted. There was no one there.

Her teeth started to chatter, and the tears fell freely over her cheeks. She sniffed as she began a slow, laboring jog back to her house. Her jaw ached by the time she reached the edge of the yard, and as she stepped onto the porch, her eyes caught the faintest glimmer of something in her periphery.

A flash—*from a camera?* Sawyer wondered.

It was there and then gone before she could blink, and

it was soundless, but Sawyer whirled anyway. Nothing. No person releasing a shutter, taking another shot. No car speeding away. Just...nothing.

Frustration knotted in her chest, and she used her fists to rub at her eyes, then blinked, her gaze lasering in on the landscape around her: empty houses; damp, desolate street; gravel upset where she fell.

After someone had chased her?

Sawyer shook her head, trying to clear it. She imagined the morning fog thick between her ears. Had she taken a pill last night?

Yes, yes, I must have, she reassured herself. *That's got to be it. That stuff makes me see shit, makes me paranoid. That's all it is.*

But even as she worked to convince herself, something remained, something nagged at her periphery, and the feeling of unease settled like a stone in her gut.

When she sunk her key into the lock, her father was on the other end, pulling the door open. He grinned until his eyes fell on his daughter, fell on the bright red raspberry on her chin.

"What happened to you?"

"I—I fell. Someone was chasing me and I fell."

Andrew Dodd opened the door wider and pulled Sawyer inside. "Who was chasing you?" He looked over her shoulder. "Who would be out at this time in the morning?"

Sawyer sniffed. "I don't know."

"Do you know who it was?"

She shook her head.

"Was he in a car, on foot?"

Sawyer shrugged again. "On foot, but I didn't really see him. I saw a shadow, and like, a camera flash. And I heard the footsteps. He was keeping pace with me."

Andrew smiled then. "Keeping pace with you? Sawyer, are you sure you heard someone? It's a little creepy out there with all the empty houses, I know. Don't you think maybe your imagination was working overtime and you just scared yourself?"

Her father was trying to be gentle, but the anger boiled in Sawyer's belly. "You don't believe me."

Andrew cocked his head. "Sawyer..."

"I'm not making this up, Dad." Sawyer paused, sucking on her teeth. "Oh my God. You think this is about the night-mares, don't you?"

"You mentioned they were back, and Tara mentioned she saw the Trazodone out on your nightstand again when she was straightening up."

"Why the hell was Tara in my room?"

Andrew quirked a fatherly eyebrow. "Now, Sawyer, Tara was just helping out."

"You mean helping herself to my business. Besides, the stupid nightmares came back right after Kevin died, Dad. Not now. And today, I was outside, I was running, I was *awake*!"

"I know, I know." He held up his hands, palms forward.

"I'm sure you think you really did hear something, but, Sawyer, there's an eleven-foot iron fence around this whole development. And the gates are closed at night."

Sawyer crossed her arms in front of her chest, hugging herself, thinking of the footsteps, the headlights from the previous night. "But they aren't locked."

———————

Sawyer tried Chloe's phone a second time after she got out of the shower, but there was no answer.

"Hey, it's me again. I just wanted to make sure you were doing okay after last night. I got your text that you made it home okay with Ryan, but I'm still worried. Call me. Besides, I want to know if we're still on for the game tonight. I totally understand if you don't want to, though; I'm not really sure I'm up to it either..." She clicked her phone shut, feeling slightly uneasy, and made her way down the stairs. Though she had gotten up and run this morning, the heft of too many sleepless nights and the drug-addled fog started to become overwhelming. She poured herself a giant mug of coffee and sank down at the kitchen table, her mind ticking.

Could the person who hurt Chloe be my admirer?

There was no reason why, Sawyer thought, as she worried her bottom lip. Chloe was her best friend; she would never hurt Sawyer. Sawyer gulped, her saliva burning her throat— she would never hurt Sawyer the way Kevin had. The thought was errant, rushing through her subconscious, and she rolled onto her side, pulling her knees up into a fetus position.

The first time, it was barely a shove. It happened so fast that Sawyer wasn't even sure it had. Kevin had his arms around her immediately, steadying her, kissing her, telling her it was an accident. And she believed him. He loved her so much—he told her all the time. He called her all the time. It was powerful, he said. His passion for her consumed him, and sometimes he didn't even know what he was doing. He never meant to hurt her.

No one would have understood.

Sawyer squeezed her eyes shut, and Kevin's face, his fervent eyes, flashed in her mind. Then it was Cooper, his hand so gently clutching hers, and her lips burned, guilty.

The only palm in Pacific Palms Park was four feet high and sat at the gated opening to the development. With its abandoned, chipped-paint guard shack and grass that was more yellow than green, it didn't look like much of a park, either. Sawyer veered through the once-white latticework gates and snaked around the neighborhood of prefab houses rooted to cracked concrete. When she pulled up to the Coulter house, Chloe was already outside, pacing the carport.

"Hey," she said when Sawyer pulled her car to a stop. "What took you so long? I thought you were coming straight here."

Sawyer cocked an eyebrow. "Keeping tabs on me now?"

"Yeah, I'm the jealous boyfriend."

Chloe laughed, the comment innocent and flippant to her, but it struck Sawyer. She forced herself to laugh it off. "Are you ready to go?"

"No, and neither are you."

Sawyer looked down at her jeans and black T-shirt ensemble. It wasn't exactly couture, but she thought it would pass for football attire.

"You look nothing like a Fighting Hornet fan."

Sawyer tried to smile; this would be the first football game she would attend since Kevin's death. As it was, Chloe had had to beg Sawyer for ten minutes straight to come to the game. "It's a big one," she reminded her friend, "and you're going to have to go to a football game again sometime."

Though she didn't love the idea of going to the game and was less than enthused about dressing up for it, Chloe was hard to turn down when she was beaming at Sawyer, her enthusiasm boundless—and catching.

"Come on in," Chloe said, "unless you mind slumming in the double-wide a minute."

Sawyer grabbed the screen door behind Chloe. "It's not a double-wide. It's manufactured housing."

"Whatever it is, it comes with wood paneling and Astroturf."

They stepped into the living room—a perfect square of wood paneling and shag carpeting, the smell of a thousand cigarettes ground in. The windows were covered with heavy drapes in a nauseating pattern of swoops and flowers, and the only light was coming from the enormous TV. It took up nearly one whole wall, and Chloe's grandmother was in the chair directly opposite it, a cigarette clamped in the corner of her mouth. Though it was midafternoon, she was still in a housecoat and slippers, and Sawyer knew that the old lady only changed for church or for bingo.

"Hey, Nan, you remember Sawyer." Chloe clapped the back of her grandmother's chair.

"Hi, Mrs. Coulter."

Mrs. Coulter took a long drag of her cigarette, her cheeks hollowing. The glow from the television flashed over her as she sat stiffly on her chair, making no move to answer her granddaughter.

"Come on." Chloe grabbed Sawyer's arm and dragged her toward the back of the house.

"Where are your parents?"

Chloe shrugged. "You mean Stepford Mom and New Daddy? Hell if I know. Let me just get my purse." She grabbed a wide leather bag, stuffed a black sweatshirt into it, and began fiddling with something on the top of her bureau.

Sawyer studied Chloe's wall, plastered with photographs—mostly of the two of them, mugging for the camera, cheering at Hawthorne games. She pointed to one. "What's this one from?" It was a glossy photo of Sawyer in a windbreaker. She was in mid-run, her face contorted with effort, misted with sweat. Her ponytail sailed behind her, and the strain on her face was evident. The shot was so close up that there was very little in the background except a mottled gray blur.

Chloe squinted. "I don't know. One of your million track practices. One of the million times you blew everyone else out of the water." She smiled.

Sawyer squinted. "How'd you get it, though? It's super close. I don't even remember it being taken."

"That's probably because you were running like your life depended on it—you know how you are." She held her forefinger and thumb a quarter inch apart. "Just the tiniest bit competitive. And I don't know when it was taken; it's been on my wall forever."

Sawyer shrugged. "I guess I never noticed it."

Chloe mirrored her shrug. "Guess not. So"—she held up two long green ribbons—"are we ready to root, root, root for the home team?"

"Okay first of all, that's baseball."

"And second of all?"

"Shut up and turn around so I can put this in your hair."

Chloe handed Sawyer her hairbrush, and Sawyer brushed Chloe's short hair into a thin ponytail, wrapping the green ribbon around it. Then they switched places and finished off with some Fighting Hornet temporary tattoos and a set of matching school tees.

"Oh, wow, we need to get going—we're going to miss kickoff!"

Sawyer glanced up at the clock, surprised that she had been at Chloe's house for over an hour. She was even more surprised at the sudden excitement she felt about going to the football game—she had forgotten how good it felt to be the old, school-spirited Sawyer.

"Let's go!"

Chloe pulled her bulging bag over her shoulder and pushed Sawyer out of her room.

"Where are you two off to?" Chloe's mom stopped the girls in the hallway, and Chloe flinched. Chloe and her mother were roughly the same size, but where Chloe's blond hair was thin and fine, her mother's was a constant yellow-orange nest of peroxide and oversleeping. Sawyer knew that Ms. Coulter wasn't particularly old, but her skin had the papery-thin look of a woman much older, her milky blue eyes gave way to crow's-feet, and her lips were constantly wrinkled as she sucked desperately on a Marlboro Light.

"When did you get home?" Chloe asked.

"About a minute ago. Where are you going?"

Chloe flicked the green ribbon on her ponytail. "To the White House, Mom."

Her mother rolled her eyes, and Chloe pushed past her—a bit roughly, Sawyer thought—and beelined for the front door.

"I'll be back in a couple of hours, Nana," Chloe called over her shoulder.

Sawyer noticed that the woman in the chair did nothing

but blink at the television screen as her granddaughter sailed out the front door.

The girls pulled into the Hawthorne High parking lot in record time. Sawyer had managed to hang on to that one surge of excitement by cranking up the radio, her and Chloe singing like tone-deaf maniacs to every car on the highway. But once she killed the engine and saw the lights flooding the football field, her heart started to pound. Chloe noticed the nuanced change in Sawyer and threaded her arm through Sawyer's.

"Don't worry, S. It's going to be okay. And if it's not, we'll leave. Simple as that."

Sawyer wanted to respond, but there were no words. She nodded mutely and let Chloe lead her toward the bleachers.

"Oh look, how truly fabulous. There's Maggie, shaking her pom-poms."

"She's not—oh, you're horrible, Chloe. And totally right."

Maggie had her pom-poms in hand but wasn't lined up on the track with the other cheerleaders. She was bent over the metal railing, batting her eyelashes and shaking her Fighting Hornet to a group of senior guys sitting on the front bench.

"Didn't I tell you this would be a fabulous night?"

Chloe and Sawyer found a spot halfway up the bleachers. The view was obstructed by students randomly getting up to dance or hug a newcomer or shimmying out toward the aisles. Sawyer liked it that way.

The game started late, so the girls were just in time to see the cheerleaders do some sort of memorial cheer to Kevin—Sawyer would never have guessed that pom-poms were a good way to honor the dead—and the football team bow their heads in a group prayer, ending with an all-hands-in explosion of "Number twenty-one!"

Chloe grimaced at Sawyer. "I'm sorry. I didn't realize there would be so much"—she gestured wildly with her hands.

"Don't worry about it," Sawyer said. "I'm sad, but it's not like I'm not reminded of Kevin every day."

Chloe threw her arms around Sawyer and squeezed her, giving her a loud smacking kiss on the cheek. "You're the best."

The game was halfway through the second quarter when Sawyer said, "Hey, I'm going to grab a hot dog. You want?"

Chloe shook her head. "Are you kidding me? With *something* going on out there on the field? I'm seriously riveted to this game right now."

"Something tells me you might be more riveted to Ryan's ass than to the actual game going on."

"Potato, potah-toh." She handed Sawyer a crumpled bill. "Can you get me some Red Vines?"

"Be back in a jiff."

Sawyer picked her way down the bleacher steps, doing her best to avoid an avalanche of Styrofoamy popcorn and pools of sticky soda.

"Hey," she heard when she hit the lowest level.

Sawyer spun, grinning up at Cooper. "Hi. I didn't know you were going to be here."

"What kind of Hornet would I be if I wasn't at the big game?"

"You're just full of school spirit, aren't you, Cooper?"

"Rah, rah. Where you headed?"

Sawyer waved her dollars. "Snack shack."

"Woman after my own heart. Mind if I join you?"

"Sure, but it might cost you."

Cooper raised his eyebrows as he fell in step with Sawyer. "Is that so? Just what do you have in mind, exactly?"

"A Snickers bar."

Cooper's mouth dropped open, even as the edges of his lips turned up. "Oh, so you mean it's going to *cost me*, cost me?"

"Isn't that what I said?"

They reached the order window, and Sawyer placed hers—a hot dog with everything, two Diet Cokes, a pack of Red Vines. And Cooper placed his—a hot dog with everything, a Coke...and a Snickers bar.

"What can I say?" he said with a smile like spun sugar. "You've got some kind of hold over me." He handed her the Snickers bar, his fingers lightly brushing over her palm as he did so. That same tiny electric jolt that Sawyer hoped she would never get used to flashed through her.

"Um, are you here alone?"

Cooper shrugged. "With some of the guys from the track team. But our seats are pretty crap. I might be looking for a spot to move to."

Sawyer wrinkled her nose. "Our seats are pretty crap too."

"That's what I meant," Cooper corrected, "our seats aren't crap enough. Maybe I can sit with you?"

Sawyer laughed, loving the zing of heat that went through her each time Cooper looked at her. It only took one step onto the bleachers, though, for that delicious warmth to be replaced by a gut-wrenching guilt. She slid into her spot next to Chloe, Cooper sandwiching Sawyer.

Chloe blinked at Sawyer. "I only asked for Red Vines."

"Shut up."

Chloe burst out with a laugh that Sawyer thought was a little too loud. She looked from Chloe to Cooper and back again, wondering if perhaps her best friend was a little jealous of Cooper. Sawyer had had a hard time juggling her time between Chloe and Kevin, with Chloe being the one who lost out most often. She said it didn't bother her, but Sawyer knew that it did.

The three watched the game in silence until the buzzer rang and the football team trotted back to the locker room. The cheerleaders danced across the field, shaking their butts to some song with muddled words and a throbbing bass. Just as the song ended, the girls ran around and started to tug on an enormous white canvas.

"Ladies and gentlemen," came across the PA system, "please turn your attention toward the screen being unfurled on the center field. The ASB would like to present a short video in memorial of Kevin Anderson."

Chloe and Sawyer exchanged an eyebrows-up glance, Chloe's full of concern. "Are you okay with this? Or do you want to leave?"

Sawyer worked lightness into her tone. "Are you telling me you're over looking at Ryan's butt?"

Chloe rolled her eyes. "I wasn't looking at Ryan's butt. At least not the whole time. But seriously, we can leave."

Sawyer shook her head, steeling her jaw. "No, I'm okay."

"Promise?"

"Yeah." Sawyer rubbed her palms on her jeans and turned to Cooper. "How was your hot dog?"

"It was everything I've always wanted in a snack, plus nitrates."

The first few bars of music crackled over the PA system, and Sawyer sucked in a deep breath, glancing up at the screen just as one of Kevin's baby pictures flashed nine feet tall in front of her.

There was a pang of hurt, but nothing she couldn't handle. When a shot of a teenaged Kevin in his football uniform flashed, Sawyer felt the hot dog bulging in her stomach, making her nauseous. At least that was what she told herself, not willing to admit to the guilt—and to a slight twinge of fear.

The slideshow continued the whole length of the song, and Sawyer watched, strangely riveted, her emotions rising and crashing with every other picture. As the photos got closer to the end of Kevin's life, Sawyer felt her heart start to pound; she felt sticky and hot underneath her thin Hornets T-shirt. The people in the bleachers seemed to lean in on her, lean closer toward her, leering, staring. Anxiety burst in her chest, tendrils, like needle pricks, racing through her.

"I have to get out of here." She stood up and shimmied past Chloe, past the row of students, and ran down the bleacher stairs, taking them two at a time as she neared the bottom. Once she was at the snack shack, she was in the midst of a full-blown panic attack and she backed into the cool, dark space under the bleachers, doubling over and working to suck in bursts of cold air. Her skin felt too tight, and she felt overwhelmed, guilt, anger, sadness, and panic washing over her in body-racking waves. She didn't even know when she started to cry.

"Sawyer?"

She could barely make out his form in the darkness underneath the bleachers, but she recognized his voice. "Cooper?"

"Yeah. You took off like a shot. I tried to catch you, but you disappeared into the crowd."

"I'm sorry, Cooper, I'm just..." She shook her head, hating the way her words sounded, choked by her tears. "Crazy," she finally whispered.

Cooper carefully picked his way toward her in the darkness. Sawyer felt his fingers first on her wrist, then walking up her arm. His touch gave her goose bumps even though her body was seizing in a panic.

Before she knew it, she was slumped against Cooper,

his arms around her, fingers laced at the small of her back. And she was crying. Huge sobs that left a wet spot on his chest, and Sawyer hiccupping and coughing. She broke their embrace, feeling the immediate cold of Cooper's absence on her chest.

"I'm sorry." She stopped crying, using her fist to push away the tears on her cheeks.

Cooper stepped into her, his arms wrapping around her again, cautious, this time not pulling her close. "Don't be. He was your boyfriend, Sawyer. You loved him. It's okay to be sad."

A tremble, so heavy it made her teeth chatter, started in Sawyer's body, and she began to cry all over again.

I did love Kevin, she thought, *once.* But she hadn't for a long time. Toward the end, he kissed her as often as he slapped her, and a severe hatred had started deep in Sawyer's chest. She wanted to break up with him; she had tried a dozen times, but each time he drew her back in with promises, pleas, and threats.

I'd kill myself if you ever left me, Sawyer, Kevin had said when they laid, bodies intertwined, on the grass. *I could never live without you.* At the time she had found the sentiment passionate and deep and a true statement of their unyielding love. But eventually it became a threat that she found so real it filled her with dread—with guilt. He needed her. Kevin Anderson needed her so much he couldn't live without her.

It made so much sense, then.

The tears stopped abruptly, and this time it was Sawyer who pulled Cooper toward her. She crushed him against her chest, and her lips, chapped from crying, found his. She kissed him hard, with passion and blazing anger for something she had missed. Her lips parted and her tongue slipped into his mouth just as her arms slipped around his neck, clawed at his back. She didn't know why, but she *needed* this. It was almost as if she needed Cooper to wipe the taste—or the memory—of Kevin away.

Cooper groaned when Sawyer leaned into him, her body fitting smoothly into his angles, that burning zinging racing through her bloodstream, firing every synapse in her body. She wanted Cooper Grey.

Her eyes flashed open as her mind started to slow, to clear. That was when she saw the figure under the bleachers with them. It moved slowly, tentative at first, so much so that Sawyer wasn't sure she'd even seen it. She broke her lips from Cooper's and narrowed her eyes. Then Logan stepped into the light.

His face was set hard, his eyes having obviously witnessed the way Sawyer had torn into Cooper—the Sawyer who had told Logan that she just wasn't ready to date.

He blinked at her, and Sawyer thought she saw the light catch, glistening on the moisture on his bottom lashes. He turned to walk away, and Sawyer felt herself consumed with guilt and shame.

"Logan," she called. "Logan!" She stepped away from

Cooper and ran after Logan, but by the time she stepped into the light-flooded mezzanine in front of the snack shack, Logan had disappeared into the hordes of kids lumbering around. "Logan?" Sawyer tried again.

Cooper came up over her left shoulder, wiping his mouth with his hand. His cheeks were flushed, and his eyes looked slightly dazed. "Was that Logan kid watching us?"

Sawyer looked at Cooper, her mouth open. Bathed in the stadium lights, she didn't know what to say. Finally, she shook her head, looked him in the eye, and said, "I'm sorry, Cooper. We really shouldn't have done that."

SIX

There was an electric hum in the air when Sawyer pulled her car into the student lot on Monday morning. Nothing was overtly different; the same cheerleaders were tightening the same bouncy ponytails in rearview mirrors, an impromptu football game had broken out in the back forty, but still something seemed different—alive with an energy that sent Sawyer's hackles up, sent an uncomfortable prickle of fire roaring through her.

Sawyer caught up with Lemon Valour as she beelined toward the brick gym, head bent as her fingers flew over her pink jeweled phone.

"Hey, Lemon, what's going on?"

Lemon looked up, apparently surprised to see Sawyer standing there.

"You didn't hear?"

Sawyer shrugged and Lemon stopped, slipping her phone into her jacket pocket. "It's Mr. Hanson."

Sawyer felt all the breath leave her body; her skin pinched and suddenly felt too tight, too hot.

"Wh—what about Mr. Hanson?" Immediately she felt his feverish, sour breath on her neck, felt his arms tightening around her waist, and she broke out into a full-body cold sweat. "There were police cars parked out front. Were they here for—did he get—"

Lemon nodded and used her index finger to poke at her eyeliner. "Yep. He's dead."

"What?" Sawyer sputtered.

"Dead." Lemon said it so matter-of-factly. Then her cell phone chirped a jaunty, ridiculous ringtone, and she snatched it up, pressed it to her ear. She cut her eyes to Sawyer.

"Nice talking to you, S. GTG. There's grief counselors in the main office if you want to get out of trig."

The click-click-click of Lemon's heels rang out hollow in Sawyer's ears as she stayed rooted to the asphalt in the student parking lot.

Mr. Hanson is dead?

Dead.

The word throbbed in her mind.

***

Sawyer picked her way through the student commons. The final bell hadn't rung yet, so kids still milled around, some red-nosed and breathing into tissues, most looking around, blank-faced and unaffected. She found Chloe sitting on one of the outside tables, legs swinging as she stared off into space, a hard expression on her face.

"Hey, Chloe, what's going on?"

Chloe sniffled, her nose a deep red. "Mr. Hanson is dead."

"Yeah, I heard that. Hey, are you okay? I didn't even know you knew Mr. Hanson. I mean other than the occasional ogle." She tried to chuckle, tried to force some lightness into the conversation.

Chloe remained stone faced. "He is—was—the faculty advisor for honor society last year."

"Hey, how's your forehead? Did your parents say anything?" Sawyer tried to touch Chloe, but the girl shrank away.

"Can you believe they're saying the guy was murdered?"

Sawyer's stomach wobbled and thunked to her knees. "Murdered?"

Chloe sliced her index finger across her neck.

"His throat was cut?"

"Maybe. I've heard that, that his lover's husband came and shot his dick off, that his gay lover shot his dick off, that that weird kid who smelled like feet and corn chips and always wore that black hoodie from last year came back and stabbed him. Oh, and that he slipped and hit his head on a bust of Cesar Chavez." Chloe shuddered. "Anyway, our teacher is dead. That's scary, huh?"

Sawyer swallowed thickly and nodded. Chloe didn't know the half of it.

Principal Chappie sped through the commons at that moment, and Sawyer caught up with him.

"Hey, Principal Chappie—is it true that Mr. Hanson"— Sawyer couldn't say the word, couldn't believe that she had to use the word *died* again in her teen lifetime—"passed away?"

Principal Chappie stopped, a look of practiced sympathy on his lined face. He put a soft hand on Sawyer's arm, his touch so light Sawyer could barely feel it through her sweater.

"Yes, Ms. Dodd, I'm afraid so."

"Well, what happened?"

"I don't think I should—"

"Please." Sawyer could hear the desperation in her own voice. "Please? I think it would help everyone." She waved an arm, indicating her fellow students. "There are all sorts of horrible rumors going around, and I think it would make the student body feel better to know the truth about what happened."

Principal Chappie seemed to consider this, but his jaw remained fixed.

"Otherwise our parents might be concerned. They probably wouldn't want us to be here."

A nervous blushed bloomed on Principal Chappie's cheeks. "Our students aren't in any danger, Ms. Dodd. But I suppose we should let everyone know what happened to allay these rumors. I don't want anyone to get the wrong impression, and I certainly don't want to concern any parents. We'll make a formal announcement."

"So…?" Sawyer raised her eyebrows, and Principal Chappie looked like he was thinking, choosing just the right words.

"It seems that Mr. Hanson died of anaphylaxis."

"Anaphylaxis? Like, an allergic reaction?"

Principal Chappie nodded quickly. "Yes."

"Don't most people who are allergic like that carry EpiPens?"

Mr. Chappie shrugged. "I'm not sure. But he must have consumed something unwittingly that contained peanuts, perhaps in the teachers' lounge. He was very allergic."

Sawyer felt her eyes widen. "So it happened here? At school?"

Principal Chappie dropped his voice. "Unfortunately, yes. That part we'd like to keep under wraps. I don't think the general population needs to know every detail. Can I count on you, Sawyer?"

"Uh, sure, Principal Chappie. I—I won't be saying anything about that."

"As you understand, we'll be canceling this afternoon's track meet and all other student activities this week."

Sawyer nodded mutely, stepping away.

"So?" Chloe hissed, grabbing her arm. "What did you find out?"

"Mr. Hanson died of anaphylaxis."

"What was it? Like a spider bite or bees or something?"

"He was allergic to peanuts."

Chloe's eyebrows went up. "Why would he eat peanuts if he was allergic to them?"

"I don't know. Hey, your mom's allergic to bees, right?"

"Yeah, why?"

"Does she carry an EpiPen?"

Chloe nodded. "All the time. Pack of Marlboros, picture of Tom Hanks, EpiPen."

"Don't you think Mr. Hanson would have had one of those things?"

Chloe shrugged. "Why? A peanut or peanut product must never enter the hallowed halls of Hawthorn. Pretty sure it's on the flag. Or the school charter or something."

"It just seems weird to me that Mr. Hanson wouldn't have had an EpiPen if he was that allergic."

"Maybe he didn't get to it in time. You have to do it like, right away. I know; my mom's doctor made me come in and learn how to do it. When I was six, my mom stumbled in drunk at four a.m. and I stabbed her in the thigh. I thought she got stung."

"In the middle of the night?"

Chloe shrugged. "Anyway, so what are you saying? Someone force-fed Mr. Hanson peanuts?" Sawyer shook her head, and Chloe frowned. "Maybe he had a death wish," she said on a turn.

Ice water rushed through Sawyer's veins and she let out a tiny, involuntary shiver.

Or someone else did, she thought.

Sawyer walked to her first class in a daze, the world moving in a slow motion of blurs and unintelligible sounds. Police officers passed by, and grief counselors ushered students into rooms with the blinds drawn. Sawyer sucked in a quivering breath when she went to her locker, butterflies changing to bat wings inside her stomach. She rolled the combination and steadied herself to find—*What?* She wondered. *Mr. Hanson's head? Another cryptic letter?*

"Grow up, Sawyer," she mumbled under her breath.

She tried to laugh and shrug off the enormous sense of foreboding and gave her locker door a good, hard yank.

All of her books, crumpled papers, and curl-edged photos of her and Kevin poured out onto the hall floor.

"Whoa," Logan said, jumping back. "Avalanche."

Sawyer looked at Logan, flushed, feeling heat and sweat prickle at her hairline. "Sorry about that."

She dove to the ground when Logan did, the two thunking foreheads in the process. Logan rolled back, rubbing his, grinning.

"I'm so sorry," Sawyer said.

"Hey, it's all right. Are you okay?"

Sawyer began stacking her books, nodding maniacally, eyes searching for any hint of mint green. "I'm fine. I'm just really—really—"

Logan reached out and laid a hand on Sawyer's shoulder. It was as delicate and uncertain as his eyes. Sawyer realized she liked them and allowed herself to breathe. "Sorry, I'm just jumpy."

"Yeah, it's not every day someone drops dead on campus."

Sawyer glanced up at Logan. The words sounded odd and rough coming out of his mouth. He glanced back at her, a hint of a smile at the edges of his lips. "I mean, you know."

Sawyer went back to gathering her books. "Yeah, yeah I guess so."

Logan stayed hunched down but was silent for a beat. He licked his lips and said, "Hey, I wanted to thank you again for the ride the other day."

"Don't mention it." Sawyer jammed the last of her books back in her locker and slammed the door shut. "Sorry again, Logan, but I've got to get to class."

"Right." And then, "Oh, wait. Hey, Sawyer—is this yours?"

Sawyer stopped without turning around, her stomach gone leaden. She didn't want to see what Logan was offering her. He stepped in front of her, grin still wide, eyes still soft. He offered Sawyer a songbook. "This is yours, right?"

Relief flooded over her in waves. "Oh. Right."

"Sawyer Dodd?" The voice that came over the PA system was deep and gravelly and bounced off the plethora of sterile metal and linoleum in the hallway. "Sawyer Dodd to the administration office, please."

Sawyer's eyes went up to the overhead speaker.

"Sounds like someone might be in trouble," Logan tried

to joke, but Sawyer couldn't find the humor. He flushed red immediately and looked at the floor. "I'm kidding. I know you're not—you know, the kind of kid who gets in trouble."

"Thanks, Logan. Apparently, I've got to go." Sawyer turned, songbook clutched to her chest, and Logan kept step with her.

"How about I walk you?"

"That's really okay."

"Too late." Logan gestured toward the fall leaves taped to the open door of the administration office. "We're here."

Logan turned and offered Sawyer his awkward salute, and she was left standing in the hallway, watching his back as he headed down the hall.

"Sawyer Dodd to the administration office, please." The overhead speaker squawked again, this time slightly more insistent. Sawyer blew out a sigh and pushed the door open.

The administration office was a cavalcade of students zigzagging through the bright orange half doors that separated the back office from the front. Most of them carried file folders or thick stacks of copy paper while they went about their work study office duties.

Sawyer cleared her throat. "I'm Sawyer Dodd," she said to no one in particular. The girl at the closest desk blinked at her and blew a bubble the size of her head. She sucked it in, eyes still focused on Sawyer. She pressed the black button on the intercom in front of her, and Sawyer could see her wad of gum protruding in her cheek.

"Sawyer Dodd?"

"That's me."

"Oh." The girl looked surprised to see her. "Principal Chappie wants to see you."

"What about?"

The girl shrugged, went back to chewing her gum. She pointed to a bank of chairs lined up in front of Mr. Chappie's closed office door. "You can wait over there, please."

Sawyer hiked up her backpack and did as she was told, sliding her feet out in front of her. She absently studied the toes of her sneakers, then clapped the sides of her big toes together, a pleasing cloud of red clay dust puffing off the soles.

Sawyer looked at her shoes, looked at the fine red powder that now littered the gray, industrial-grade carpet. Her skin started to prickle and she sat up straighter, her left hand slowly reaching out in front of her. Her fingers flicked. She imagined reaching under her bed in the dim, near-dawn light. She remembered her fingers falling over the soft leather of the single metallic flat as she looked for her sneaker. She remembered rolling the hard buds of dirt under her index finger.

Then she remembered the photograph that Detective Biggs had slid across the table to her.

Sawyer's throat constricted. Her tongue darted out to lick paper-dry lips. *How had the shoe—just one shoe—ended up under her bed?*

Her body started to tremble, a slow, painful jitter. *How did the mud get there?*

Sawyer remembered the hollow ring of Detective Biggs's voice when he mentioned that someone might have been there when Kevin was killed. That a woman may have pushed the passenger seat back, gotten one shoe stuck in the mud when she slipped away.

One metallic, mud-covered flat.

Sawyer doubled over and held her head in her hands, her mind racing, trying to go back to that day, trying to go back to the day she had spent the last three weeks desperately trying to block out.

Had she taken a pill? Had she blacked out or blocked it out?

Her breath caught in her throat as her heart tried to hammer its way out of her chest. She shook her head.

No. There was no way. I would have remembered...right?

She felt the wind on her face, the moist, biting sting of the wind as she jogged down the hill, picking up speed as she put precious distance between her and Kevin.

"I was running," Sawyer mumbled. "If I was running, I wasn't wearing flats."

She thought back, clamping her eyes shut, trying to remember the way it felt each time her foot hit the ground. Before a track meet she would pinch her eyes closed and concentrate on the feeling of her feet falling in perfect quick-time rhythm, hitting the red clay of the track just softly enough to propel her forward one more step.

How did her foot feel?

"Ms. Dodd?" Principal Chappie poked his head out of his office, his voice shaking Sawyer out of her revelry. She sighed as her mind failed to grasp the image of her leaving that night.

"I'm right here," Sawyer said, standing up slowly.

Principal Chappie stood aside and ushered Sawyer down the hall. He pushed open the door and she followed him in.

"Sawyer," Principal Chappie said, arm extended. "This is Ms. Alum, the grief counselor."

Sawyer swallowed hard, looking from Principal Chappie to the tiny, dark-haired grief counselor who couldn't have been more than five years older than she was. She had heavy black lashes over wide, eager, brown eyes and a pin-tucked charcoal suit that was all at once businesslike and sexy.

"I don't need to see a grief counselor, Principal Chappie. Sorry, Ms. Alum. They already make me see a psychologist twice a week. I'm really kind of grief-counseled out." Sawyer hiked her backpack up her shoulder and turned to go, but was stopped when she came chest to tweed-coated chest with a mustached man, his stubby fingers clutching a black leather notebook.

"And this is Detective Biggs."

Sawyer's breath hitched. "Oh."

Heat washed over her cheeks and Sawyer fought to stay cool, thinking that the detective could somehow sense her guilt, her confusion over the night, over the muddied shoe underneath her bed.

"Hello, Sawyer."

Sawyer forced her muscles to move and felt her head bob in a semblance of a nod.

Detective Biggs offered a smile that wasn't really a smile, his teeth a faded, nicotine yellow. "I'm sorry we have to meet again this way. Under these kind of circumstances."

"Yeah," Sawyer said, licking her bottom lip as her pulse started to speed. Up until Kevin's death, she had never even seen a detective that wasn't on television. Now, she seemed to have her own personal one.

Detective Biggs stared at her, and Sawyer felt the insane urge to bolt. She didn't want any of this to be happening. She wanted to be normal again, to be staring at the clock in biology class, deciding which dress to wear to prom.

"Can you take a seat, please, Ms. Dodd?" Principal Chappie's voice was kind.

Sawyer took a small step back, the detective's eyes still on her. His face broke into what passed as a smile for detectives, Sawyer guessed. "There's nothing to be afraid of, Sawyer."

Sawyer didn't like the way the detective used her name when he spoke to her, holding it in his mouth and then pressing out the syllables. Sawyer sank into a chair opposite Ms. Alum, and Detective Biggs sat down next her, pulling out the same leather notebook he'd had at Sawyer's house. Sawyer vaguely wondered if he bought them by the case. "This is just some routine questioning, you understand."

Sawyer looked at the ring of faces around her: Ms. Alum's was pretty but pinched with an attempt to look both serious and sympathetic; Principal Chappie's lips were pressed together and he kept rubbing his thumb over the face of his watch, his impatience evident; and Detective Biggs looked as though he'd just waddled out of a cop show with a few crumbs of powdered sugar at the edge of his mouth, his caterpillar eyebrows sharp Vs.

"Routine questions about what?" Sawyer wasn't sure she'd actually asked the question. The voice that came out was subdued and strange, and though she couldn't understand why, she felt herself flush, felt her knees weaken and the all-too-familiar salivating that came before vomiting.

"Oh God. I'm sorry, but I think I'm going to be sick."

Ms. Alum patted Sawyer's back soothingly. "Shall I take you to the ladies' room?"

Sawyer shook her head, and Detective Biggs pushed a Styrofoam cup of water into her hands. She took a small sip, her eyes flashing behind the cup.

"I think I'm okay," she said finally.

Seated there in the school conference room, Sawyer worked the rim of a Styrofoam water cup with her fingernails for a full minute. No one said anything. Finally, Ms. Alum broke the silence. "Are you feeling better?"

Sawyer nodded.

"It's perfectly normal to have visceral reactions to emotionally charged situations."

Sawyer nodded again, letting Ms. Alum's textbook conversation drift over her. "There's just been a lot going on."

"You mean because of Kevin."

It had become the stock answer and Sawyer gave the stock response: a mute nod followed by a watery-eyed stare—a brokenhearted teenager mourning the death of her first love.

Ms. Alum reached out her hand as if she wanted to pat Sawyer's, but she thought better of it, or remembered the litigious nature of school parents, and folded her hands in her lap. "Do you want to talk about him?"

"No."

"Then how about Mr. Hanson?"

Sawyer swallowed heavily, feeling the need to vomit again. "Why are you asking me about him?"

"We're asking everyone. I understand that Mr. Hanson was a popular teacher among the junior class. You had him for Spanish sixth period, is that right?"

"Yes."

"His death must come as quite a shock and especially to you, after what happened."

Sawyer felt her jaw tighten. "You mean because my boyfriend died? Because I'm fragile and they make me take drugs?"

Redness bloomed in Ms. Alum's cheeks. "No, that's not it. And antidepressants are nothing to be ashamed of, Sawyer. They're medicine for an illness that you have. You'll get better."

She batted her big eyes, and Sawyer felt slightly sorry for the curt way she bit off her words.

"I'm just here in case you want to talk, to share any feelings of unfinished business or if you want to talk about how you are feeling."

Sawyer pinched a piece of Styrofoam from her cup. "I feel fine."

"Okay," Ms. Alum said slowly, "then you won't mind answering a few questions for Detective Biggs."

"Wait, what? Why do I need to answer more questions?" Sawyer spun around in her chair to focus on Detective Biggs, trusty notebook still poised in one hand, pen in the other.

"Again, I'm sorry we have to meet again this way. I'll try my best to make it quick and painless."

"Are you allowed to do this?" Sawyer asked, suddenly nervous, gripping the armrests of the cheap leather chair she sat in.

"Principal Chappie got the okay from your parents."

"From my parents? My mother is an attorney. There is no way she'd let you question me especially when I don't know anything—anything about Mr. Hanson." She began gathering her backpack. "I need to get back to class."

Detective Biggs pushed the end of his pen against Sawyer's arm. "Your mother was at home when we called."

"No, she—Tara? You mean Tara. You talked to Tara, my stepmother. She can't—she can't say what I should do." Sawyer felt her words trailing off. "She doesn't know what I can do."

"Your father called back and agreed. I spoke to him personally. Is there a reason you don't want to talk to me today, Sawyer?" Detective Biggs's deflated balloon cheeks pressed up into a weird smile. "You're not in any trouble. We're just trying to get a clear picture of what happened in the hours before Mr. Hanson's death."

Sawyer pulled her sleeves down over her hands, fisted them. "Then why are you asking me?"

"Mr. Hanson had his grade book open to your file. It looked like he was making notes. Did you talk to him about that?"

Sawyer just shook her head, staring at the sweater wrapped over her knuckles.

"Did you see Mr. Hanson after school, Sawyer?"

Sawyer felt the same prickle of disgust crawl up the back of her neck. "Yeah. Just for some"—she paused, sucked in a steadying breath—"just for some homework help."

"About what time was that?"

Sawyer shrugged. "Two, almost three o'clock, I guess."

"And can you tell us what transpired when you saw Mr. Hanson for homework help?"

"What transpired?"

"What happened, Sawyer?"

Sawyer tucked her knees to her chest. "Nothing. He gave me my test. I got a bad grade. He told me how I could improve it."

"And how was that?"

Sawyer bit her lip. "Um, extra credit."

"Extra homework, worksheets, stuff like that?"

Sawyer nodded. "Uh-huh. Stuff like that."

"And how was Mr. Hanson when you left him?"

Lecherous, Sawyer wanted to reply, *blue-balled.* Instead, she just shrugged. "Fine, I guess."

"No signs of respiratory distress?"

Sawyer wagged her head, bit her thumbnail. "No."

Detective Biggs wrote something on his notepad, tapped the end of his pen against it as if considering his next question carefully. "Was he eating anything? Did he have any food on his desk that you could see? Did he offer you anything to eat?"

"No. Nothing that I could see," Sawyer said. "And he was fine when I left."

Biggs puckered his lips. "And you didn't give him anything? A snack, a cookie or—"

Sawyer felt herself gape as terror seized her heart. "You think I did this?"

"No, no," Ms. Alum broke in.

"We're just trying to get a clear picture of—"

"Of what *transpired,* I know. But I didn't do anything. I didn't force-feed him peanuts or anything. Is that what you think?"

"We know that you wouldn't do anything deliberate like that. But just so I know, how did you know it was peanuts Mr. Hanson consumed?"

Sawyer's mouth fell open. "I—Principal Chappie told me."

Principal Chappie's eyes widened, pinning Sawyer. "But everyone knew it," Sawyer backpedaled, "everyone knew that was what Mr. Hanson was allergic to. He had a no-peanut sign up in his classroom."

"A no-peanut sign?" Detective Biggs asked.

"You know, like, Mr. Peanut with a red slash across him." Sawyer made the sign of a circle and a slash with her hands, then felt immediately ridiculous doing so. "Everyone knew," she finished softly.

"That's fine, Sawyer, thanks. Now, after you met with Mr. Hanson, did you drive home right after school?"

"No. I mean, yes. I took a kid home. I dropped him off and then, yes, I went home too."

Detective Biggs pressed his lips into a thin, hard line and read over his notes, which Sawyer guessed must have been a series of no's and nothing else. "Okay, well, that's all I need from you."

Relief washed over Sawyer. "That's it?"

"Yeah." Detective Biggs's grin was kind, almost fatherly. "Unless there's something you want to admit to." He chuckled, the buttons on his shirt vibrating.

Sawyer pushed back in her chair. "No, thanks."

As she wound her way out of the conference room and through the administrative office, Sawyer breathed deeply, peeling her suddenly damp T-shirt from her back. Her heart rate had just slipped back to normal when she heard someone calling out to her.

"Oh, Sawyer! I was about to send a note to you." Mrs. Cambert, school secretary, from the top of her silvery bun to the bottom of her sensible shoes, smiled up at Sawyer. She slid an enormous bushel of blooms toward Sawyer. "These came for you."

Sawyer blinked at the velvety red roses, blooms as big as fists interspersed with sprays of eucalyptus and tiny budding baby's breath. She felt the smile press across her face. "These are for me?"

Mrs. Cambert plucked a small white envelope from the foliage and pressed it into Sawyer's hand. "That's your name, isn't it?"

Sawyer nodded at her name typed across the front. "Sure is." Sawyer snaked one arm around the glass vase and clutched it against her hip, still smiling. "Thanks so much, Mrs. Cambert." She stepped into the hall and rested the vase on the edge of the water fountain, sliding a finger under the envelope's seal.

She took one look at the enclosed mint green card and sucked in a sharp whoosh of ice-tinged air.

Sawyer—
    You know I'd do anything for you.

It wasn't the message that scared Sawyer so much—it was the curled piece of plastic that slid out with the card. With fingers shaking, she unfurled the thin label.

"Arachis oil?" she mumbled to herself. "What the heck is—" Sawyer's heart stopped when she read on: *100% Cold-Pressed Gourmet Peanut Oil.* A black circle was drawn in Sharpie around something in the bottom corner. It was flanked by a hand-drawn smiley face. Sawyer squinted.

Caution: allergen.

SEVEN

The tremble that started at Sawyer's fingertips spread through her entire body until her teeth were chattering and her bones, it seemed, clattered against each other. Her throat closed to the size of a pinhole, and she struggled to breathe, feeling the blood rush to her head in a thunderous pounding that brought tears to her eyes.

Is this what it's like to suffocate?

She clamped her eyes shut and tried to focus on bringing her sensibilities back under control.

Is this what it was like for Mr. Hanson?

Vaguely, she felt the vase slip from her fingers, heard the echo of glass shattering on the floor, the water pooling at her feet. The roses scattered, bloodred petals scarred with shards of glass, cut, torn, turning in on themselves.

"Ms. Dodd?" Sawyer heard from a thousand miles away. "Ms. Dodd?"

She felt the slight weight of a hand on her shoulder, felt her eyes try to focus on the figure before her. She worked to move her mouth, her body, but all she could do was ball the peanut oil label up in her fist, the telltale crinkle of the cellophane screaming for everyone to look at her, to look at the girl who could cause a man to die.

"Can we get the nurse in here?" Detective Biggs was yelling over his shoulder, his hand firm now, holding Sawyer up.

"I'm okay," she finally forced her mouth to say. "I'm okay. I just slipped and—"

The school nurse rushed out next, a pin of a woman who doubled as a lunch lady and a part-time librarian. Her lips were pursed, her eyes slanted in that sympathetic way, the pink sweater buttoned over her shoulders flying like bat wings.

"Oh, Sawyer." She looked at Sawyer and then at Detective Biggs. "She's had a rough couple of weeks. Shall I call your father, hon?"

Sawyer stepped back, sliding out of Detective Biggs's reach, her sneakers crunching on the broken glass. She licked her Sahara-dry lips and nodded. "Yes, please. I think I need to go home and lie down."

Nurse Tucker slid a motherly arm across Sawyer's shoulders and pressed her hand against Sawyer's cheek. Her fingers were soft and cool, and Sawyer longed for comfort, for her own mother. "This must be too much for you. First Kevin, and now Mr. Hanson," she clucked, tucking Sawyer's head underneath her chin. Then, she dropped her voice into a totally audible whisper, her chin jutting toward Detective Biggs. "Her boyfriend was Kevin Anderson, you know. The one who died in the accident. It was so tragic."

Sawyer didn't have to look to know that the detective nodded knowingly. For the last three weeks, people had exchanged glances whenever Sawyer was around, glances that spoke volumes, glances that reminded Sawyer that she was now and forever would be attached to Kevin's death— more so than she ever was to his life. A lump strangled what breath was left in Sawyer's throat and she doubled over, coughing and heaving.

"Oh, honey!"

"No." Sawyer wagged her head, using her fisted hand, peanut oil wrapper locked inside, to wipe her eyes, her nose. "Can you just let my dad know that I've been excused? I need to go home right now."

"I don't think you're in any condition to drive, Sawyer. I'd be happy to run you home," Detective Biggs said.

"But I have my car."

Nurse Tucker made a dismissive motion with her hand, her mob of tiny bangles clinking as she did. "The detective is right. You shouldn't be driving. You can lie down in my office for a while to calm down if you'd like."

Sawyer looked from Nurse Tucker to Detective Biggs, the

array of shattered glass and broken roses on the floor behind him. "I think I'd like to go home now, please."

Detective Biggs kept silent as they left the administration building and walked out to the parking lot. Sawyer was grateful for the silence; every time the detective sucked in a breath and looked like he was about to speak to her, her skin tightened, every muscle in her body seemed to collapse in on itself and she had to look away. Biggs seemed to get the message and repeatedly just cleared his throat.

He gestured toward his car, and Sawyer stood at the passenger side door, hands hugging her elbows, until he clicked the lock.

Detective Biggs drove a big, gray, unmarked cop car that smelled like cigarettes and McDonald's. Sawyer wrinkled her nose when she got in.

"Sorry," Detective Biggs said, a hint of sympathy in his voice, "my partner is a smoker."

Biggs cleared the passenger seat of a stack of coffee-stained files and crumpled fast food wrappers and Sawyer sat down, her body stiff, her hands clutching the straps of her backpack.

They pulled out of the school driveway and onto the street when the rain started to fall. Heavy droplets thunked against the hood of the car. Sawyer liked the sound, thought it was soothing. She liked the way the rain marred the windshield before the wipers took it away. If she squinted, she could pretend they were somewhere else, that she was some*one* else.

"I hate the rain," Detective Biggs said.

"Take the Old Oak highway, please."

"Oh, right." The detective nodded, puckering his lips as if considering something. "So, I guess Kevin was pretty popular at school."

Sawyer hiked her backpack onto her lap and wrapped her arms around it, her hands disappearing in the long sleeves of her sweater. "Uh-huh."

"Done much unpacking?"

Sawyer looked at the detective, but he didn't look at her. His eyes were focused hard out the windshield, guiding the hulking car over the slick black highway.

"Not really." She vaguely wondered if he knew about the shoes—maybe he had a spy or a bug or something. She tightened her grip on her pack. "Not since you were there."

"Tragic about what happened with Kevin. I really hate to see something like that."

Sawyer nodded, replaying the rest of the conversation in her mind. It was the same one every time an adult tried to talk to her: Tragic about what happened. Such a waste. Just goes to show you that nothing in life is guaranteed; we're all mortal.

"Kevin much of a drinker?"

Sawyer blinked. "What?"

"It was a drunk-driving accident, right? Was Kevin a drinker?"

Sawyer shook her head, feeling her ponytail tag the side

of her cheeks. "No, not really." She began to wonder why none of these questions had come up the day Detective Biggs appeared at her house.

"But he was definitely drinking that night," Biggs said matter-of-factly.

She remembered that night. It was raining then, too, big quarter-sized drops that pelted her forehead, that made the fresh cut under her eye sting. She felt the pain of that cut again, remembered the way Kevin's eyes looked when he noticed the blood. He studied the dime-sized drop that clung to his class ring. He didn't look at the red velvet drop that bubbled under Sawyer's eye.

Sawyer remembered seeing Kevin's face, and it was blurry, soaked. She watched him roll up on the balls of his feet, saw his fingers curl, one by one in molasses slow motion until they were fisted. Sawyer felt her body instinctively recoil, start to flinch.

A flash of something flitted through his eyes at that moment. It was almost—joy. Amusement. He made a fist, her body instinctively flinched, and he liked that. As if he enjoyed the fear he'd cultivated in her. Anger, harder than fear, roiled through her body. He always let her believe it was her fault.

Not tonight.

Kevin's fingers were still wrapped in that tight ball. He wouldn't raise that fist to her, but he gritted his teeth, his eyes narrowed and spitting a kind of wicked anger she had come to recognize.

"*Leave me alone, Kevin.*" *She heard her own voice and it rang out loud, clear, and strong through the rain that night.* "*I'm done with you.*"

As she sat in the car she searched her memory for the quaver that must have been in her voice, for the shrinking fear she knew she must have felt. *She turned around and Kevin reached for her, clamping a hand on her wrist. He squeezed, digging his fingernails into her flesh. She wouldn't wince. She wouldn't cry out.*

"*Don't you dare run away from me,*" *he spat.*

She shrugged him off violently. "*I said leave me alone.*"

He gave her a hard shove, but Sawyer kept her ground.

"*Screw you, then!*" *he yelled to her back.* "*I don't need you. I made you. No one knew who the hell you were until you started dating me, you little slut.*"

Sawyer still felt the sting of those words as she clenched her jaw and hugged her backpack a little tighter, feeling the sharp edges of her books dig into her chest.

She heard the plink! *and spritz of a beer being opened, then felt the whiz of the bottle as it soared past her left ear, leaving a spray of cold beer soaking her shoulder, dribbling down the naked skin on her throat and collar bone.*

"*I'm so done with you,*" *she said, surprised at the calm finality in her voice.*

Kevin shrugged and took a pull on the beer he was holding. "*Then what the hell are you still doing here?*"

She felt the adrenaline in her legs even now as she

remembered her slow jog away from Kevin, his beer bottles, and his car. *The rain had started to let up, and she could hear the crinkle of leaves and twigs underfoot as she ran. She picked up speed and her hood slipped back. What remained of the drizzling, spitting rain rushed into her eyes, beer mixed with rain, and Sawyer kept running, kept going even when she heard Kevin's tortured voice on the wind. "Sawyer!" he was yelling. "Sawyer, stop!"*

"You're way out there, aren't you?"

"What?"

Detective Biggs jabbed a finger toward the rain-drenched windshield. "The housing development. It's way out there, huh? I guess I didn't realize it when we came out before."

"We?"

"Officer Haas and me. He didn't come in. He was handling some paperwork in the car."

Sawyer remembered the fluorescent glow of Officer Haas's cigarette as he lifted it to his lips when Sawyer drove up to her house.

"Oh."

She paused, listened to her heart thrum out a metered beat. "Um." Sawyer's fingers started working the woven strap again on her backpack. "Detective Biggs? If someone—if something happened to someone and you—I mean, if I were to have…" Sawyer let her words trail off when the detective turned and smiled at her.

"Take a deep breath and start again."

"I think I'm the reason why Kevin is dead."

The words came out in a single, breathless string, and the second they were out, Sawyer desperately wished she could suck them back in. She stared straight ahead, eyes focused on the white dashes of the roadway, not daring to look at Detective Biggs.

"Were you in the car with Kevin?"

"No."

Detective Biggs rubbed a big hand over his bald head, keeping one hand resting on the top of the steering wheel. He didn't look at Sawyer. "Do you know where Kevin got the alcohol?"

Sawyer shook her head. "Not really. Sometimes he'd just take it from the fridge."

"But you didn't supply him with it."

"No, sir. But I—I may have been the reason he was drinking."

Detective Biggs put his other hand on the wheel, smoothly guiding the cruiser through the heavy iron gates of Blackwood Hills Estates. "Did you force him to drink the alcohol?"

"We were fighting. He was mad at me. I think that's why he was drinking." She licked her lips. "I'm sure that was why."

A half smile cut across the detective's face. "You didn't force Kevin to get behind the wheel, Sawyer. You didn't force him to drink and drive." He looked at her, all amusement gone from his face. "That was his decision."

Sawyer continued working the strap, her fingertips feeling raw from the course fabric. She wondered if she should mention the notes, mention the *other* reason she felt responsible for Kevin's—*and now Mr. Hanson's?*—death. She thought about the crumpled peanut oil wrapper stuffed in her jeans pocket, thought of the fact that regardless of what Detective Biggs said, if Sawyer hadn't broken up with Kevin that night, he wouldn't have been drinking, he wouldn't have gotten behind the wheel of his car. He wouldn't have died.

"I didn't force anyone to do anything," she mumbled.

───────

Sawyer's cell phone started blaring the Notre Dame fight song the second she stepped through her front door.

"Hi, Dad," she said into the phone. "I just walked in the door."

"The school nurse called me. How are you feeling?"

Sawyer shimmied out of her jacket, dumped her backpack on the floor. "Better now."

Her dad was silent for a beat and Sawyer imagined him on the other end, reclined in his black leather chair, fingers steepled as he wrestled with his thoughts. Sawyer sighed.

"What is it?"

"You know, Sawyer, you only saw Dr. Johnson that one time after Kevin's death—"

Sawyer felt a red-hot coil of anger low in her belly. "But

I saw him every week of your and Mom's divorce. And every week of your trial separation."

"I know, hon, but this is different. He really helped you, right? Maybe you should consider..." He let his words trail off, and Sawyer cradled her cell phone against her shoulder, arms crossed in front of her chest.

"Maybe you should consider that I didn't sleep well last night." She pulled aside the front curtain, her eyes sweeping the bare street, the ominous-looking bones of the half-built houses surrounding her. "It's impossible to sleep out here. It's so damn *quiet*."

"Language, Sawyer."

Sawyer rolled her eyes and let the curtain drop back over the plateglass window. "It's darn quiet, Dad."

"Your mother and I just think it would be a good idea for you to check in with the doctor."

"You talked to Mom about this? When did you talk to her?"

"We worry about you, Sawyer."

"So, if I see Dr. Johnson and let him know that it's too—" she paused, sucked in a sharp breath "—*darn* quiet around here and that I got a headache today from lack of sleep, you and Mom will drop this?"

She heard her father draw in a steady breath. "We just want to do what's best for you. You've been through a terrible tragedy."

Sawyer mouthed the words "terrible tragedy" as her

father said them and rubbed her eyes. "Fine. I'll make an appointment later. I just want to take a bath and go to bed right now, okay?"

"That sounds good. Tara and I have a birthing class, so we're going to be home late. We could always postpone, though, if you want us to be home with you."

"You can't postpone a birthing class. You're kind of on a time crunch with that one. I'll be fine, Dad. Like I said, bath and bed just sounds really good to me right now."

"Okay, honey. I'll call you again before we head out. Love you."

"Love you too."

Sawyer clicked her phone shut and tossed it onto the couch, sinking down next to it. She rested her head on the stiff, new pillows Tara had picked out—some weird hemp weave stuffed with something hypoallergenic and renewable—and spied a mammoth spray of baby-pink roses on the kitchen counter.

Baby *girl* pink roses.

She groaned, snatched up her backpack and coat, and plodded to her bedroom. Sawyer had the water running in her attached bathroom (a perk of the new house), when she opened her laptop and dialed up her mom.

"Hi, Mom."

The face that smiled back at Sawyer from her thirteen-inch screen mirrored her own: deep brown eyes, high cheekbones, a determined nose, but her mother's face had a tiredness that tugged at Sawyer's heart. Angela Dodd's hair had always been a few shades darker than Sawyer's, something that gave her a hard, no-nonsense edge in the courtroom; now Sawyer noticed the fringe of gray around the temples. It softened her.

"Sweetheart! I only have a minute to talk—I'm between clients—but I'm glad you called."

Sawyer glanced at the clock on her screen. "Isn't it almost time to knock off?"

Her mother smiled apologetically. "There is no quitting time around here. We've got a huge trial coming up." Angela leaned toward the screen, studying her daughter. "You look good. Healthy. How are you?"

Sawyer cocked her head, rubbing small circles on her temples with her index fingers. "Seriously, Mom, please don't fall into shrink mode."

Her mother's eyebrows went up, and Sawyer watched her pick up a carton of Chinese takeout and dig into it with a pair of chopsticks. "Shrink mode?"

"You know." Sawyer dropped her voice into a high-pitched, saccharine-sweet tone that dripped with insincerity. "How are *you* doing? How does that make *you* feel?"

"Can't a mother worry about her daughter?"

Not from 3,000 miles away. The thought bounced around Sawyer's mind before she had a chance to stop it, and it left a pang of guilt—and pain—niggling at her heart.

The divorce hadn't even been finalized when Angela Dodd packed up her closet and her office and moved to

Philadelphia. The offer—senior partner at one of the top law firms in the country—was epic; at least that was what she told Sawyer. It didn't come as a complete surprise to Sawyer, nor did it seem all that different. Her entire childhood her mother would generally pepper her head with kisses as she walked out the door each morning, Sawyer with a bowl of cold cereal in hand and cartoons on the television. Angela usually had a cell phone pressed to her ear as she mouthed for Sawyer to "be good" and "listen to Daddy." By the time she'd come home at night, hair mussed, briefcase groaning with unfinished briefs, Sawyer would be in bed.

It wasn't that she was a bad mom. Angela Dodd taught her daughter to be strong and self-sufficient; she was nurturing and doted on Sawyer—when she was around—but Sawyer always got the distinct impression that her mother's career, not her husband or her daughter, was her first love.

Sawyer swallowed hard, another memory of Kevin flashing in her mind.

They were stretched out on the living room floor, "studying." Not a single book was cracked, but Sawyer's lips were chapped and the feel of Kevin's lips on hers, his fingers on her bare skin, made her whole body buzz. He pulled away, a sly smile on his face, and brushed a thumb over her bottom lip.

"I should probably get going. Your parents are going to be home soon."

She looked into his eyes; the twilight breaking through the blinds seemed to make them glitter and shine. She shrugged. "No one will be home for hours."

Kevin wagged his head, his eyes still locked on hers. "I don't see how your parents could leave you alone for a minute, let alone whole days at a time." His hand dipped to her collarbone, tracing the curve there until Sawyer's whole body erupted in gooseflesh. "I can barely get through two periods without seeing you."

She didn't know why, but the idea that Kevin wanted her near him—that he needed to see her—was the most incredible feeling to Sawyer. Her parents had their jobs, their crumbled marriage, but to Kevin, Sawyer was all there was.

"I love you so much, Kevin."

Sawyer shook off the memory, hammering down the disgusting need that sprang up. "I'm fine, Mom. Dad didn't need to call you."

Angela feigned innocence, and Sawyer shook her head. "Cut out the Meryl Streep. He told me he called you."

"We talk, Sawyer. And we worry. Besides, Dad told me that one of your teachers passed away. I'm really sorry to hear that."

Sawyer gripped her bedspread, pressing the puckered fabric between forefinger and thumb so hard her finger went numb. "It was an accident," she said, her voice a hollow whisper. "He had an allergic reaction to something he ate."

Or was fed.

Angela cocked her head, her eyebrows pressing together.

"That's terrible, sweetie. Is there going to be some sort of memorial? Did they cancel classes or anything?"

"Look, can you just tell Dad that you talked to me and I'm okay?"

Sawyer's mother opened her mouth—to protest, Sawyer guessed—but Sawyer held up a hand. "I'm going to make an appointment to see Dr. Johnson, who will also tell you that I'm fine. But please, until then? I'm fine. I'm adjusting. I have friends and eat vegetables and don't cut myself. And"—Sawyer pointed a silencing finger—"I'm not selling myself for drugs or sex or Beanie Babies."

"Beanie Babies?" Sawyer's mother shoveled some chow mein into her mouth and grinned, chewing steadily. "How do you even know what those old things are?"

"I pay attention in history class. Do we have a deal?"

There was a shrug on the other end of the line. "You certainly seem like the old Sawyer."

Sawyer squinted at the screen. "What are you eating? Did you make your famous call to the Chinese restaurant tonight?"

Angela jabbed at her screen with her chopsticks. "Now I know you're the old Sawyer. And the deal is you only have to eat vegetables until you're eighteen. Then you're a legal adult and can fill up on takeout and Red Bull like the rest of us."

"Oh, the joys of adulthood. So, vegetables, yes, cutting, no, et cetera. Do we have a deal?"

"About vegetables? We made that deal when you were ten."

"Mom." Sawyer felt her nostrils flare, even though deep down her mother's razzing felt familiar and comforting. Almost like things were normal.

"Okay, okay. But I want you to check in every day, and I want to hear how your appointment goes."

Sawyer crossed her arms in front of her chest. "Doctor-patient confidentiality, prosecutor."

Angela smiled. "That's my smart kid. Oh." There was an off-screen tone and Sawyer's mom leaned toward it. "That's my next client. Love you, baby, be good. I'll talk to you soon."

"Bye." Sawyer's screen went blank and she sighed, closing her laptop. "Bye, Mom, love you too."

Sawyer sunk chin deep in strawberry-kiwi-scented suds and blew bubbles, then rubbed her eyes. The house settled—*even new houses did that*, Sawyer assured herself—with a spine-tingling creak, then dropped into steady silence. Sawyer groaned, leaning her head against the cool marble slope of the tub.

"Note to self," she said out loud, her voice reverberating through the sterile, tiled room, "unpack stereo ASAP."

The bathroom was still, the tub water unmoving. Sawyer breathed in and out in long, supposedly calming breaths until there was a soft thump against the front door. Sawyer shifted in the tub, cocking her head to listen; when no sound responded, she cupped her hands and dug into the hot tub water, dripping it over her head.

There was another thump.

Sawyer stiffened, her heart and her mind racing. *Probably just a branch*, she told herself, *or a bush*. Sawyer was able to comfort herself with that thought for a breath before she realized that there were no branches or bushes outside—just a desolate wasteland of spray-painted outlines of someday-grass and orange-topped landscape flags.

Despite the hot water, Sawyer felt a chill that covered her skin with gooseflesh. She stood up, snatched her robe from the hook by the door, and slipped into it. Her wet feet left damp imprints on the heavy pile carpet as she stepped out of the bathroom, tiptoeing to the landing, her breathing shallow and forced.

"Hello?"

There was no answer.

Sawyer leaned over the staircase, her fingers wrapping tightly around the banister. She swallowed. "Dad? Tara?"

The silence of the house pressed against Sawyer's chest and her stomach played the accordion while her breath hitched in a throaty rasp. She silently prayed for the comforting noises of a populated neighborhood—car alarms, children shrieking, a thumping car stereo bass.

But there was nothing but the silence.

Had Sawyer been wearing pants she might have peed them when she heard the knock on the front door. It was determined, insistent, loud. The hollow sound bounced off the house's high ceilings and half-furnished rooms. She ran downstairs and pressed her eye to the door's peephole, her heart thundering against her chest the whole time. Finally she sighed—a great, bone-jellying sigh—when she saw the dirt-brown uniform of an annoyed UPS guy, his head enormous and distorted through Sawyer's fish-eye peephole.

"Yes?" she called through the still-closed door.

She watched the UPS guy check his handheld device. "Tara Dodd?" he asked the door as he gestured to the package he held.

Sawyer yanked the door open, tightening the belt on her robe as she did so.

"Sure," she said. "Sorry about that. It's just—" She shrugged.

The UPS man offered an easy smile. "I get it. Pretty freaky around here with all them empty houses."

You don't know the half of it, Sawyer thought. Instead, she reflected the man's smile and said, "Totally."

He looked over his shoulders. "You the only one who lives here?"

Sawyer quirked an eyebrow, half nervous, half fearful. "Um, no. My dad. And brother. Big...brother. And we have a dog." She vaguely considered appropriating a growl or yelling, "Stand down, Chomper!" over her shoulder into the empty house.

"No, I meant up here." He waved his one free arm. "It's just, I've never delivered anything out here before."

"Oh." Sawyer swallowed. "There's people," she said vaguely, pushing more of her body behind the door. "Tons of people. They probably, you know, use FedEx or something." She held out a hand, her eyes gesturing toward the box. "Can I?"

"Oh, right. Sorry." He gave her an embarrassed once-over, took her signature, and pressed the package into her hands. Sawyer shut the door and leaned against it, breathing heavily until her heartbeat returned to a normal, nonlethal pace.

Maybe a dog named Chomper wouldn't be such a bad idea, she thought to herself.

EIGHT

Sawyer blinked in the sunlight as the morning show DJs cackled on her nightstand. She slapped the alarm off and sat up in bed, rubbing her eyes and finally focusing on the spray of baby pink roses on her bureau. They were the same ones from the table downstairs, and Sawyer frowned as she passed them and stepped into the bathroom to get ready for school. When she headed downstairs, Tara was seated at the kitchen table, yesterday's UPS box splayed open in front of her, packing peanuts surrounding her plate of half-nibbled dry toast.

"Morning, Tara."

Tara pushed her plate aside, wiping toast crumbs from her swollen belly. "Good morning, Sawyer. Are you feeling any better? You were dead to the world by the time we got home last night."

Dead to the world?

Sawyer grimaced but tried to hide it with a friendly smile. She nodded. "Yeah, I'm feeling way better. How about you?"

Tara groaned, resting her head in her hands. "Is it that obvious?"

"A little. You don't usually look so…green." Sawyer felt bad immediately when she saw the blush wash over Tara's cheeks. "Sorry. Is—is there anything I can do for you?"

"Short of delivering this baby, I don't think so." She began the mammoth job of pushing herself up from her chair. "How about I get you some oatmeal, hon?"

Sawyer felt herself bristle involuntarily. Only her parents—her *real* parents—called her "hon."

"No, thanks."

Tara's face fell now that she was standing. "Nothing?"

"I'm okay. You should sit down. Oh, and you didn't need to bring the flowers to my room. They're nice, but you should be the one to enjoy them."

Tara pulled a cup from the cupboard, poured herself a glass of water. "Why? They're yours."

Sawyer blinked. "What do you mean?"

"They came for you yesterday."

Sawyer's stomach started to roil, and she swallowed hard. "For me? Was there a card?"

Tara frowned. "I didn't see one. But the delivery kid asked for you specifically. He said, 'These are for Sawyer Dodd.'"

"It was a kid? Like, my age?"

Tara drained her water glass and shrugged. "Yeah, about your age, I guess. Why? Do you have a secret admirer?"

Sawyer's eyes went wide, and Tara held up her hands then clapped one on her mouth. "Oh, Sawyer, I didn't mean—I mean, I know you and Kevin were together for a long time and—I was just being silly."

Sawyer took a step back, threw her backpack over her shoulder. "I need to get to school."

***

Chloe was sitting on the stone wall that surrounded the school when Sawyer spotted her.

"Hey," Chloe said, launching herself from the wall. "You didn't call me last night."

"What? Oh, sorry."

"And I didn't see you after school."

"I went home early. I wasn't feeling well."

Chloe offered her a sympathetic look. "You know you can talk to me, Sawyer."

"My parents want me to talk to the shrink."

Chloe rolled her eyes. "Still?"

"Again." Sawyer stopped walking and turned to face Chloe. "Hey, do you know anyone who would send me flowers?"

Chloe folded a stick of gum into her mouth. "What kind of flowers?"

"Roses."

"No, like, romantic flowers or sympathy flowers or, I don't know, 'sorry your dad and stepmom are breeding' flowers."

Sawyer tried not to smile. "This is serious. And I don't know what kind of flowers. Just...roses."

"Color?"

"First red and then pink."

Chloe waggled her eyebrows. "Two bunches? Ooh la la. Red is the color of love. And pink is appreciation."

"How did you know that?"

Chloe shook her cell phone. "Information superhighway. So you're loved and appreciated. What did the card say?"

Sawyer bit her lip and glanced at her friend. Normally, she would tell Chloe everything—every crush, every intimate detail of her dates with Kevin—but her admirer and the notes he left her felt bigger than all that. "No," she lied. "No note."

Chloe blew a bubble and sucked it in. "What about that Cooper guy? You said he sent you a flower, right?"

Sawyer nodded. "Yeah, but why would he send roses right after he sent me a flower?"

"Maybe he didn't want to send you the flower. Maybe Meddling Maggie forced him into it. Face it: a buck is a small price to pay to get her to shut up."

Sawyer thought of Cooper, of his shy smile, of the way Sawyer knew next to nothing about him. "It's a possibility, I guess. Oh. There's the bell. See you in choir?"

Chloe nodded and popped another bubble. "Sure."

Sawyer was digging in her backpack when she bumped into Logan.

"Oh, hey, Logan. I'm really sorry. It seems like I keep doing that to you."

Logan's smile—and his cheek-pinkening blush—went all the way up to his eyes. "That's okay." He didn't move, and Sawyer stared at him for a beat.

"Um"—she pointed over his shoulder—"you're kind of blocking my locker."

"Oh." Logan jumped out of the way. "I'm really sorry."

Sawyer spun her lock as students milled around her. She felt motion everywhere as she was jostled and bumped, but she also felt the stillness. Logan remained behind her, eyes boring into her back. She turned slowly, gripping her history book.

"Can I help you with something, Logan?"

"Um..." He twisted his hands in front of him, then jammed them into his jeans pockets. "Did you get the roses I sent?"

Ice water shot through Sawyer's veins. She had the overwhelming feeling of heat and cold all at once. "What did you say?"

"The roses. I sent them. Did I get the right house?"

Sawyer put her book down. "You sent me flowers."

"Roses. Pink roses. Just to say, you know"—Logan looked at his feet, kicked at the school-issue linoleum flooring—"thanks and all."

"How do you know where I live?"

Logan shrugged, a small, shy smile on his lips. "You said it was the new housing development past the market. I knew it was called Blackwood, and once you're in there, it's not that hard to find. Only full house in the place, right?"

Sawyer nodded, hearing the roar of her blood as it pulsed. "You only sent the pink roses?"

Logan stared blankly at her. "That's all they were supposed to be. Why? Did they bring something else? I don't have much money, so..."

Sawyer held up a hand. "So all you sent was the pink roses?"

"I'm sorry, I thought that would be good enough—"

"No, no"—Sawyer's heart caught on a giggle—"sorry, that's really sweet. They were fine, really pretty. I just— am a little—thanks, Logan. That was nice. You really didn't have to."

Sawyer switched her books and slammed her locker shut, shivering at the cold sweat that sprung up under her clothes.

"And I was wondering if..."

She turned to Logan once more. He was twisting his fingers again, the pink in his cheeks replaced by a flaming, all-out red. "Wondering if," he started again, "you'd want to go out sometime?"

"Oh. Oh." Sawyer felt sorry for the kid, but the idea of dating anyone—Cooper included—suddenly seemed frivolous, precarious, dangerous.

And maybe deadly.

"I really appreciate you asking, Logan, but the truth is, I'm just not ready to date again. And besides"—she took a step toward him, leaning in conspiratorially—"you really don't want to be with me. I'm—I'm a little messed up." She smiled apologetically. "Maybe, you know, when I'm up to it."

The smile didn't fade from Logan's face. He nodded at everything she said, and Sawyer recognized the look, the smile, as the pasted-on kind, the kind that a second-place winner keeps on her face until she can break down in private. Sawyer's heart felt a pang of guilt, but when Logan shrugged and nodded, she felt better for keeping him safe.

The school day continued and passed uneventfully but Sawyer was still on edge, scrutinizing everyone who chanced a glance at her and jumping at the slightest sound, cringing each time she rolled her combination lock, pulled open her locker. She was changing for a lone run on the track in the nearly empty girls' locker room when she heard the heavy doors press open. Sawyer straightened, that same piercing finger of fear tracing her spine.

"I can't stand her," she heard.

"You know she didn't really care about Kevin. He was her ticket to popularity. I mean look at her; she came right back to school afterward. I was practically shattered, and we weren't even dating anymore." Maggie sniffled as she rounded the bank of lockers and came upon Sawyer. Maggie's groupies hung close to her, arms crossed, throwing glaring, challenging looks at Sawyer.

"Why do you care so much about what I do, Maggie?" Sawyer wanted to know.

Maggie batted innocent lashes. "I don't know what you mean. We were just having a private conversation among ourselves. Were you possibly eavesdropping, Sawyer?" She wrinkled her pixie nose. "Such a bad habit."

Sawyer pulled on her sneakers and slammed her locker. "Whatever."

"You know Kevin was never really that into her," Maggie said, her voice low but just loud enough to stab at Sawyer.

"Go to hell, Maggie. He left you for me. So, if he wasn't all that into me, he must have been completely over you even when you were dating." Sawyer crossed her arms in front of her chest and cocked her head, feigning sympathy. "Ooh, that must have hurt."

Maggie's mouth fell open, as did the mouths of her cronies. "You are such a bitch!" Maggie yelled, nostrils flared, wide eyes moistening.

Sawyer shrugged and walked out of the locker room, hearing the girls closing in on Maggie, patting her back and cooing, "She doesn't know anything" and "She's a totally jealous bitch, Maggs," behind her.

When Sawyer set foot on the track—leaned in and let herself run—she finally felt free, felt weightless, felt untouchable. The strain of Kevin's death, of the note, of

Maggie, and of Sawyer's soon-to-be stepsister poured off of her as the sweat started to leave her pores. Suddenly, she didn't feel needled or pinned down, and by the third lap she was shrugging off the note and the flowers—a coincidence, she told herself—*an ill-timed coincidence.* But no matter how fast or how far her legs pumped, Sawyer couldn't outrun the tiny, niggling voice in the back of her head— *but what about the peanut oil label? But what about the "you're welcome" note?*

Sawyer clenched her fists and pumped her legs harder, punching at the air as she whizzed down the track. The heat that broke in her legs was punishing, but she relished the aching feeling. It made her feel alive.

No one knew about my relationship with Kevin, she reminded herself. *No one knew about what happened with Mr. Hanson.*

She was looping the track again, closing in on the bleachers, when she saw him up on one of the top benches, oversized coat on, hood pulled up. She slowed to a steady pace and studied Logan. He didn't look up at her from his perch, just kept his head on the notebook he was scribbling on. He looked up once and caught Sawyer's eye; she saw his eyes grow, his cheeks redden. He immediately dropped his head, and his hand went back to his pencil, working on his notebook. Sawyer ran past him, but something weighed on her.

Logan was there when she left Mr. Hanson's room.

But I didn't say anything...but maybe he saw?

Her throat went dry and she coughed, her diaphragm closing in on itself painfully. Her legs seemed to spin uncontrollably, and she found herself falling. Her arms went out instinctively and she was chest-flat on the red clay track, dust floating up in choking clouds. Sawyer rolled onto her back, sputtering, choking, coughing. Suddenly, someone blocked her light.

"Are you okay, Sawyer?"

Sawyer blinked, then squinted. "Logan?"

He offered her a hand, and Sawyer looked at it for a beat before taking it, allowing him to pull her to her feet. She was surprised at how strong he was. Sawyer brushed the red clay dust from her damaged knees and coughed again. "I'm okay."

"Let me get you something to drink."

Logan disappeared, returning immediately with an icy bottle of water. He popped the cap and gave it to Sawyer, studying her as she drank. She took a large sip and held it in her mouth before swallowing, the cold liquid soothing the ache in her diaphragm.

"Thanks," she said, breathing out icy breath. "That's just what I needed."

"You're fast," Logan said, smiling.

Sawyer nodded. "What are you doing out here?"

Logan looked sheepish. "I missed the early bus again. But it's not like I expect you to drive me home or anything. I didn't know you'd be out here running. Sometimes I like to come out here and think or write or whatever."

Sawyer gestured to the red notebook tucked under Logan's arm. "Is that what you were doing? Writing?"

"Something like that. Anyway, I'm really glad you're okay. That was kind of a big spill. Kind of a Logan-style spill." Logan's smile went from sheepish to goofy and lopsided, and Sawyer had to smile back.

"Thanks, Logan," she said, "I'm really fine though. I just got distracted. I tend to bail when distracted. You sure you don't need a ride home?"

Logan seemed to focus on something just over Sawyer's shoulder. She watched his goofy smile falter, saw his face pale.

"Logan?"

He pasted on a smile again, this one far less goofy, far less authentic. "No, thanks, Sawyer. I'll be fine. I've got to go."

"Hey." She reached out and grabbed the edge of his sweatshirt. "Are we okay?"

"Us? Yeah." He still didn't look at her. "I get it. You're not ready to date." He turned on the last word and Sawyer almost thought she heard the word "me." But he was already halfway up the bleachers by the time her brain processed it. She watched Logan snatch up his backpack and hop down from the bench, disappearing into the slatted shadows beneath the bleachers.

"That kid's a weird one."

Sawyer whipped around, sending a spray of ice water careening out of the bottle over her wrist, slapping her already soaked T-shirt and leaving a wet trail on Cooper's chest. "Oh, crap."

Cooper's eyebrows went up. "Sorry, I didn't mean to scare you."

Sawyer's heart was in her throat, still doing a choking pound. "You didn't," she squeaked. "Okay, maybe you did." Her eyes went to his wet chest. "Sorry—sorry about your shirt."

Cooper was dressed almost identically to Sawyer: he was wearing the green and white Hawthorne High track uniform, fearsome, fisted, fighting hornet smack in the middle of his nylon tank top. Sawyer took a second to notice Cooper's chest—and his broad shoulders, the bubbly muscles in his bare arms. "Why are you wearing a track uniform?"

"Because this is what the track team wears...right?"

"You're on the team? You're a runner?"

"I was at my old school. I thought I'd give the track team a try here. Coach let me on without trying out. My old times were pretty good, I guess."

Sawyer studied Cooper, the way the thin material of his shorts fell over his tanned legs; they were thick with well-defined muscle. He didn't have the powerful, sinewy legs of a runner.

"I know," Cooper said on a smile, "I don't look like I can run." He seemed to be reading her mind, and Sawyer felt an involuntary shiver run through her. A dark cloud passed over Cooper's face. "Are you okay? Let me get you my sweatshirt."

"No." Sawyer put her hand on Cooper's arm. "I'm fine. I'm just wearing a refreshing beverage."

Cooper slid back into that easy smile. "I prefer to drink mine, but whatever works for you. So, Ms. Nonbeliever"—he jutted his chin toward the empty track—"a friendly jog? Or an all-out race?"

Sawyer nodded and breathed deeply, testing out the ache in her diaphragm. The water seemed to have done the trick, and she had never been one to back down from a challenge— according to her father, it was both her best and her worst trait. She leaned over and set the water bottle on the bench, looking at Cooper through the dusting of long bangs that fell over her forehead.

Then she bolted.

She was on the track in a split second, legs pumping, wind slapping against her face when she heard the tail end of Cooper's "Hey! Cheater!"

She vaguely heard his footfalls as he entered the track, could hear his huffing breath as he closed in on her. He was panting by the time he came up on her left shoulder.

"Is this how you win all your races?" he panted. "By cheating?"

Sawyer kept up her steady pace, her breath shortening. "So you know I win all my races?"

"And now I know how!" Cooper balled his hands into fists and put his head down, going head first into the oncoming wind, his sneakers kicking up bursts of red clay dust as he passed Sawyer by a hair. Then it was a shoulder, then a full body length. Sawyer felt the fire in her legs, felt her lungs expanding, and she blew by him. She crossed the finish line and hooked her arms over the bleacher gate, blowing on her nails when Cooper finished a few seconds behind her.

"What took you so long?" she said without looking up.

Cooper knotted her in a playful headlock. "Cheaters. Every one of you Hawthorne Honeys!"

Sawyer backed out of the headlock, laughing. "Honeys?"

A blush flitted over Cooper's cheeks. "Honeybees. I meant honey*bees*."

"We're hornets!" She gave Cooper a hard hornet sting with her index finger, and when he came at her, she cringed. It was automatic; muscle memory burned in from dating Kevin, from never knowing just what it was that would set him off. She burned with shame.

He stopped. "Hey, I'm sorry."

"What?" Sawyer felt a nervous twitter rush through her. She licked her dry lips and forced a laugh that sounded false even to her. "I was kidding. Let's get some water."

Cooper followed her out to the center of the field, Sawyer suddenly stiff with embarrassment—*was she afraid of everyone now?* Cooper stayed silent, walking behind her.

They headed back toward the locker rooms, and Cooper sucked the last of the water from his bottle, stuffing the empty in his bag. "I guess this is where I leave you."

Sawyer cocked an eyebrow. "What does that mean?"

"It means that I don't usually shower in the girls' locker room." His eyes went over her head, gesturing at the *Women's Locker Room* sign.

"Oh," she said on a sheepish grin, "right."

They stood in awkward silence for a beat before Cooper nodded, gave her a mannish chuck on the shoulder, and promised to beat her next time around the track. Sawyer grinned and was grinning still when Cooper disappeared into the men's locker room; she went into hers.

The locker room was empty when Sawyer walked in, her half-dry track shirt stuck to her jog bra, her cheeks red hot and flushed. She slipped out of her clothes and into a towel and flip-flops, grabbing her shower bag and turning a shower on as hot as she could get it. When steam poured out of the stall, licking her knees and pressing against her chest, she slipped inside, letting the hot water rush over her, soaking her skin. She imagined it seeping into her aching muscles, dripping over her head and into her brain. She wished she could wash away the violent memories of Kevin, but knew the memories ran deep—so deep that she cringed even when she didn't want to—and soon the water that rushed over her cheeks was salty with tears. She slumped against the shower stall and doubled over, letting herself cry until her stomach ached, until her skin was red and raw and overheated from the searing water. Finally, she turned the shower off and rewrapped herself in her towel, shuffling to her locker.

That's when she stopped dead.

The locker room was silent—so quiet that it seemed to hum with the vibe of desertion—but Sawyer's locker seemed to scream. The word *whore* was spray-painted in an angry red across her locker door.

NINE

Sawyer stumbled back, foot over foot, clutching her towel around her but feeling the icy chill of the cold locker room air as it crept up her naked thighs. She swallowed repeatedly and knew that she would have to open her locker—what she would find, she wasn't sure—wasn't sure she wanted to know. Steeling herself, she used numb fingers to spin her locker combination, slowly pulling open the door. She let out a great whoosh of calming air when her locker contents appeared undisturbed—the usual jumble of school clothes tossed in a careless heap, a sneaker jammed with her bra, her jeans inside out and balled up.

Looking over her shoulder, she quickly shuffled the wrinkled clothes out, putting her hand through the hole in her jeans.

Hole in her jeans?

"Holy shit!" Sawyer spat out the words—in anger or sheer surprise, she couldn't be sure—and held what was left of her jeans out in front of her. The waistband was still intact—the rivets, the zipper, the zippy little 7 logo—but that was it. The denim was shredded and wagged in long, primitive tongues, the fabric edges already starting to fray. The crotch was torn out completely, and one of the pockets fluttered down like a broken moth when she shook the tattered fabric. She dropped the jeans and went for her T-shirt, her sweater—both had met the same fate, as had her running clothes. Her bra was a mess of overstretched cotton, the inner pads busted embarrassingly open, spilling out their little tufts of fluff. Her panties were gone.

Sawyer's stomach twisted, and she felt the need to vomit; she doubled over, hand still clutching desperately to keep her towel closed, and dry heaved, coughing until her eyes watered, her nose ran.

"It's just a stupid prank," she whispered when she could catch her breath. "A stupid prank. Probably Maggie."

She used the back of her hand to wipe her eyes and nose, and stood up straight, feeling the burning anger roil through her.

"Bitch." She said the word through clenched teeth, yanked out her sneakers, and slammed her locker shut. She listened to the phone ring after she speed-dialed Chloe.

"Speak and ye shall be heard," Chloe said, smacking on something on her side of the phone.

"You'll never guess what that—that bitch Maggie did!"

"Regale me."

"First of all, I'm in the locker room. Second of all, I'm wearing a towel."

"Okay…"

Sawyer took a lung-cleansing breath. "Ask me why I'm wearing a towel."

"I'm assuming it had something to do with a shower, but why, Sawyer, are you wearing a towel?"

"Because Maggie shredded my clothes!"

"Shredded them?"

"Shredded. Think coleslaw. Sans mayo."

"She shredded your clothes? Were you wearing them at the time?"

Sawyer sunk down on a bench, scooching forward so her towel would blanket her naked skin against its cold aluminum. "No, I was in the shower. I ran late today and Maggie was there—here—before I got in the shower, then when I got out, she had spray-painted my locker and shredded my clothes."

"Like coleslaw?"

"Like coleslaw."

"That bitch!" Chloe spat.

"I know."

"We have to stop her. We have to fight back—fight fire with fire."

Sawyer hung her head. "I don't want to do that," she

muttered. "Maybe I'll just put a complaint in with Principal Chappie."

"A complaint? As in a note in his complaint box? That's a horrible idea, Sawyer. Horrible! That's not fighting fire with fire; that's fighting fire with *paper*. Fire kicks paper's ass!"

Sawyer sighed, fingering the fringed end of her towel. "I need to get going."

"Do you want me to bring you some clothes? I can be there in a few minutes."

"No, that's all right. If I don't get on the road now I'm going to be stuck in traffic."

"Not if you hit the freeway naked," Chloe giggled.

Sawyer smiled in spite of herself. "Thanks, but I've got a towel."

"Très chic."

"See you tomorrow?"

"Of course."

Sawyer hung up her phone and plodded to her locker, shoving the shredded remains of her clothes into her backpack and pressing it against her chest. She tried to inch the towel down for a more demure look; it was either a school-wide glance of butt cheek or super cleavage, and she decided to go with the latter as she sucked in a deep breath and peeked out the locker room door. Luckily, the school was nearly deserted, so Sawyer picked her steps carefully, trying her best to stay close to the walls and out of public view. There was a student council meeting going on in the English room, desks dragged into a semicircle, students semi-interested in their speaker, and Sawyer tiptoed past, feeling both the draft from her nakedness and the heat from her embarrassment. She made it to the school's double doors and was ready to take off in a full sprint when someone yanked the door open.

"Cooper!" Sawyer folded over herself, hands splayed over her toweled private parts.

Cooper paused, obviously taken aback. "Um, hi?" He tried his best to avert his eyes, finally staring up at the ceiling. "Did I—did you—I'm sorry, I just have no idea what to say." His head inched downward, and Sawyer caught him eyeing her towel. "We just didn't have this kind of thing at my old school."

The shake started low in Sawyer's gut and before she could stop it, tears were rolling down her cheeks and she was pinching her naked knees together. Cooper's eyes went big.

"Are you okay?"

Sawyer just nodded, unable to speak. The laughter was racking her whole body, the terror of the situation replaced by the sheer ridiculousness of it. "I'm wearing a towel in the middle of school."

"Yeah." Cooper shrugged out of his hoodie and looked away while Sawyer slid into it. He started to laugh with her when she didn't stop. "Um, do you always run around school buck naked?"

Sawyer wagged her head before a snort escaped. That made her and Cooper laugh harder. Finally she straightened up, taking deep gasping breaths.

"I'm sorry," she said, shaking her head.

"Don't be," Cooper quipped, his eyes running over her bare legs.

"Someone shredded my clothes. I was in the shower, and they shredded everything. My track clothes, my school clothes, everything."

Cooper went suddenly serious. "Sawyer, that sucks."

"Almost as much as making a break for it in a school-issued towel."

"And a fine sweatshirt."

"Yeah." Sawyer giggled again. "Thanks for that."

Cooper jerked a thumb over his shoulder. "Can I drive you somewhere? To the mall or something?"

"No. The only thing better than cruising around here in my altogether would be hitting the mall this way. I'm just going to head home."

"Oh, right. Sure."

They stood in awkward silence for a beat.

"So, maybe, once you get some clothes on we could go out or something sometime."

Sawyer's cheeks burned despite her lack of clothing, and her heart did a traitorous double thump. Before she could open her mouth, before she could say that she would love to, she was pelted with bitter guilt. A kiss—two kisses—she could pretend didn't happen. But she couldn't fall for Cooper. She was supposed to be in love with Kevin. She was supposed to be the mourning girlfriend. Still, the zing she felt while looking into Cooper's eyes was undeniable, and she wanted to say yes.

"I'm sorry. I can't. I"—she looked down at her bare toes on the cement—"I have to get going."

She pushed past Cooper and took off at a sprint, pumping her legs until the heat roiled through them, ignoring the searing tears on her bare feet as she cleared the blacktop. When she was safely in the driver's seat of her car, engine on, heat on full blast, she started to cry. The tears came slowly at first, little rivulets of angry sobs, but as she thought over the notes, the flowers sent to her house, the shredded remains of her clothes, the tears got heavier, her breath got shorter. Her body hiccupped, caught in the wretched fist of guilt— and fear.

At home, Sawyer changed into sweats and pulled her shredded clothes from her backpack. As she did, a single white business card floated out of her bag, settling on the floor like a flag of surrender. She picked it up and turned it over in her hands, rubbing her thumb over the raised gold insignia of the Crescent Hill Police Department. She sucked in a slow breath and dug out her cell phone; she yipped when it chirped in her hand.

"Oh, crap, Chloe, you scared the shit out of me."

"And a holy hello to you too."

"I'm sorry." Sawyer tossed Detective Biggs's card on her bureau and flopped onto her bed. "I'm just completely freaking out."

Chloe clucked sympathetically. "Oh, sweetie. Maggie is really getting to you."

Sawyer nodded. "I'm thinking of calling the police."

"On Maggie?"

Sawyer pinched the bridge of her nose, feeling a headache coming on. She struggled with how much to tell Chloe. She didn't want her best friend to worry about her. She also didn't want to have to tell Chloe everything—everything she'd been hiding. "Just…there's a bunch of stuff going on and Maggie, well, she—it's complicated, Chloe."

Chloe paused, considering. "If you can't explain it to me, how are you going to explain it to the police? I mean, what are you going to say?"

Sawyer sat up, hugged a pillow to her chest. "I'm not exactly sure." She stopped then, holding the words in her mouth. "Maybe I'll tell them that someone is stalking me."

The words were out and hung in the air, oppressive, *real*. Sawyer felt the itch of tears at the corners of her eyes, the pound of the headache that came with, and pinched the bridge of her nose. "He knows stuff about me, Chloe, about people—people in my life." She sighed. "I don't know. Maybe I'm blowing the whole thing out of proportion?"

Chloe's breath sounded weighted. "I don't think you're blowing anything out of proportion."

Sawyer thought back on the notes now safely tucked away in her underwear drawer—the notes and the peanut butter label.

"He sent me a peanut butter label after Mr. Hanson died."

Chloe gasped. "Sawyer, that's evidence! You've got to turn that over to the police!"

"It's evidence *against* me, Chloe. I'm the one with the label."

"But he sent it to you. You have to tell them that! They'll believe you. I mean, why would anyone believe that you wanted to hurt Mr. Hanson?"

"Because…" She paused, sucked in a deep breath. "The other day, after class. I think he—I think he may have—like, come on to me. What if the police think I"—she dropped her voice, swallowed heavily—"killed him?"

"Wait, what? Mr. Hanson came on to you? Like hit on you?"

"That's not really the—"

"Why didn't you tell me, Sawyer? God, I can't believe you had to go through something like that alone. I mean, are you sure?"

Sawyer's stomach wobbled. "No. I mean yes."

"He is—was, I guess—really friendly. Maybe you misinterpreted it? What happened exactly?"

Anger pricked in Sawyer's gut, and she felt herself narrow her eyes. "I shouldn't have to explain to you—or prove anything to my best friend. Are you saying you don't believe me?"

"No, of course I believe you, sweetie. I was just asking because—"

The anger blossomed. "Because the medication makes me a little loopy? God, Chloe, I thought you would be the one person to understand."

"I do, Sawyer, and what I was going to say was that, you know, he drove Libby home that one time, and he is always super helpful with the honor society. He talked to everyone."

"*Was* always super helpful."

"What?"

Sawyer licked her lips. "He *was* always super helpful. I'm sorry I'm snappy. It's just—I almost wasn't sure it was a pass either. But I know how I felt and it was gross. I felt gross afterward. Like I needed a shower. Or a shot of penicillin."

"Are you going to tell the police that?"

"No. I can't, Chlo—they'll think I did something to him."

"But the note! And Kevin! He was your boyfriend. Why would you kill your own boyfriend?" Chloe's voice hitched on a sob. "You loved him. He was head over heels for you."

Sawyer wanted to confide in Chloe, but how could she after she'd kept Kevin's feelings, his abuse, hidden for so long? The lie—even the simple lie of omission—sat in Sawyer's gut like a fat black stone. "Yeah," was all Sawyer could answer.

The next morning Sawyer dressed quietly and slipped out the door while Tara and her father were still sleeping. By 7:00 a.m. she was parked in front of the Crescent Hills Police Department, listening to her heartbeat and watching the automatic glass doors of the station swing open and shut as officers came and went. Her hands felt clammy gripping the steering wheel, and her fingers itched to click the key in the ignition, to start the car and drive away.

On a deep, steadying breath, Sawyer got out of the car and stepped into the police department, blinking in the harsh, fluorescent overhead lights. She wasn't sure what she expected of a police department, but this wasn't it. The main office was relatively quiet and heartlessly businesslike, with wall-to-wall gray industrial carpeting and dusty silk plants interspersed between modern metal desks manned by uniformed officers. Sawyer started to nervously tug at the strap of her purse.

Maybe this wasn't such a good idea.

"May I help you?"

The officer who smiled down at her had a head of close-cropped dark hair that made his bright green eyes stand out. He was tall and pale and there was something incredibly familiar about the lopsided smile he offered.

"Can I help you?"

Sawyer bit her lip. "Um, maybe? Yeah. I guess."

"Okay...how about we start with your name?"

"I'm Sawyer." She wasn't sure if she should put out a hand to shake or just wave. She chose the latter. "Sawyer Dodd."

"Are you a student, Ms. Dodd?"

Sawyer nodded, not sure why that would matter. "Yeah, at Hawthorne."

The officer nodded and smiled. "I thought I recognized you. My brother goes to Hawthorne. I'm Stephen Haas."

"Haas? You're Logan's brother." Sawyer did a mental head slap. "Detective Biggs mentioned his partner but I didn't realize—I didn't put two and two together, I guess. I remember Logan saying that his brother was a cop, though."

"You can call me Stephen." He nodded, offered Sawyer a hand. "So, you are a friend of my brother's?"

Sawyer nodded. "Kind of. He has the locker under mine, and I drove him home from school once."

Stephen cocked that half smile again and pointed at her, green eyes narrowed. "Ah, that's right. You're *that* Sawyer Dodd."

"Uh, yeah."

"My little brother kind of has a—let's just go with mammoth—crush on you."

Sawyer's cheeks flushed red, and she felt the heat go to her ears. "Oh."

"So, what can I do for you?"

"Oh, right. Actually, I was looking for Detective Biggs. Is he in?"

Stephen checked his watch. "He probably won't be in for another couple of hours. Is there something I can help you with?"

Sawyer chewed her bottom lip. "Well not to be rude but no, I don't think so."

"Okay, let me put it this way: Detective Biggs won't be in for another couple of hours, and even then, it's pretty likely you'll be talking to me. I'm his liaison."

Sawyer smiled in spite of herself. "Liaison? That sounds very French."

"Why don't you follow me over to the conference room and you can tell me what's going on. I can start the case file for Detective Biggs."

Sawyer's fingers still worked the strap of her purse, and she felt herself shift her weight from one foot to the other. "Well..."

But Stephen Haas's face was so earnest, so open, that Sawyer smiled thinly and followed him into the conference room.

"So," he said, whipping out a yellow legal pad, "what can I help you with?"

Sawyer's eyes followed the blank lines on the notebook, and she licked her parched lips, fisted her hands, which seemed clammy once again. She cleared her throat. "Well," she began, feeling her mind whirl with everything that had happened—and how preposterous it would sound. "Maybe I'm making a big deal out of nothing." She stood. "You know, I should really just go."

Stephen laid a gentle hand on her forearm. "Sawyer, if whatever is bothering you is enough to make you drive all the way down to the police station at seven o'clock in the morning, it's something I want to hear about. Besides"—he flashed that sweet, relaxed smile of his—"I'll be the judge of whether or not we send in the SWAT team or the guys in the white coats with the straitjackets."

Sawyer sunk back down, still nervous, but feeling a genuine smile twitching at the edges of her lips. "Well, Detective Biggs came to my house a few weeks ago—just after my boyfriend, Kevin Anderson—died in a car accident."

Stephen nodded. "Kevin Anderson. It was a drunk-driving accident, right?"

Sawyer pinched her lip. "Yeah. But they think someone else was in the car. Someone who escaped. They think it was me."

Stephen's eyebrows rose. "And was it?"

"No. No. We got in a fight that night and when I left him, he was drinking but he was alone."

"Okay. But I don't see how this is—"

"And the Monday after his funeral," Sawyer went on, her eyes fixed on the faux wood grain veneer on the conference table, "I got a note. It said, 'You're welcome.' And there was a newspaper article with the note—it was the one about Kevin's death."

Stephen leaned back in his chair, sucking in his breath and tapping the end of the ballpoint pen on the still-blank notepad. "Sounds like a prank to me. A prank in really bad taste."

"And then my Spanish teacher was killed."

"Uh, Mr. Hanson, right? Logan told me about that. But he wasn't murdered; he died of an allergic reaction."

"Yeah, but then I got another note. Oh, and before that, we were at a party and someone attacked my best friend, Chloe Coulter."

"Can you spell that last name?"

Sawyer bit her nail. "Maybe you shouldn't write that down."

Stephen raised his eyebrows. "Why shouldn't I write it down?"

"It's just—we were out, late—and Chloe's parents don't know."

"If this was an attack, Sawyer, this is pretty serious. Tell me what happened."

"It was serious. Someone cut the brake lines on Chloe's mother's car. And Chloe walked outside—"

"Where did this happen?"

"Oh, at the Rutgers' house. But maybe you shouldn't—"

"Let me guess. This girl's parents didn't know they were hosting a party?"

"It was a guy, actually, Evan. Evan Rutger. And no."

Stephen sucked in a breath. "Okay. Just tell me what happened and we'll figure out who to talk to—if anyone—after, okay?"

Sawyer nodded. "Okay, I guess. Anyway, someone hit Chloe in the head."

"Was she injured badly?"

"Not very. But enough. He drew blood."

"So you know it was a male."

"No, not—I mean, that's what Chloe said, but she also said she really didn't get a good look at him."

"Did anyone call this in?"

Sawyer shook her head again, feeling slightly ashamed. She should have made Chloe call the police that night. "No. Chloe didn't want to get in trouble."

"Okay, so your friend got attacked. Did she receive any of these notes?"

"No, she didn't."

"Has anyone messed with your car? Have you seen anyone who fit the description of Chloe's attacker?"

"No."

"So there really isn't any reason to believe that the same person is targeting both of you?"

"No." Sawyer frowned. "I guess not."

Knowing that her best friend wasn't a target of Sawyer's admirer should have made her feel better, but the thought that two horrible people were on the loose in Crescent Hill wasn't any more comforting.

"So you said you got a note after your teacher passed away." Stephen cocked his head. "Did you bring any of these notes?"

Sawyer wagged her head. "No. I didn't really plan on coming here this morning."

"Do you recognize the handwriting, or was there a postmark? Anything recognizable?"

"No."

"Well, Sawyer, I understand your concern and I appreciate you bringing this to my attention, but I really think this is just—"

"A coincidence? A prank? Someone sent me flowers, too, at school. And then someone spray-painted my gym locker—right after making coleslaw out of my clothes while I was in the shower."

Sawyer listened to the tension rising in her voice and cringed inwardly. Everything she was saying *did* sound preposterous, coincidental—like a prank. Someone was playing with her—was capitalizing on the horrid things that had happened and trying to freak her out. Sweat beaded along her upper lip and she sighed.

"Maybe you're right. This is probably just a really bad prank."

Stephen pressed his lips together in a sympathetic smile and patted Sawyer's hand as it rested on the table. Her eyes followed his hand.

"I'm sorry that someone would do this to you, Sawyer. Kids can really suck. And from what I hear from my brother, your class has a particularly mean streak."

Sawyer thought of Logan sitting in her car in his sweatpants and forced a smile. "I guess so."

"He's mentioned some kids—your late boyfriend included, sorry—who have pretty much tortured him from the time he set foot on campus."

Sawyer dug her fingernail into the table's veneer.

"Is there anything else I should know about these incidents? I'll write a report just so we have something on file, should there be any more—"

Sawyer's eyes flashed and her whole body stiffened, the thought of another note, another murder, like a steel fist to her gut. Stephen seemed to read her immediately. "Not that there will be any more incidents."

She thought of the peanut butter label and shook her head. "No, sir."

"Call me Stephen. Or Officer Haas, at worst. Not sir."

Sawyer nodded wordlessly and stood when Stephen checked his watch. "Shouldn't you be getting to school? If you leave now, you can just make the last bell."

"Yeah." Sawyer gathered her purse. "Thanks."

As she left the police station she felt an overwhelming sense of relief—fueled by stupidity—and the tiniest bit of calm. *Yeah,* she convinced herself as she drove the distance to Hawthorne High, *it's just a prank. A stupid, bad-natured prank. I'm not responsible for anything.*

She repeated the mantra even as she guided her car into the parking lot and pulled it into park. She gathered up her backpack, a twinge of confidence bolstering her movements. *Just a prank…* The words resonated in her head and seemed to fill her with a modicum of calm. But somewhere, deep down, Sawyer knew the calm wouldn't last.

TEN

Sawyer was feeling slightly more comfortable after homeroom and had nearly forgotten the notes, the flowers, and the shredded clothes by the time she got to second period. When she walked into the choir room, she was downright giddy thinking of her solo, appearing in her new choir costume. Chloe bounded over to her.

"Hey! You're smiling. Kind of like an idiot." She poked Sawyer in the ribs and grinned. "Anything I should know about?"

Sawyer shook her head, feeling her soft brown hair tumble over her shoulders. "Nope. I'm just feeling pretty decent today."

"Good to know."

"Ladies and gentlemen." Mr. Rose strode through the

door, hands up as though he were conducting the students' conversations. "Tone it down now. I suspect you all have been looking over—and loving—our new set list." He shuffled some papers. "We're going to start today with the third number first so we can work on everyone's solos." His eyes flashed to Sawyer's and she gulped, then clapped a hand over her mouth.

"Oh, crap. I forgot my sheet music," she murmured.

"Huh?" Chloe asked.

"My sheet music." Sawyer's hand shot into the air. "Um, Mr. Rose? Can I run to my locker for just a sec? I left my sheet music in there."

Mr. Rose sat down at the piano and nodded, waving absently toward the door. "Hurry."

Maggie rolled her eyes as Sawyer shimmied past. "And the whole world waits for Sawyer Dodd," she muttered just loud enough for Sawyer to hear.

Sawyer pushed into the deserted hallway and, head down, beelined toward her locker. She looked up just in time to avoid a collision with Cooper.

"Oh, hey." He flushed a blotchy red from exposed neck to forehead and then broke into an uncertain grin.

Sawyer looked from Cooper to her locker—less than three paces away—and back to Cooper again. "What are you doing out here?"

He waved a pink hall pass. "Bathroom break."

Sawyer bit her lip and pointed over Cooper's right shoulder. "The boys' room is in corridor C."

Cooper's smile looked uncomfortable, forced. "I thought I'd take the long way. Trig is killing me."

Sawyer cocked an eyebrow and crossed her arms in front of her chest. "The very long way."

"What are you doing out here in the middle of class? I mean, besides general interrogation." Cooper's voice was light, amused, but there was an edge to it that made Sawyer feel uncomfortable.

"Forgot something in my locker," she said.

"Oh, your locker is in this corridor?"

Sawyer nodded, unease traveling the length of her spine. "All the junior lockers are."

"Right. We were all kind of mixed up at my old school." Cooper dangled the hall pass again. "Well, I should be getting back to class. Someone's going to catch on that it doesn't take this long to pee."

Sawyer said nothing while Cooper hurried past her down the hall. He headed away from corridor C, away from the bank of math classrooms behind them. When she finally turned to her locker, Sawyer spun the lock, feeling a weird sense of calm and dread. *If there is a note, Cooper is suspect number one,* she told herself.

She immediately thought of their conversations, of the delicious heat that crept through her when his lips were on hers. She thought of the softness in his eyes and felt herself slump. "God, I'm freaking paranoid."

Cooper would never do anything to hurt me. He—she

paused in mid-thought, about to utter the word "loves." *He likes me,* she corrected herself.

Even people who like—or love—you can hurt you, her conscience warned her. Sawyer ignored it.

"Prank," she muttered out loud, as if trying to convince herself. "Stupid prank."

But there was nothing amiss in her locker, and her sheet music, her track clothes, and her photos were exactly as she had left them. She slammed the metal door, her heart thumping in a way she could barely remember—normally.

She whistled the chorus of her new solo as she skipped back to class.

———

"So, I figure I'll head home and change, and then drive over around five. Sound okay?" Chloe asked.

"Yeah, that sounds good. I say we do an all-night bad-movie chocolate fest. If I get through chem today, I'm totally going to need it." Sawyer had turned to head to her locker when Chloe laid a soft hand on her forearm.

"Hey, Sawyer"—she licked her lips—"I'm really glad you're—you're feeling better."

Sawyer felt a lump grow in her throat, but this time, it didn't have the sharp pang of despair that she was now so used to. Instead, she smiled—genuinely—and pulled her best friend into a hug. "Me too. And you too."

Chloe pulled back, confusion flitting across her face.

Sawyer cocked her head, gently brushing her fingertips over Chloe's forehead, over the still-healing cut above her best friend's eye.

"Oh, right."

"Hey, Chloe, speaking of that. Did you—did you ever go to the police?"

Chloe shook her head. "I told you—my mom would kill me. Besides"—she wrinkled her nose—"Ryan was able to get the car towed without anyone being the wiser. His dad owns that garage out on Forest, you know."

Sawyer nodded. "But someone attacked you, that's pretty—"

Chloe put her hands on Sawyer's shoulders and squeezed gently. "It's over, Sawyer. No big deal."

Sawyer wished she had an ounce of her best friend's bravery. Maybe then she wouldn't nearly jump out of her skin every fifteen minutes or scrutinize cute guys who were just trying to be nice to her.

"I worry about you, Chloe."

Chloe began to annunciate. "No. Big. Deal. Car is fine." She pointed to her forehead. "Noggin made of stone or some such other hard material."

Sawyer laughed. "I guess. And hey, I guess with the car at Ryan's dad's, you two got to spend some extra time together, huh?"

Chloe's eyes rolled to the ceiling and a sly smile formed on her lips. "A lady never tells…"

"Which is why you should be spilling everything."

"Nothing to tell, S. Don't you think I would have given you every sordid detail by now if there was?" She winked. "Best friends don't keep secrets."

Sawyer felt her smile falter, just for a second. "Yeah. You're totally right."

"All right, gotta run. See you later, sweet cheeks." Chloe skipped through the double glass doors on her way to PE while Sawyer spun her locker combo and yanked out her chemistry book.

"You!"

Maggie's voice cut through the din of students in the hall.

"What's Maggie going on about now?" Sawyer murmured to herself.

"I'm talking to you!"

Sawyer felt a bony finger jabbing below her shoulder blade. She gripped the sides of her locker and breathed in what was supposed to be a calming breath. Maggie poked her again.

Sawyer spun around, eyes in mid-roll. "What do you—" Sawyer stopped when she saw the note clenched in Maggie's hand. It was the same pale-green paper, the same size and shape, and judging by the fury in Maggie's eyes and the flush on her cheeks, Maggie had read it.

"Where did you get that?"

"You shoved it in my locker, you bitch!"

Before Sawyer had a chance to process what Maggie

had said, she felt Maggie's palms against her chest, giving her a hard shove that landed her against the cold metal of her locker. Her lock stung the back of her neck, and Sawyer winced.

"You think I'm a whore?" Maggie continued without missing a beat, waving the note in Sawyer's face. "You think I'm a slut? Kevin only left me for you because he heard you were easy. He heard you were blowing half the guys from here to your stupid new housing tract."

Maggie's face was inches from Sawyer's, and her voice had reached a frenzied pitch. Her eyes were wild, her nostrils flared, and that was what Sawyer was focused on when Maggie hit her.

The slap was clean and stinging against her cheek, and for the second time in her life, Sawyer felt cornered, threatened. Her eyes watered, and she pressed herself against the cold metal lockers.

"You don't know the first thing about me and Kevin!" Maggie spat. "He cheated on you with me!"

A tiny bubble of anger percolated low in Sawyer's stomach. She stopped listening as Maggie went to slap her again. She grabbed Maggie's wrist, feeling the heat roiling into a full fire in her gut. No one was going to hit her again, not ever.

"Don't you touch me," she said through gritted teeth.

"Don't send me those damn notes," Maggie screamed back. When her other hand came up against Sawyer's head

Sawyer grabbed that, too, and gave Maggie a hard shove. Maggie stumbled over her own feet, over the group of kids who had ringed them to watch, and fell hard on her butt on the linoleum. The note slipped out of her hand, and Sawyer watched its graceful arc as it slid behind Maggie and came to rest against the bank of lockers.

Maggie's fury was palpable. "You bitch!"

"What's going on here?"

Principal Chappie's baritone voice made the kids scatter like marbles until only Sawyer and Maggie were left, Sawyer pressed against her locker, Maggie looking like a wounded dove on the floor. Sawyer watched Maggie's chest pulse as she blinked hard until huge mascara-colored crocodile tears slid over her cheeks. "Sawyer attacked me! She pushed me down!"

"No, I didn't," Sawyer protested. "She came after me!" She stepped closer to Principal Chappie and Maggie stayed put, throwing an arm over her forehead as through she feared a blow from Sawyer.

"Oh, get up!" Sawyer barked at her. "You know what happened. You fell over your damn self trying to hit me. Tell him!"

Maggie blinked innocent, doe-like eyes. "I don't know what happened. I was walking down the hall and Sawyer threw herself on me like some kind of animal."

"No, I didn't! And you spray-painted my locker and tore up my clothes!"

Maggie's pitiful facade didn't crack. "I don't know what

she's talking about, Principal Chappie. She's crazy. She sent me a threatening note. I'm just…" She sniffed, and Sawyer watched Maggie's small shoulders shiver, her face crumple under another torrent of tears.

That girl could win an Oscar, Sawyer thought bitterly.

"I'm just so scared. I don't know what I ever did to her."

Sawyer gaped. "What *I* did to *her?* Principal Chappie—"

Principal Chappie helped Maggie up and cupped his chin with his hand. "You'd better come down to my office, Sawyer. Do either of you need to see the nurse?"

Maggie made a show of checking her elbows, twisting her wrists as though looking for breaks. "I think I'm okay, sir. I'd just like to get to class. I have a presentation due for English."

"Of course, Maggie. Go on ahead." Principal Chappie put his hand on Sawyer's elbow. "Sawyer?"

Anger radiated from Sawyer in waves as Maggie slipped away, head held high.

Sawyer watched her leave.

"Come on," Principal Chappie said.

"Fine," Sawyer relented, trying to loosen the tight set of her jaw. "Let me just grab my backpack." She bent down to gather her pack, then snatched Maggie's discarded note from under the locker, jamming it down in her pocket. "Okay."

Sawyer sat in Principal Chappie's office, chewing her bottom lip as he hung up the phone. "You father should be here in just a few minutes. I already told him what we talked about."

"I'm suspended," Sawyer said miserably.

"Effective immediately. But don't think of this as some kind of vacation. You will come in tomorrow morning before the first bell and report to detention while the board decides whether your punishment is sufficient."

"I didn't do anything," Sawyer said, her voice a low, nearly inaudible rumble.

"If you choose not to report to detention tomorrow, you will immediately be expelled."

"Expelled?" she gaped.

"This is very serious, Ms. Dodd. We don't take bullying lightly at Hawthorne High. Do you understand?"

She nodded, her entire focus going to the note in her pocket. Its contents radiated through her, and she played through any scenario that would allow her a few private moments to read it.

"Can I use the restroom?"

Principal Chappie pressed his lips into a stern, straight line. "Is it an emergency?"

Sawyer pumped her head, pressing her fingertips to her lower abdomen. "Cramps."

He seemed to consider a moment before picking up his phone once again. "Ellen, can you come here and take Ms. Dodd to the ladies room?"

"I can go to the bathroom alone, Principal Chappie."

Ellen, a freshman who barely cleared Sawyer's chin, was standing in Principal Chappie's doorway a beat after he hung up the receiver. "I can take you right now." Ellen's cracked lips broke into a friendly smile, showing off a mouthful of silvery braces.

"Thanks," Sawyer muttered, walking behind the tiny blond.

"So," Ellen started when they had reached the relative sanctity of the deserted hallway. "Is it true you attacked Maggie Gaines?"

"No," Sawyer said without looking at the girl.

Ellen frowned, and Sawyer saw the girl's fingers go to the hem of her T-shirt, rolling the fabric nervously.

"I'm sorry," Sawyer said, stopping to face Ellen. "I'm just in a really bad mood. It's nothing against you."

Ellen nodded, her cotton candy fluff of blond hair swirling around her freckled cheeks. "That's okay. I'm sorry about the suspension."

"You already know?"

Ellen's freckles disappeared under a wash of pink. "I kind of figured. It's a zero-tolerance policy here."

"Anyway"—Sawyer pointed to the girls'-room door— "I'm just going to—"

"Oh, right." Ellen nodded, smiled, and leaned against the adjacent wall. "I'll just wait for you here."

Sawyer jammed her hands in her pockets, her fingertips brushing the top of the note. Her stomach dropped, but she forced a small smile. "I promise not to make a run for it."

Sawyer slipped into the first stall and locked the door behind her, digging the note from her pocket. She smoothed it against her thigh and felt the hairs on the back of her neck stand up. Every beat of her heart seemed to squeeze the last of the breath out of her lungs as she read.

> Maggie—
> You're a slut! Don't think Kevin didn't tell me about you. As a matter of fact, he said you were the worst blow ever... although ALL the other guys on the football team might have a different view. We used to laugh about what a skanky bitch you were, pretending to be a sweet, innocent virgin. You aren't fooling anyone; the entire school knows what a whore you are, what a ho...

It wasn't the words on the note that caused Sawyer's distress; it wasn't even the fact that the note appeared on the same mint-green paper as hers had—it was the handwriting. It was *identical* to hers.

Sawyer bit down hard on her lower lip as she read the last line—signed,

> —Sawyer Dodd, an admirer

Her breath came out in painful gasps now, and Sawyer flopped forward, clutching the note in one hand as she pressed her head between her knees. She squeezed her eyes shut and willed her breathing to slow down, her heart to slow down, when there was a frantic beating on the girls'-room door, followed by a crack of hallway light as the door opened.

"Sawyer? Is everything okay?"

Sawyer pushed herself up and used the heel of her hand to brush away the tears that had inexplicably started to fall. "Yeah," she said, clearing her throat, "I'm good." She kick-flushed the toilet for good measure and beelined to the bank of sinks, keeping her head bent so Ellen couldn't see her flushed cheeks. She splashed her face with cold water and Ellen's eyebrows went up, her lips curling into a sympathetic coo.

"Are you worried about what your parents are going to say?"

"Um, yeah, a little bit," Sawyer said, meeting Ellen at the door. "But time to face the music, I guess, huh?"

Ellen fell into step next to Sawyer. "You know, if you need anything, you can call me. I know we don't really know each other, but I can get your schoolwork for you or something."

"That's okay," Sawyer said, "you don't even know my classes."

"Oh, no worries. I can pull your schedule from the office. It's no big deal."

Sawyer felt a small bit of heat clawing at the back of her neck, but she wasn't sure why. "No, that's all right. I really appreciate it though, thanks."

Andrew Dodd didn't say anything to Sawyer as they left Principal Chappie's office and walked to the visitors' lot.

"Dad," Sawyer tried once they got to the car.

Andrew held up a silencing hand as he sunk his key into

the lock and slid into the front seat of the car. Sawyer flopped into the passenger seat next to him, dumping her backpack on the floor.

"Dad, I didn't do anything. Maggie threw herself on me! And I didn't even write that note." She paused, and when Andrew didn't respond, she crossed her arms in front of her chest and slunk down in her seat, staring out the front windshield. When her father made a left turn away from the highway toward Blackwood Hills Estates, she frowned. "Where are we going?"

"You're going to see Dr. Johnson."

Sawyer straightened up, anger and betrayal tearing through her. "What? Dad, I told you I had nothing to do with this. Maggie is a freak—and someone sent her a note and they said it was from me but it wasn't."

Andrew raked a hand through his thinning hair then rubbed his eyes. "Sawyer, Tara's on bed rest. She's gone to her mother's house."

Sawyer felt her eyebrows rise. "What? Why?"

Her father turned to look her full in the face now. His eyes were narrowed and cold, and his cheeks were flushed a hot red. "Really, Sawyer? Really?"

"Dad, I have no idea what—"

"Save it. God, Sawyer, I just don't know what to do with you anymore. I mean, I know you lost your boyfriend, and my marriage and this baby have been hard on you, but, really, grow up. What you did—" He gripped the steering wheel until his knuckles turned white and he continued looking straight out the front windshield. "You know what? You're about to be late for your appointment. I'll be right out here in an hour, and I expect you to be here."

Sawyer opened her mouth to say something, but the tension was oppressive. Instead, she swallowed back tears and slipped out of the car, making a beeline for Dr. Johnson's empty waiting room.

"Sawyer Dodd," she said to the woman at the front desk. "I guess I have an appointment."

The dark-haired woman smiled serenely. Without checking her computer or datebook, she gestured toward Dr. Johnson's office. "You can go right in."

Sawyer hiked up her shoulder bag, suddenly feeling very small and very unprotected as she walked into Dr. Johnson's posh office. She had been there a handful of times before— just after Tara and her father married, and then again after Kevin's death.

"Ah, Sawyer, so nice to see you again." Dr. Johnson was dressed in his signature "don't think of me as a doctor, think of me as a buddy!" khakis, with a light-colored button-down that showed off his trim physique. His sleeves were rolled up to his elbows, showing off well-toned forearms tufted with blond hair. He was a good-looking man, but Sawyer never trusted anyone who steepled their fingers and "mm-hmm, mm-hmmed" as much as he did.

"Have a seat."

She did, tentatively, dropping her purse on the floor. "Why am I here?"

"Why don't you tell me?"

"I wouldn't have asked if I knew," she said, feeling the hot fist of anger forming in the pit of her stomach. "Some chick at school jumped me and my father picked me up and dumped me here. It wasn't even my fault."

Dr. Johnson pressed his lips together. "So you don't want to talk about the nursery."

Sawyer felt her lip curl. "What about the nursery?"

The doctor cocked his head in what was supposed to be a comforting look, Sawyer guessed, but it just looked like condescension to her. "So we're not going to talk about it?"

"What are you talking about?"

Dr. Johnson picked up the cell phone on his meticulously kept desk. He scrolled through a few screens and then handed it to Sawyer.

She gasped.

"Oh my God. Who did this?"

The pictures were of the nursery that Tara had so carefully put together with her organic fabrics and the soothing, butter-colored walls, the white slatted crib with its layette that matched so perfectly. Only it wasn't. Now the calm of the pale yellow walls was interrupted by angry slashes of red paint that dripped in sad streaks, leaving pools on the carpet. Slats of the pristine white crib were kicked in on each other, showing the blond wood underneath. The layette was torn and slashed, bubbles of organic cotton fill bubbling out. What wasn't destroyed was splashed with heavy dots of red paint, giving the image that something truly terrible had happened there—or was about to.

Sawyer gaped at Dr. Johnson. "They think I did this."

The doctor waited.

"That's why I'm here, isn't it? My dad thinks I've gone over the edge and I—I want to hurt the baby." She shoved the phone back at Dr. Johnson. "I didn't do this. You know I wouldn't do this, Dr. Johnson, you have to tell them."

"Sawyer, a lot has happened in your life in a very short time. It's understandable that you would feel some anger."

"I'm not angry!"

"You were in a fight today at school."

"I told you she jumped on me. I didn't do anything! I had to push her off of me—that's all. I didn't mean for her to fall."

"Did you mean to send her the note? Uh…" He pushed his glasses up onto his forehead and picked up his phone, reading from it. "Maggie, You're a slut! Don't think Kevin didn't tell me about you. As a matter of fact, he said you were the worst blow ever…although ALL the other guys on the football team might have a different view."

Sawyer's eyebrows rose, as did the heat at the back of her neck. Her hand immediately, almost subconsciously, went to her jeans pocket, where Maggie's note was stashed.

"How do you know what the note said?"

Dr. Johnson looked surprised. "Your principal sent me a picture of it."

Sawyer frowned. "May I see it?"

The doctor handed over his phone. "Is that not the note you sent to Maggie?"

Sawyer read over the note pictured on the screen. The text was the same, but the paper was slightly different. "Principal Chappie had this?"

"Yes. I suppose Maggie brought it to him. You know she was suspended as well. Now tell me—"

"Maggie was suspended too?"

"That's what zero tolerance means, Sawyer. Both parties are immediately—"

"I didn't write that note."

Dr. Johnson smiled, lips pressed together. "That's beside the point. Maggie was still suspended as well."

"No—I mean, that's fine, whatever. But the note. I didn't write that. I try my best—every day—to stay out of Maggie's way. She's the one who's been harassing me. She spray-painted my locker." Sawyer paused, considering. "It was the same color paint that was on Tara's wall. And Maggie shredded my clothes, just like the layette. Maggie must have done this too!" Even as she said the words, they didn't ring true. Sawyer wasn't even sure that Maggie knew her stepmom was pregnant, let alone where she lived or what kind of schedule her family kept.

She felt the blood drain from her face.

"Someone is watching me, Dr. Johnson. Someone is trying to hurt me—and my family."

Dr. Johnson pressed back in his chair, did his psychologist-approved hand steeple. "Sawyer, I can't do anything to help you unless you're honest with me."

"I *am* being honest. I didn't do any of this."

Dr. Johnson blinked slowly. "If you can't be honest with me, you need to at least be honest with yourself. How does the impending birth of your half-sibling make you feel?"

"I feel pissed," Sawyer said, springing up, "but not at the baby. I'm pissed at whoever is making my life hell." She snatched up her shoulder bag. "And I'm going to find out who's doing it." She turned on her heel and went for the door, slamming it hard behind her.

Dr. Johnson didn't try to stop her.

ELEVEN

Sawyer was pacing on the sidewalk outside Dr. Johnson's office when her father pulled up. "Can you just take me back to the school to get my car?" she asked him.

Andrew Dodd nodded silently and Sawyer slipped in beside him, her hands gripping the strap of her bag, her heart thumping. "Dad, I—"

Sawyer stopped dead when her father made no indication that he heard—or was willing to listen to—her. His icy silence, his eyes fixed on the street in front of them was answer enough, and Sawyer kept her mouth shut, her hand on the door handle the second Mr. Dodd's wheels crunched over the gravel in the Hawthorne High parking lot.

"I didn't do this," Sawyer said before getting out of the car. "I promise, Dad. I'll prove it to you." She snapped the car door shut and Andrew revved the engine, sliding smoothly out of the parking lot without response.

Sawyer was walking to her car when she heard Chloe calling out to her.

"Hey, Sawyer! What happened to you?"

"Therapy."

"Lucky."

"You can go talk to someone if you need to, Chloe. There are counselors at school, even."

Chloe blew out a sigh. "Yes, but I prefer my therapy in retail form. Mall?"

Sawyer shook her head. "Didn't you hear? I got suspended. I'm pretty sure that translates directly to 'Sawyer Dodd will be homebound until she's seventy-five.'"

"Damsel in distress."

"Yeah. Come throw pebbles—or jelly beans—at my window. Or better yet, throw a prince on a white horse at it."

Chloe grinned. "I'll see what I can do. So, see you later?"

"God willing."

———

Sawyer walked into the house, sliding off her shoes in the foyer, feeling the need to be silent even though her father's car wasn't in the driveway and the entire house stood still and silent. She crept slowly up the stairs, each footfall landing with the heavy thud of her heart, her blood rushing in a deafening torrent as she walked to the baby's nursery. The door was closed, and Sawyer pushed open the door slowly, ice-cold air whooshing over her bare arms, making her hair stand on end.

"Oh, shit."

The pale green curtains that had once seemed so sweet and dainty with their zoo-animal border looked menacing with their severe shreds as they were sucked and expelled from the window, edges catching and tearing on the broken glass. She had seen the kicked-in slats of the crib in Dr. Johnson's cell phone picture, but up close the crib looked like a smile with broken teeth that had caved in on itself; the oozing red paint was as viscous as fresh blood and made Sawyer's stomach lurch. She clapped a hand over her mouth and heaved, relieved when nothing came out.

The baby mattress exploded with downy fiberfill, and Sawyer ran her fingers over the soft batting, her nail catching on a sharp corner. She snatched at the corner and pulled out a folded piece of paper, the same familiar green, the identical weight.

She sucked in a breath sharp as a dagger.

After everything I've done, you go to the police? You are ungrateful, Sawyer Dodd. You will pay.

She dropped the note, and this time she did heave, vomit and bile searing the back of her throat, burning in her nostrils. She ran to the bathroom and fell to her knees, the thrumming pain of the cold tile against her kneecaps nothing compared to the cramping in her stomach, to the pounding of her head as she gripped the cool sides of the toilet bowl, hurling, sweat, tears, and snot mixing in a relentless whirl.

When there was nothing left, Sawyer trudged to her own bedroom and crawled into her bed, slipping under her blankets still fully clothed down to her sneakers, and fell into a fitful, restless sleep.

The shrill ring of the telephone roused Sawyer. It was coming from somewhere around her, and she woke up confused, disoriented. It was dark; she was in her bedroom, and the phone was jammed in her pocket.

She answered on the last ring.

"Hello?"

"Sawyer!"

"Chloe?" Sawyer fumbled to sit up, to find her alarm clock. "What time is it?"

"Just after midnight. You have to get over here."

"Over where? It's midnight?" Sawyer kicked off her covers and stood up, going to her bedroom window and blinking at the single yellow streetlight that cast an ominous glow through her picture window. "Are you downstairs?"

Chloe's brother's car—mostly a Buick with three Ford hubcaps and a Rolls-Royce emblem glued on the hood—was parked askew in Sawyer's driveway. She could see Chloe, cell phone pressed against her ear, sitting in the driver's seat, her eyes fixed on Sawyer's second-story window.

"What's going on?" Sawyer wanted to know.

"Just get down here."

Sawyer looked behind her; her bedroom was untouched, nothing moved from the moment she crawled under the covers. "I don't know if I can. Someone—Maggie—"

"That's why you have to come down here."

Sawyer hung up the phone and tiptoed to her closed door. She was already in trouble; sneaking out wouldn't affect her cause for better or for worse, but when she opened her bedroom door she noticed her father and stepmother's bedroom door was open as well. The bed was still made; her father had not come home after leaving her at the school. Sawyer sighed and made a beeline out the front door.

"So, what's going on?" she asked as she sat in Chloe's passenger seat.

Chloe turned the key in the ignition, and her brother's car chugged to life, the stereo blaring and scaring Sawyer half to death.

"Sorry," Chloe said, reaching out and turning it down. "It's the only car I'm allowed near since the brake line incident. You okay?"

"No," Sawyer said. "What's this all about?"

"Maggie," Chloe said without tearing her eyes from the road. She guided the big car down the sloping hills of the estates and through the heavy iron gates, steering smoothly— if twenty miles over the speed limit—onto the highway.

"What about her?"

Chloe swallowed slowly, and for the first time since she had gotten into the car, Sawyer noticed that her best friend's blue eyes were impossibly wide, covered with a glossy sheen. Her makeup was crisscrossed with tear tracks, and the edge of her nose was red. "She killed herself."

"What?" Sawyer stomped an imaginary brake on her side of the car and turned her full body to face Chloe. "What do you mean?"

Chloe's eyes started to moisten again and she took her hands off the wheel, pressing her palms over her eyes. "Maggie's mom called my mom. They found her tonight."

"Chloe!" Sawyer gripped the wheel and pulled the car back into their lane as a big rig horn wailed next to them.

"I hated her, but I can't believe she—she—"

Chloe sniffed, and Sawyer felt the same lump growing in her throat. "She committed suicide?"

They drove in silence for a beat before Chloe turned off the highway, down a forested off-ramp that Sawyer recognized as the one nearest Maggie's house. They drove down a long, winding street that was bathed in a starlit darkness until the angry slashes of emergency lights gashed the night, orange, red, and blue cutting through the Buick's windshield as they veered to a stop.

"Oh my God," Sawyer breathed.

The cul de sac was littered with cars—some Sawyer recognized from the student parking lot at Hawthorne, most she didn't know—and police and emergency vehicles with open doors, officers and paramedics staggered around with notepads or listening to squawking shoulder radios. An officer stepped in front of a shard of yellow headlight, and Sawyer clicked off her seat belt, launching herself out of the car. She barely heard Chloe calling in the background.

"Stephen?"

Officer Stephen Haas stopped in midstride. He smiled when he saw Sawyer, but she could see that the grin held no joy, was wooden, meant to be offered to strangers and mourners in such situations.

"What are you doing here, Sawyer?"

Sawyer's eyes cut to Maggie's house ablaze with lights and then back to Stephen. "Maggie was my..." She pressed the word out over her teeth, reminding herself that it had been true, once, "My friend. What happened?"

Stephen swallowed slowly, his Adam's apple bobbing as he raked a hand through his hair. He dropped his voice and Sawyer stepped closer to him. "There's nothing official yet, but off the record"—he touched Sawyer kindly on the shoulder, an almost fatherly gesture—"I'm sorry to have to tell you this, but your friend Maggie killed herself tonight."

Sawyer felt the firm fist in her gut, felt all the air go out of her body. "She *what*?"

Now Stephen's fatherly touch on her shoulder dipped to her elbow, his fingertips closing tightly around her arm as he led her to a slightly less populated area. He cocked his head when he brought Sawyer to a stop, dug his notepad out of his front shirt pocket.

"Did you know of anyone who was bothering Maggie?" he asked her.

"Bothering Maggie?" Sawyer crossed her arms in front of her chest, suddenly, strangely aware of the chill in the night air. "No one ever bothered Maggie." *She bothered everyone else*, she stopped herself from saying.

"She didn't leave a note." His eyes flashed, almost asking if he could trust Sawyer. "But she had previously mentioned to a family member that she couldn't take the bullying anymore."

"Maggie *was* the bully."

Stephen's shoulders went up. "She didn't see it that way."

"What? That's—no. You can even ask Logan—he would know. Maggie practically ran the school."

There was a heavy metal clanging, and the heartbreaking wail of misery. Stephen looked over his shoulder, and Sawyer's eyes followed his as the front door of Maggie's house was pushed open wide and a gurney was pushed out, the unmistakable shape of a body covered in a black vinyl body bag strapped on top. Maggie's mother, her face screwed up in agony, clawed at the bag, her husband grabbing her shoulders, trying to hold his anguished wife back.

"She obviously didn't think so," Stephen said.

Sawyer felt her fingernails digging half moons into her

palms well before she realized she was fisting her hands. "Can you tell me—can you tell me how?"

She stopped before she could complete her sentence—*can you tell me how Maggie killed herself?* Because even though she knew the words, she couldn't form them, couldn't let them cross her lips, because teenagers weren't *supposed* to die. They weren't supposed to kill themselves.

The muscle in Stephen's jaw jumped as he looked Sawyer over hard, obviously wondering what he should tell. "I'm sorry," he said finally, "I can't do that."

He turned to walk away, and Sawyer jumped after him, her hands clawing against the navy blue of his heavy shirt. "Please." It was half whisper, half gasp. "I need to know."

Stephen's eyes trailed down to Sawyer's fingers and she unleashed them, one by one. "Please," she whispered.

"Officer Haas!" The stern voice cut through the light-pocked night, and Sawyer whirled. Detective Biggs was striding toward them, his pants pulling up at the ankle as he rushed, showing off his thin, slouched socks, the tufts of black hair poking out of them.

"Sawyer." Detective Biggs regarded her cautiously. "I assume you knew Maggie." He cocked his head, a mask of sadness tingeing his big cheeks pink. "I'm sorry for your loss."

Sawyer nodded, numbness overtaking her as her eyes swept over Maggie's parents, embracing, shaking under the weight of their eldest daughter being moved slowly into the back of the waiting van, the word CORONER painted in bold, straight letters on the side.

"I have to go."

Sawyer snapped herself back into the passenger side of Chloe's brother's car.

"What did you find out?" Chloe wanted to know.

"Can we just leave, please?" Sawyer's voice sounded strange and hollow.

Chloe frowned. "Sure. I guess so. Did you—"

"Please, Chloe?" Sawyer shook her head, swallowing slowly. "I just want to go home."

Chloe nodded, big blue eyes wide and focused on the dim street in front of them. "Sure. Let's just head home."

———

Sawyer's father had come home sometime—during the night or in the morning, Sawyer couldn't be sure—and left again, leaving a terse note on the countertop.

WILL BE LATE TONIGHT. FOOD IN THE FREEZER. DAD.

Sawyer crumpled the note and tossed it in the trash; she hadn't slept all night, and her stomach had been in knots since she saw the paramedics wheeling Maggie's body away. She drove to school with the radio off and the windows rolled up tight, convincing herself that if she could just stay in the tiny, closed confines of the car, none of this would touch her.

There would be no more notes.

No shredded surprises.

Sawyer took the exit that fed her into town; she slowed in front of the police station and turned into the parking lot. Her heart started to thump when she glanced through the large plateglass windows and saw Stephen in the lobby, talking to Detective Biggs.

I should stop, she told herself. *I should go in and find out what happened to Maggie.*

Sawyer pulled her car to a stop but kept her hand on the key, the ignition quiet.

After all I've done for you…

The words of the note flashed in front of her eyes.

He knew.

Sawyer's hackles went up, and a cold sweat pricked at her hairline, at her upper lip. Her saliva was sour, her tongue limp and heavy in her mouth.

He could be watching me now.

Sawyer turned in her seat, her eyes scanning the back seat littered with discarded sneakers and crumpled homework papers, a few paper cups from the Sonic drive-through on the floor.

She swallowed hard and then looked outside. The parking lot was choked with cars, but all of them sat empty. The bushes that lined the manicured lawn in front of the building were clipped too low, and the plants and trees were too sparse to hide a person. Sawyer should have felt better, but unease still cloaked her like a blanket.

When someone rapped on her windshield, Sawyer screamed.

"Sorry!" Stephen's eyebrows shot up. "I'm sorry, I didn't mean to scare you."

Sawyer opened her door and smiled sheepishly up at Stephen, her heart thundering in her throat. "No, I—I'm just a little freaked out is all."

"Is everything okay?"

Sawyer looked at Stephen, weighing the eager look in his eyes, the friendly, open set of his smile.

She could tell him.

Ask him to keep it a secret.

You'll pay, Sawyer Dodd...

"Everything's fine. I just thought I would stop by here and say thank you...to you. Thanks for listening to me. Everything is fine, though. I should go."

Sawyer snapped her car door shut and flicked the key in the ignition before Stephen had a chance to answer. She pulled out of the parking lot leaving Stephen behind her, watching her taillights flash as she sped from the lot.

"It's a juice box, not a male model," Chloe said when they were sitting in the lunchroom.

"What? Oh. Ew." Sawyer put down the juice she was drinking and rolled her eyes at Chloe. "You're gross."

"Sorry. Just trying to inject a little lightness into the day,

I guess." Chloe's smile was wistful but held no joy. "How's detention?"

Sawyer shrugged and shook her head, distracted.

There had been the pale drone of sad, whispered stories on campus since Sawyer stepped into the Hawthorne High student lot: *Is Maggie really dead? Did she really hang herself in her closet? I didn't know she was so depressed...*

A semiofficial rumor—some kid was related to someone at the county coroner's office—said that Maggie had hanged herself, that she was found in her own closet, a belt wound around her neck. Rumor or not, the idea that Maggie—or anyone, for that matter—could loop something around her neck and *kill herself* made Sawyer's blood run cold.

It had only gotten worse as the school day progressed, and every time Sawyer saw the red, puffy eyes of a fellow student, she was thrown back to Kevin, back to the Monday after his death when she trudged through the molasses-smeared memory of her heavy feet, her guilty heart.

Sawyer chewed her bottom lip. "Do you think she really did it?"

Chloe unwrapped her spork, stabbed at a dish of electric-looking orange pieces. "Did what?"

"Killed herself." Sawyer's voice dropped into a hoarse whisper. "Do you really think Maggie killed herself?"

"Well...yeah. She hanged herself, S. She was in her own closet." Chloe shuddered. "It's just awful."

"But—" Sawyer started and then stopped, snapped her mouth shut when Chloe looked up at her questioningly.

"What are you thinking?" Chloe asked.

A hot blush washed over Sawyer's cheeks and she shrugged, shoulders to earlobes. "Nothing, I guess."

Sawyer gathered up her lunch tray, unease settling over her. Maggie had harassed her every day for the last year and a half straight. Could it be a coincidence—or a message?

TWELVE

Sawyer dressed carefully, pulling on a simple black sheath dress and dark tights. There was a cold bite in the air, and when she stepped outside, goose bumps littered her bare arms. She shivered, sunk her key into her car door, and slid inside.

She was at Maggie's house twenty-three minutes later.

Sawyer parked across the street and watched the mourners crossing the Gaines's well-kept lawn. The front door to the house opened and closed rapidly as people slipped inside, their black clothes blending them together into a faceless mourning mob. She sucked in a painful breath—each time she breathed lately, she felt a sharp stab of pain in her abdomen—and kicked open the car door.

"I can do this," she told herself. "I need to do this."

Sawyer took a shaky step onto the concrete and willed her legs to carry her across the street. She paused on the Gaines's front porch when a chilled breeze cut across the lawn, carrying with it the supersweet smell of lilies. It made Sawyer's head hurt, made her remember the last time she had slipped into the black dress she now wore. The last time was at Kevin's funeral.

The warmth enveloped her the second she stepped through the door. People were packed into the living room and spilling into the kitchen, clothes in shades of mourning black and muted grays, eyes uniformly red and puffy. There was a spread of barely touched luncheon meats and cold salads that people silently poked at; no one seemed to be talking, but the quiet hum of conversation was everywhere.

Sawyer beelined for a tall, thin woman in a long-sleeved black dress. Though her eyes looked weary and her cheeks were sunken, she shared the same thick, blond hair as Maggie, the pale in her eyes a distant match to the bright cornflower blue of her daughter's.

"Mrs. Gaines," Sawyer breathed, "I'm so sorry."

Elaina Gaines's eyes raked over Sawyer and softened as a fresh wave of tears spilled over.

"Sawyer! We haven't seen you in ages." She threw her arms open and embraced Sawyer in a stiff hug, her thin, spindly arms gripping Sawyer tightly. "Thank you for coming."

Sawyer nodded, swallowing heavily. "Of course. Maggie and I were..." She struggled to say the word since so much time—and animosity—had passed between the two girls. But the photograph, two bone-thin girls in oversized helmets, grinning toothless smiles, was still in a simple frame on the mantel: Maggie and Sawyer as third-graders, arms entwined, showing off their Best Friends Forever embroidered bracelets. Sawyer felt the burn around her wrist from the bracelet she never wore.

"Is there anything I can do for you?"

Mrs. Gaines just wagged her head, pressing her hands to her cheeks. "No, thank you. I'm just so—we're just so—" The woman looked away helplessly, her shoulders racking under her silent cries. She sniffled finally and breathed deeply, using the heel of her hand to wipe at her tears. She forced a small, polite smile.

"The new choir uniforms are lovely."

Sawyer cocked her head, confused. "Yeah, they finally got it right this time."

"Maggie was so excited to wear hers. She loved to sing." Mrs. Gaines's eyes shone. "She sang like an angel."

Sawyer nodded, the words "she did," coming out soft and breathy. Guilt tugged at her heart as she remembered the exchange she'd had with Maggie about the solo.

"We plan on burying her in the dress."

Sawyer felt all the air leave the room. She knew Maggie was dead. She knew that she had killed herself in a horrible way, but the idea of her being dead and *buried* left a burning hole in Sawyer's gut.

Maggie was really dead.

"I just wish Mr. Rose had decided to add some color to the dresses. The cut is so nice, but the black is so drab."

Sawyer began to focus on the dresses—the rack of plastic-wrapped garments and Mr. Rose's sheer joy over them. Anything not to think of Maggie *buried*.

"The sashes are red," Sawyer heard herself mumble.

"Sashes?"

Sawyer made a motion around her waist. "The dresses have a big red sash that goes around the waist."

Mrs. Gaines's eyebrows pressed together as she chewed on her bottom lip. "There was no sash on Maggie's dress. It was still in the plastic bag when we—when we—" Her words dissolved into tears, and Sawyer patted her shoulder, unsure how to comfort a woman who had lost her child.

"Maybe it just fell out at school or something," she said, feeling inadequate and dumb.

Mrs. Gaines swiped at her tears again and steadied her shoulders. "You know who would love to see you? Olivia. She's around here somewhere." Mrs. Gaines started to crane her neck, and Sawyer laid a soft hand on her arm.

"I'll go find her," she said softly.

Olivia was sitting on the bottom stair, balancing a paper plate heaped with untouched ham and a congealing macaroni salad of some sort on her lap. She was holding a biscuit in her hand, tearing absently at it, the crumbs littering her plate, her pinched-together knees.

"Olivia?" Sawyer was surprised when the girl looked up at her. She had grown into her freckles and big ears and was nearly the spitting image of her older sister. She had Maggie's eyes, the gentle sweep of her nose. Her hair was a slightly paler version of her sister's, worn in the same long, layered style.

"Sawyer?" There was a faint shimmer of light in Olivia's eyes, and she dropped the hunk of bread she was holding and reached out to hug Sawyer. "What are you doing here?"

Sawyer sat down next to the girl. "Maggie was my friend."

Olivia started working the biscuit again. "She hated you."

It wasn't a surprise or a shock, but Sawyer still felt the sting of Olivia's words.

"After the whole Kevin thing," she finished.

Sawyer nodded. "It was a big misunderstanding. I wish Maggie knew—could have known—that. I just wanted to pay my respects."

Olivia nodded without answering, staring at the blank white wall in front of her. "I found her, you know."

"What?"

"Maggie. I found her in the closet. We were fighting the day before. I was wearing a pair of her jeans. She swore at me, told me never to touch her stuff. I was going in to put the jeans back...and there she was." Tears pooled on Olivia's bottom lashes. "There she was. Only, she wasn't."

Sawyer began to tremble, tears rimming her eyes. "My God, Olivia, I'm so sorry."

"I thought she was just being silly. She used to say if I kept taking her stuff without asking, bad things would happen." Olivia shook her head. "I thought she meant to me."

"Oh, Olivia, no." Sawyer slid an arm around the girl's shoulders and pulled her into her.

"How could she do that?"

"I—I—" Sawyer stammered, then felt the question burning her lips. "Was there a note?"

Olivia turned to look at her, her eyes glossy. "You mean like a suicide note?"

"Yeah."

Olivia swallowed and shook her head slowly. "No, nothing. And the weird thing is, she seemed fine—totally fine that day, that week." The girl shrugged, a fresh torrent of tears wobbling over her pink cheeks. "She never seemed like anything was bothering her."

"What is *she* doing here?"

Sawyer's head snapped up as the nasally voice cut through the din in the room.

"You, her!" Sawyer looked up to see Libby, one of Maggie's henchwomen, pointing right at her. Libby's eyes were as tear-drowned as everyone else's, but anger bloomed a bright red on her cheeks. Sawyer blinked at her, at the crowd that was craning to see.

"Libby, I—"

"You what?" Libby spat. "You wanted to make sure you'd finished the job?"

Sawyer felt herself gape. "What? What are you talking about?"

"You're the reason Maggie's dead. You—you tortured her, like, every day. You stole her boyfriend and then flaunted it in front of her. Maggie was so nice, and all you did was act like a bitch to her. And this is what happened. Maggie was so desperate to be friends with you again, but you kept right on bullying her." Libby sniffed, tears raking over her cheeks.

"No, no, that's not true. That's not how it was at all." Sawyer's heart started to pound, the blood behind her eyes a painful throb.

"You hit her the other day. You attacked her and knocked her down."

Sawyer stood up so quickly that Olivia's flimsy paper plate flipped off the girl's lap, spilling barely touched food on her lap and the staircase. Libby glared at the mess and then at Sawyer, crossing her arms as if that said it all.

Sawyer pointed to the plate. "That was an accident. And so was the fight in the hallway. Maggie picked the fight with *me.*"

Libby's eyes were spitting fire. "Convenient."

"What's going on here?"

Maggie's mother pushed through the crowd—who were all staring at Sawyer—and looked up at Sawyer, her red eyes questioning.

"Go ahead, Sawyer, tell Mrs. Gaines how you treated poor Maggie. What you did right before she died."

Sawyer felt a bitter, metallic taste in her mouth as heat engulfed her. The crowd in front of her started to shimmer as tears pooled behind her eyes and raked down her cheeks. "I didn't," she squeaked, her eyes locked on the anguish in Mrs. Gaines's eyes, "I didn't do anything to Maggie."

It was a croaked whisper while Sawyer backed through the crowd to the front door. "It wasn't my fault. It wasn't..." Her words were lost in Libby's last screams, in the coos and whispers of the crowd that tried to defend and calm. She had her hand on the doorknob, the stares around her accusatory, seeming to suck the breath out of Sawyer's lungs. "It's not my fault," she whispered.

Even she had a hard time believing it.

Her cheeks burned, and her stomach seemed to collapse in on itself as she stepped out of the house.

Could this—Maggie—*be the message her admirer was talking about?*

No. No.

Maggie did this to herself. She—But even in her own head, Sawyer couldn't form the words. Maggie *killed herself.*

Sawyer couldn't breathe. She couldn't see as tears flooded her eyes, and that was why she slipped on the porch step and fell, chest to chest, against Cooper.

"Oof!" he groaned.

Sawyer stepped back, Cooper's muscled arms holding her taut and upright.

"What are you doing here?" she asked.

His dark eyes took her in from head to toe. "Same thing you are, I suppose."

Sawyer noticed Cooper's black suit, crisp white shirt, and simple tie. Had he been dressed this way for any other occasion, she would have complimented how his broad shoulders looked under the nicely tailored jacket.

"I didn't even know you knew Maggie."

Cooper shrugged. "She was in a few of my classes. I just thought it would be nice to…"—his eyes went around Sawyer, to the closed door behind her—"pay my respects, I guess."

Sawyer nodded. "Me too."

"It's nice that you came here. I mean, I remember you told me about what happened between the two—or, three, I guess—of you."

Sawyer's eyebrows went up. "Oh, right. At Evan's party."

Cooper's finger was gentle as it brushed against Sawyer's cheek. She felt a warm shiver go up her spine and then the hot blush of embarrassment.

"Yeah." She used the heel of her hand to roughly swipe at the tears. "Sorry. Maggie and I had our issues, but I have to remember that we were friends." *Once.*

Sawyer immediately set to work stomping out the voices in her head—reminding her that Maggie said Kevin was cheating on her, letting her know that if it hadn't been for her, Maggie might still be alive this minute.

"Sawyer?"

"Oh, sorry, Cooper. What did you say?"

"I said I was just going to go in for a minute. I don't really know Maggie's family. Do you want to come in with me? Maybe afterward we can grab a cup of coffee or something."

There was nothing Sawyer wanted more than to be far away from Maggie's house and everyone in it. But coffee with Cooper…actually, anything with Cooper sounded good. Sawyer looked at Cooper's earnest eyes and paused, considering. She took a tentative step, then stopped. "Can I ask you something?"

"Yeah, sure."

"The other day, when I saw you in the hall?"

"You mean when I was going to the bathroom?"

Sawyer sucked in a breath. "You weren't going to the bathroom. No one walks completely across campus to go to the bathroom."

Cooper opened his mouth to say something but Sawyer stopped him. "And you weren't sneaking out of trig. You were on the other side of the school. Why were you in that hall?"

Cooper laughed, but it sounded forced, rough. "Wow. Nosy much?"

Sawyer didn't falter, looking at him hard.

A light blush crept across his cheeks. "Okay, I wasn't sneaking out of trig. You're right." He held up a finger. "But I was on my way back from the bathroom." Cooper blinked, looking suddenly shy. "I was in class. It wasn't trig. It was home ec."

Sawyer narrowed her eyes. "This isn't 1957, Cooper. Hawthorne doesn't even have a home ec class."

"I wish that were true. But Hawthorne does, and it's taught by Ms. Oliver in room 257, in the arts building. Third period. And if you're a transfer student hoping to take something more manly—anything, actually, that doesn't involve an apron or a ladle—you're shit out of luck." He shrugged. "It was the only open elective."

Sawyer tried to hold her lips steady, but they kept creeping up. "You're in home ec? You were lying to me because you didn't want me to know you're in home economics?"

"Yeah." Cooper lowered his voice. "And I'd appreciate it if you didn't let it get around. It's hard enough being the new guy without everyone knowing that I can't bake a soufflé to save my life."

Sawyer laughed, then clapped a hand over her mouth, relief flooding over her. "A soufflé, huh?"

"Hey, if you don't believe me, come over sometime. I can make you a roasted potato frittata that will rock your world. All the girls in class were jealous."

"Sounds like you're going to make someone a lovely wife someday, Cooper."

Cooper batted his eyelashes and pursed his lips. "Someday my prince will come along," he said in a high-pitched voice. "Hey, so, why the questions though? Is someone keeping tabs on me?"

Sawyer bit her bottom lip, the light playfulness slipping from her body. "Um, no. I was just wondering is all."

Cooper nodded. "I see. So, that coffee?"

Sawyer's mind tumbled. "I—" She glanced over her shoulder at Maggie's closed door and could almost feel the hate and blame seeping through it. She looked at Cooper and warmed when she remembered his lips on hers, his kisses deep, sincere, and sweet. She wanted to go with him. She wanted to climb in his car and drive with him wherever he wanted to go—to drive away and never come back.

Sawyer's cell phone vibrated and she snatched it up, semi-thankful for the break. "That's Chloe," she said, looking at the readout and then looking at Cooper. "I can't go for coffee," she said suddenly, pressed back into her normal Sawyer-stance. "But not because of the home ec thing. No, that's—I'm a modern woman. Just—maybe some other time for the coffee."

Disappointment flickered across Cooper's face and tugged at Sawyer's heart. He tried to hide it with that easy smile. "Sure, yeah. Another time. Totally."

They stood in a beat of awkward silence before Sawyer started to turn.

"Um, I guess I'll see you around later?"

He nodded. "Not if I see you first."

It was an old and cheesy joke, but Sawyer had a hard time laughing.

THIRTEEN

Sawyer gripped the steering wheel, her knuckles going white as she sped past the police station, then made a U-turn around it. She wanted to go to the police, to talk to Detective Biggs or Stephen Haas, but somehow her admirer knew she was there once.

He would know again.

She sighed and drove away, aimless. Though when she found herself pulling into the Hawthorne High student lot, she wasn't surprised.

A slow drizzle started to fall, and Sawyer grabbed a zip-up hoodie that lived in her back seat. She slid it over her goose-pimpled flesh and zipped it up to her neck. When she slid the hood up over her hair, Kevin's scent—cologne and a football field's worth of cut grass—enveloped her. She closed her eyes and breathed heavily, the weight of remembering heavy on her chest.

Kevin's fingers slid down her bare arm and laced with hers. She turned to him, startled—they were still a brand-new couple, and the topic of PDA hadn't been broached yet—but Kevin's eyes were warm, held that playful crinkle that she loved so much.

"What are you so nervous about?" he asked, squeezing her hand and pulling her closer. "You're with me now."

Sawyer caved to the gentle pull and snuggled into Kevin, who brushed a soft kiss over her lips. The fire that started in her belly ran through her bloodstream, warming every limb. I want to feel this way all the time, *she told herself.*

They broke their embrace—too soon, in Sawyer's opinion—and turned the corner toward the cafeteria. They were still hand in hand, shoulders pressed together, heads bent as they whispered and giggled and breathed in the comforting scent of one another.

They nearly ran headlong into Maggie, whose gasp was sharp, her cold eyes more so as they shot daggers at Sawyer. She and Libby stood in the hallway directly in front of them, blocking the cafeteria doors.

"Bitch," Maggie whispered between pursed lips.

Sawyer stiffened, tried to shake Kevin's hand from hers, but he held tight. Sawyer went from fear to guilt as she noticed Maggie working to look hard, angry—but the glossy sheen on her eyes gave her grief away.

"We broke up months ago," Kevin muttered. Whether it
was a reminder to him or to Maggie, Sawyer couldn't be sure,
but the sweet, warm feeling she reveled in was gone, replaced
by something else—something wanting and steel-cold.

"Maggie, I'm really sorry—"

"Shut it," Libby spat at her, linking arms with Maggie.
"The least you could do is not flaunt your new relationship"—
she cut the word, hard—"right in front of her face. You're
trash, Sawyer Dodd. You two deserve each other. You two
and your trailer trash third wheel, Chloe."

Sawyer stiffened, the old anger boiling up again. Maggie,
Sawyer, and Chloe had been friends—but that was a long
time ago. Maggie and Kevin had dated, too, but that was also
a long time ago. Sawyer had nothing to be ashamed of, to feel
guilty about. At least that's what she told herself when Kevin
tucked her under his arms, guiding her into the lunchroom,
Maggie's ice-cold glare left in their wake.

Sawyer swallowed back a sob and jammed her hands in
the sweatshirt pockets, crossing the parking lot and ending at
the edge of the football field. The drizzle had dipped into a
thick, gray mist now that dotted her face with a cold sheen,
but she liked the cold, slick feeling, the slight discomfort
giving her something else to focus on.

Maggie hadn't left a note. She hanged herself; she must
have talked to Libby about the way she was feeling. Sawyer's
stomach lurched painfully. Whether or not her admirer was
involved, Maggie's death was her fault. She either caused it

or drove her to it. The tears rolled down her cheeks now, dripping from her chin and disappearing into the well-kept lawn as she crossed it, her heels barely sinking in but causing a muddy, sucking sound. She crossed her arms in front of her chest and hugged herself tightly until her feet were moving faster, even though her calves and her feet protested against the ache of her shoes. By the time she had reached the stands, mud spattered her calves and the hem of her dress; her shoes were ruined and snot ran over her lips, mixed with tears, and dribbled down the front of her sweatshirt. She didn't care.

The sound of a car engine roaring to life was muffled but discernible, and Sawyer whipped around. She hadn't noticed the other car in the lot. It wasn't one she recognized—a red Celica, sporting three mismatched hubcaps and a rust stain that ran the length of the trunk. She couldn't see who was inside, either, but she knew they were in a hurry. The driver didn't turn on the headlights as he stamped on the gas, the Celica's tires spinning once on the slick asphalt before they dug in and lurched the car forward with a high-pitched squeal.

Sawyer pulled the sweatshirt tighter across her chest and jogged back to her own car. Her heart lodged in her throat when she saw the folded mint-green envelope tucked under her windshield wiper. Her breath came in short gasps and she ran to the look where the car had gone. Was he her admirer? Was he waiting, watching right now, getting off on her terror?

The car was long gone and Sawyer spun back to her own,

her fingers on the note. It was damp—not quite wet—and Sawyer's hand recoiled.

Had it been there as she left Maggie's house?

She slid into the driver's seat and glanced out the front windshield. The small note was visible, but to a distracted driver...

She yanked the note out, fingers shaking.

No one will ever hurt you again, Sawyer.

Not while I'm watching you.

———————————

Sawyer drove home in a fog, the raindrops starting with a gentle patter on the hood of her car, then moving to a loud rumble by the time she drove into Blackwood Hills Estates.

When she stepped through the front door, her father and Tara immediately stopped talking, looking up at Sawyer with eyebrows-up stares. Tara was curled on the couch, her belly swollen and huge, her bare feet tucked underneath one of the hemp pillows that Sawyer hated so much. Her father was leaning against his wife; the one hand that was tenderly massaging her back stopped and held her protectively.

Sawyer felt sick to her stomach. The image of her father and stepmother afraid, accusing, was almost too much to take. Her eyes started to water.

"I'm so sorry, Tara," she said, "but I promise you—"

Tara held up a silencing hand and forced a small smile. "It's okay, Sawyer. We can work all of this out. I know there must be a lot going on that we don't understand."

Sawyer pumped her head. "Yeah. But no more. I'm going to—I'm going to figure this out."

She spun on her heels and took the stairs two at a time, peeling off her mud-soaked clothing when she got to her room. Sawyer dumped the soiled clothes into the hamper and chose a pair of warm, dry sweats, but the chill in her bones stayed with her, and she shivered, her teeth chattering as she clicked on her laptop and dug out her cell phone. While she waited for the Hawthorne High student page to load, she paced, chewing on her bottom lip and praying that she was making the right decision.

She wasn't going to the police, after all.

Not exactly.

She sifted through smiling profile pictures on the student page until she found the one that she wanted.

"Hello?" He answered on the first ring, and Sawyer recognized Logan's voice immediately and hoped that he didn't recognize hers.

She cleared her throat. "Um, hello. Can I—may I speak to Stephen, please?"

Logan paused for a beat, and Sawyer's heart clanged like a fire bell.

"Stephen?"

"Yes. Please."

"May I ask who's calling?"

Sawyer went back to pacing. "Um..."

"Sawyer? Is that you?"

She sucked in a shaky breath. "Yeah, hi, Logan."

"I didn't know you and Stephen were friends." Logan's voice had changed. It was slow, even.

"Yeah, actually. I mean, kind of."

There was an expectant pause, and Sawyer weighed whether or not she should tell Logan that she had met his brother at the police station.

But it was *just* Logan.

Who had the locker underneath hers and was watching her run the day of the shredding.

Had Stephen told Logan that Sawyer was at the police station?

"He stopped me for speeding," Sawyer blurted, "and I just have a quick question." She forced a light, cheery tone. "Is he available?"

"Yeah, I guess so."

Logan put the phone down, and Sawyer was able to breathe again. All of her nerve endings were tingling and her mouth went dry; she didn't wait for Stephen to get on the phone before ending the call. She tossed her phone and sat at her desk, pulled out a blank sheet of paper and a pen. She scrawled the words: *note 1—Kevin*, at the top, the name Logan, with a question mark just under it. After that she listed

Mr. Hanson's note, the two bunches of flowers, the message scrawled on her locker.

Logan was there when she left Mr. Hanson's classroom after he tried to force himself on her. Though she had tried to act nonchalant afterward, she knew emotion was rolling off her in waves. He was there at the track while she ran and could have easily stayed around while she showered. And he admitted that he had sent the pink flowers, that he knew her home address.

Did anyone else?

Sawyer went back to the student home page and looked herself up. She was smiling in that picture, head thrown back in mid-laugh, clad in her track uniform. The site listed her name, her class, and her phone number. Nothing else.

A Google search wouldn't help; Sawyer's mother was paranoid and had her clerks systematically comb the Internet for any mention of her family, deleting personal information from snoop sites and public records. She said she had prosecuted too many criminals who found easy prey on the Internet.

She sighed, leaning back in her chair. Her eyes scanned her bedroom, then landed on the brochure for Blackwood Hills Estates that her father had proudly pinned to her bulletin board. One side showed the entire intended housing tract, penciled sketches of happy families walking cartoonish dogs around houses that looked like hers, shaded by trees that right now were sticklike saplings. The other side was a full-color photo of the "model" house—*her* house—with the street address clearly visible.

Sawyer's breath went sour.

Logan would have known about Maggie and Sawyer's feud—everyone did—but was he capable of *murdering* her? Her heart began to pound.

No one will ever hurt you again. Not while I'm watching you.

The ringing of the phone brought Sawyer clattering back to earth. She stared at the blinking thing and felt herself start to shake. She finally snatched it up, letting out a relieved sigh when she saw the readout: Chloe.

"Oh God, Chloe, I'm so glad it's you."

"And that's how you should always greet your best friend."

Sawyer clutched at her chest, hoping to slow her heart. "Yeah, sure. Sorry, I just—I just thought you were someone else."

"Who's that? Cooper? No, wait; then you wouldn't be so glad it's me."

"What is that supposed to mean?"

"That you love him."

Sawyer flopped back on her bed. "No. He's cool, but I'm not—whatever. What's going on?"

"News."

"Juicy gossip?"

"Kind of morbid, actually."

Sawyer frowned, sitting up. "I'm not sure I can take any more morbid right now."

Chloe's voice was soft. "I know, right?"

"So, what is it?" Sawyer's heart seemed to go from powerful thump to absolute stillness with nothing in between. "Is everyone okay?"

"Yeah. I just heard they're going to autopsy Maggie."

"So?"

"Isn't that weird? I mean, she killed herself. It was pretty obvious."

"They always autopsy suicides," Sawyer said. "It's mandatory."

"How do you know that?"

"*Law & Order.*"

Chloe sighed. "And what would we do without television? I just thought it was weird, is all. Libby was blubbering about it, saying she couldn't stand the thought of Maggie being cut up."

Sawyer's stomach clenched. "It is pretty awful." She paused. "When did you talk to Libby?"

"The memorial."

Sawyer felt her eyebrows go up. "You went to the memorial? Why didn't you tell me? We could have gone together. Then maybe they wouldn't have thrown me out and accused me of killing Maggie."

"They said *you* killed Maggie?"

Sawyer licked her lips. "According to Libby, I was the

reason for Maggie's suicide. She…she never got over me and Kevin."

Chloe sucked in a breath. "Wow. Sawyer, I'm sorry. You don't believe that, do you? I mean, Maggie killed herself. Her reasons were her own. They didn't have anything to do with you."

Sawyer wished she could be as certain.

FOURTEEN

It had been nearly a week since Maggie's memorial, and things at school were slowly—so achingly slowly—getting back to normal. Sawyer's suspension had been suspended itself, no one on the administrative board willing to mull over an incident with a dead girl and one who seemed barely alive.

Lunch hours were back to being loud and raucous even if the general murmuring in the halls was peppered with guesses about the autopsy, about what may have really transpired the night Maggie died. Sawyer felt like a zombie most days and slept like the dead most nights—a thick, dreamless sleep that settled over her in heavy waves, making her feel sluggish and tired the mornings after. She wasn't taking the Trazodone regularly now. Regardless of how much she slept, she still found herself yawning, found herself resting her head on her arms, eyelids desperate for a few more minutes of sleep at any moment.

She still jumped each time the house settled, still felt her stomach do a roller-coaster drop every time she spun the combination on her locker. She found herself backing away from crowds at school, bowing out of student events. It wasn't difficult as word of what happened at Maggie's memorial had gone viral and Sawyer had reached general social pariah status. She was even starting to avoid Chloe and Cooper, partly because she didn't have the energy to try to be social or normal, partly because she thought—vaguely—that her distance was possibly the only thing that could protect her two friends.

Sawyer woke up on Thursday morning, still crushed under the weight of sleep, under the pressure of trying to chase every errant thought out of her mind. The newspaper was strewn casually across the kitchen table when she finally trudged downstairs, dressed in dark-washed jeans and a heavy gray hoodie, hair wound in a sloppy, top-of-the-head bun. Her face was freshly washed and free of makeup; the buttery pallor was obvious, as were the heavy purple half-moons underneath her eyes. The ensemble had become her signature look over the past few days. Tara was at the table already, cup of tea steaming, elbows resting in her hands. Sawyer stood in the doorway, worrying her bottom lip.

"Tara?"

Tara looked up slowly, her hair a mess of tangles and snags, her usually healthy-looking pink face a sallow yellow.

"I thought morning sickness was supposed to end in the first trimester." She rested her forehead on the table. "And in the morning."

Sawyer smiled, a small bit of guilty relief washing over her. "Well, it is morning—I'm sorry about the multiple trimester thing. How about I make you some dry toast?"

Tara chuckled mirthlessly. "Your father thinks we should name this baby 'Dry Toast.'"

"I guess it is pretty much the Dodd family cure-all." Sawyer paused, fingers kneading her palm. "Tara, about the nursery—"

Tara looked up at Sawyer and shook her head. "It's okay, Sawyer."

"No, it's not."

"You're right, it isn't, but I'm willing to look past it if you can assure you me that this is it."

"It is," Sawyer said, nodding emphatically.

"I know this has all been a bit rough for you." She rubbed her palms over her basketball of a stomach. "And fast. But I really do want us all to be a family."

"Me too," Sawyer answered, surprised to find that she actually did. She reached for the paper and Tara stopped her, her fingers gentle on Sawyer's forearm.

"The news isn't good," she said, blue eyes wide.

Sawyer reached for the newspaper anyway, her breath

hitching in her throat when she saw the glaring headline, saw Maggie's face smiling at her from the front page: TEEN SUICIDE WAS MURDER, CORONER SAYS.

"I'm sorry, Sawyer. Your father said you two had been close."

Sawyer heard Tara speaking to her, vaguely, but everything was muffled. Heat surged through her limbs, closing like hot fingers around her throat. Sawyer gripped the newspaper and willed her eyes to focus, to avoid the innocent smile on Maggie's face, to read the newsprint underneath.

Seventeen-year-old Hawthorne High School student Maggie Gaines was found dead in her home late Tuesday night from an apparent suicide. The autopsy revealed postmortem ligature marks and fibers in the teen's throat are consistent with death by asphyxiation.

Sawyer's stomach went to liquid and scanned the paper, pulling sections apart. "Is this all there is? Don't they say anything else?"

"What else would you want to know?"

"Well, do they have any suspects? Did anyone come forward or see anything?"

Was there a note?

Tara stood up and pulled a box of Chex from the pantry. "There hasn't been any more information. I've been up since four, and the news report basically says the same thing. Cereal?"

"No." She licked her paper-dry lips and snatched her book bag from the floor where she had dropped it. "Thanks." She glanced at the clock, startled. "I'm late. I've got to go."

Sawyer tore down the front walk, her blood pulsing, coursing so hotly through her veins that she didn't even feel the cold drizzle that began to fall. She started the car and zoomed out of Blackwood Hills Estates, the empty, gaping houses shapeless blurs through the Accord's rain-splattered windows.

Students were milling around outside the school when Sawyer pulled up; she beelined for the junior hall and spotted Chloe waiting under an awning, checking her watch and tapping her foot impatiently.

"I've been waiting forever for you."

"Sorry." Sawyer shrugged. "I got a late start." She swallowed. "Did you hear about Maggie?"

"*Everyone* heard about Maggie. Everyone's freaking out. They think there is some crazed killer on the loose."

Sawyer stepped away from her best friend. "Don't you?"

Chloe shrugged under her big coat. "I don't know. I don't want to think about that. What have you heard?"

"Just what I read in the paper. That she was strangled. There were fibers in her throat."

"Red fibers," Chloe informed.

"How did you know that?"

Chloe gestured over her shoulder at the pool of kids behind her. "Gossip."

Sawyer checked her watch. "Why is everyone out here? The last bell should have rung two minutes ago."

"It did."

"Grief counselors again?"

"I haven't seen them, but there are cop cars everywhere."

Sawyer stiffened, ice water going through her veins. "Cop cars? Do they think—is there something that led them back here?"

"Like what? Clues or something?" Chloe shrugged again. "I don't know. Last I saw that short, fat detective guy was going into Principal Chappie's office." Chloe leaned close, her voice dropping. "I heard that she was strangled—or suffocated or something—with the sash from her choir dress."

Sawyer felt her face pale. She thought back to Maggie's memorial, to her mother noting that there had been no red sash with her daughter's black satin choir dress.

"Red fibers," she whispered.

"Hey, let's go in."

Logan was inside the school, striding down the hallway. He pushed open the doors and smiled at Chloe and Sawyer. "Hi, Sawyer."

"Hey, Logan. It's nice to see you. What are you doing in here?" She tried to hide her unease, but her voice sounded false, insincere, even in her own ears.

"I took the early bus. I was working in the computer lab, so Principal Chappie let me stay inside."

Chloe's eyebrows shot up. "So you've been inside the

whole time? Do you know anything? Did you hear the police talking?"

"About Maggie's murder," Sawyer said.

Logan's jaw dropped open. "I thought Maggie committed suicide."

Chloe shook her head. "No, it was all over the papers this morning and on the radio. What, do you live under a rock?"

Color bloomed in Logan's cheeks. He held up his iPod. "I was plugged in all morning. Someone murdered Maggie?"

Sawyer narrowed her eyes at Logan, trying to read his expression. Was he feigning ignorance to hide his crime?

"Your brother didn't tell you?" she asked.

"Stephen? No, he doesn't tell me anything that happens at the station." Logan turned to Chloe. "So, do they know who did it? Did they catch him?"

Sawyer shook her head.

"Why? Does anyone know why?"

"She was kind of an über bitch."

"Chloe! She's dead," Sawyer snapped. She saw the hurt look in Chloe's eyes and sighed. "She wasn't very nice, but she didn't deserve to die."

A throng of kids pushed through the open door then, separating Logan and Sawyer. Just before the crush, Sawyer was sure she heard Logan mumble the words, "Like Kevin."

She couldn't shake the chill that rolled through her.

Homeroom passed with a textbook discussion of teen suicide, the teacher lecturing on how many lives are cut short by bad, spur-of-the-moment decisions. Her eyes flashed to Sawyer when she said this and went round and sympathetic; Sawyer's eyes started to water.

She raised a hand. "Can I go to the nurse, please? I don't feel so well."

Mrs. Fluke nodded her head and scribbled out a pass; Sawyer picked up her bag and stepped out into the deserted hallway. Her cell phone buzzed in her pocket, and she slid it out: a text from Chloe.

u ok?

Just need air.

brb?

Sawyer was about to text that she would be right back when the clanging of a locker distracted her. One bank up began the junior hall, where her locker was located. Principal Chappie, Detective Biggs, and an officer Sawyer recognized, with a sinking feeling, as Stephen Haas, were standing shoulder to shoulder, watching as the principal unlocked a student locker. Sawyer silently counted the rows—*one bank down, three lockers in.*

Logan's locker.

A cold sweat broke out all over her body; for the first time since the note appeared in her locker, Sawyer was able to suck in a deep, relieved breath. She liked Logan, but if there were something in his locker that incriminated him as her admirer, that pointed to him as the one who killed Maggie, Sawyer wanted him stopped. Her eyes shifted over Stephen, and she briefly wondered if he knew that this was his brother's locker.

She choked on her deep breath when she saw Detective Biggs lean over, stepping backward with something wrapped around the edge of his pencil.

It was a long, crimson sash.

"Oh no, Logan," she whispered. But she stopped cold when the men turned and Sawyer could see that it was *her* locker door that was pried open—and that the edge of the sash was still in there.

Sawyer's eyes were wide. She sucked her breath in and flattened herself against the wall, praying the bank of lockers to her left would allow her some cover. She could hear the men talking, their voices harsh but muffled. When they quieted, she chanced a peek, her stomach rolling in on itself as she did. Detective Biggs was pawing through her things. He handed out items—her chemistry book, her math book—to Stephen, who held out latex glove–covered hands. Detective Biggs slowed when he came to a large envelope Sawyer had never seen. Her breath sped up when she noticed its telltale mint-green color. Biggs slid open the envelope and pored through it, handing each piece to Stephen as he did. The article about Kevin's death. The peanut butter wrapper and what Sawyer surmised was the folded printout of the anaphylaxis web page. A large photograph of her and Kevin. The crumpled test paper from Mr. Hanson's classroom. There were a few other things that Sawyer couldn't make out, but the last item the detective pulled out made her blood run cold.

Detective Biggs sighed and handed Stephen the framed photograph of her and Maggie that had been on the Gaines's mantel. The glass was cracked, and even from where Sawyer was standing, she could see that Maggie's face had been scratched out.

Sawyer's feet were moving before she knew she was running. Her book bag thumped against her hip; she didn't breathe until she pushed through the wide double doors and felt the sting of the cold, damp air on her face.

"Oh my God," she moaned, doubling over.

The mumbling voices of Principal Chappie and the officers were coming down the hall and when Sawyer straightened up, she saw the threesome opening the door to Mrs. Fluke's classroom.

Her cell phone was chirping by the time she had unlocked her car door. It was Chloe.

> where r u? chap & police
> looking 4 u.

Sawyer sucked in a shaky breath, then started typing.

Getting answers.

The police station parking lot was nearly deserted, and for that Sawyer was relieved. She still chose a parking spot that camouflaged her car as much as possible, just in case.

"May I help you?" The woman at the front desk was in uniform, her hair clipped short and her face freshly washed.

Sawyer pasted on her best eager smile. "Yes, actually. I am from the school paper. I'm supposed to interview Officer Haas." She neglected to note which school paper, and the young officer didn't ask.

"He is not in the office right now."

Sawyer nodded. "Right, he told me that. He should have left a file for me. Some questions. Basic stuff"—she smiled brightly, willing an innocent blush into her cheeks—"about becoming a cop and all."

The officer nodded kindly at Sawyer and pointed with her pencil. "Haas sits over there. Do you know where the file is?" She craned her neck. "Looks like there's a big stack."

"Oh, yeah, he told me exactly. He said it would be right there on his desk."

"Knock yourself out."

Sawyer beelined to Stephen's desk, quickly sifting through

the stack of manila file folders, silently thanking God that the little police department had money for silk plants, but not for a digital file system.

Gaines, Maggie, was the third file down. Sawyer shoved it in her bag and was ready to leave when something else caught her eye—another folder, another file.

Anderson, Kevin.

She looked around, confident that no one was paying attention to her, and slipped that one in her bag as well.

"Finding everything you need?" The female officer was smiling at Sawyer, looking over her shoulder.

Sawyer's heart thrummed with embarrassment. "Yep, got it. Thanks."

The folders seemed to vibrate in Sawyer's bag, and her fingers itched to pull them out and examine them, but she smiled graciously at the female officer and walked slowly out of the police station. As if on cue, her cell phone began to chirp once Sawyer stepped into the parking lot. She looked at the digital readout and sighed.

"Dad," she muttered to the empty car.

She hit the *ignore* button on the phone and slid it into her purse.

Sawyer got on the highway, guiding her car down the first exit. The trees that had looked so black and ominous the night of Maggie's death looked cheery and welcoming now, and Sawyer's little Accord zipped past, her heart seeming to speed up with every mile crossed. She pulled her car to a stop across the street from Maggie's house and killed the engine, breathing in the silence.

Sawyer slid the file folders from her bag and found Maggie's, running her fingertip over the handwritten marker—*Gaines, Maggie E.* She flipped the manila folder open quickly, her stomach clenching at the two side-by-side photographs clipped to the front cover of the folder. They were both of Maggie, her long hair brushed back from her forehead, her lips pursed. In the photograph on the left, her lips were a glossy, impish pink, the edges slightly turned up. Her eyes stared straight out, daring you to look away; they seemed to hold a world of mystery, of mischief. In the photograph to the left, the glossy pink on Maggie's lip was replaced by a matte, unnatural blue. The edges that had so often turned up in a grin or a snarl were slack now, giving way to sallow-colored cheeks. Her eyes were open but the spark was gone, the mischief, the mystery faded. Her eyes stared at Sawyer, unseeing, milky white, dead.

Sawyer was surprised when a fat tear plopped on the file folder. She sniffed, willed her shaking fingers to turn the page. The autopsy report was clipped in next and read like the newspaper article—nothing Sawyer didn't know—nothing she wanted to know.

Finally, she pushed open the car door and approached Maggie's house. It stood quiet, the entire street desolate. Sawyer pushed her hands in her pocket, unsure of what she wanted to do. When she went to reach for the doorbell, she

saw the upstairs curtain twitch, a snatch of blond hair. Her
heartbeat sped up. She knocked.

Olivia opened the door a few inches, her red-rimmed eyes
zeroing in on Sawyer. "What are you doing here?"

"I'm sorry, Olivia, I know I'm probably the last person
you want to see right now."

Olivia swallowed hard and looked over her shoulder
into the darkened house. She opened the door a small bit
more and slid out. Sawyer was surprised at how small
and frail the girl looked, even though only a few days had
passed.

"I don't want my mother to see you," she said.

Sawyer nodded. "I understand."

"I know you weren't bullying her." Olivia sunk down on
the porch step, slipping her sweatshirt over her knees.

"Do you know if anyone else was?"

Olivia shook her head soundlessly, and Sawyer bit her
bottom lip. "I need to get into Maggie's room."

Olivia's eyes flashed, brows high. "Why? What do you
want from her?"

Sawyer held up her hands placatingly. "Nothing. I don't
want anything from Maggie. We may not have been friends
at the end but we were, once. We were best friends, remember? I want to help her."

"No one can help my sister anymore. She's dead."

Sawyer closed her eyes, struck by the bitterness in Olivia's
voice. "I know. I want to find out who did this to her."

Olivia looked over her shoulder again as if considering. "My mom took a pill. You have five minutes."

Sawyer nodded and followed the girl into the house.

Maggie's bedroom hadn't changed much since she and Sawyer had been friends in elementary school. The walls were painted the same billowy pink, the bed was still spread with the lacy linens that Sawyer remembered walking her Barbies on and telling ghost stories under. The only difference was the posters and pictures tacked everywhere—Libby, Maggie and Kevin, cheerleaders, bands that Sawyer had never much cared for.

That, and the silence.

An overwhelming silence permeated the whole room, as if everything in there knew that Maggie wasn't coming back.

Sawyer wasn't sure what she was looking for and touched things gingerly—Maggie's schoolbooks, her cheer uniform, the pom-poms discarded on the floor. When she turned and faced the closet, beads of sweat rose out at her hairline.

She tried hard not to think of Maggie's final moments and instead dropped to her knees, feeling around the closet floor. Her fingers closed around a woven bracelet, her heart speeding up as she brought it closer to examine it.

"Best friends," Sawyer breathed. The words were embroidered into the thing, a bracelet that she and Maggie shared the summer they spent at camp. Like Maggie's, her own was probably discarded somewhere in her closet.

"Time to leave," Olivia said from the doorway.

Sawyer slid the bracelet into her jeans pocket and stood, passing Olivia as she left.

"Did you get what you came for?" Olivia wanted to know.

Sawyer just nodded, her emotions knotted in her throat.

When Sawyer got back to her car, she noticed she had missed another two calls from her father. She ignored them and put the car in gear.

Sawyer drove home on autopilot, was at the gates to Blackwood Hills Estates before she realized where she was going. She paused briefly to glance at a car just inside the gate. It was mud splattered and parked on a stretch of untouched earth that Sawyer's dad assured her would one day be a community park. Sawyer blinked at the car, faint recognition glowing in the back of her mind. It was the same make as Cooper's, but this one had a heavily dented passenger door that seemed to be slightly open. Sadness throbbed in her throat. There wasn't much chance that Sawyer's life would go back to normal now; not much chance that a nice guy like Cooper would be interested in a girl being chased by the police. She sighed and pressed on the gas, leaving the car—and thoughts about Cooper—behind.

The rain was falling in heavy sheets now, darkening the sky and giving the bare trees and vacant homes in the tract an ominous look. Sawyer zipped past them and parked in her own driveway, car skewed. The yawning living room was awash in shadows, and Sawyer turned on every light, clearing this morning's paper from the kitchen table and laying out the file folders. On a steeling sigh, she pulled Kevin's to the top of the pile and opened it.

Stapled to one cover was the coroner's report. Sawyer winced, trying her best not to fixate on anything there—grisly descriptions of textbook body parts—body parts that had belonged to Kevin, that she had loved and caressed and brushed up against. Her fingertips brushed over the toxicology report, listing Kevin's blood alcohol level as 0.22. A heavy black X covered the box marked *legally intoxicated*. Sawyer sighed, pinching her bottom lip and peeling open the envelope included in Kevin's report.

Her stomach roiled, and she clamped her lips down hard as she spilled out the contents of the envelope. Full-color crime scene photos littered the top of the dining table, and Sawyer's fingers fumbled as she worked to gather them up, stacking each horrid image one on top of the other. Her mouth filled with blood, but she kept her teeth gritted hard, her hands fisted as she forced herself to sift through each picture, taking in every putrid detail—the crushed, buckled metal of the broken car, the splinters of blood-edged glass staining the concrete. The first few shots were exterior, and Sawyer smelled the acrid smell of hot metal, the choking stench of blood on the night air. It stung her nostrils and she flipped, fingers shaking, to the next group of photos. These were interior, and Sawyer was blinking, the itch from her tears tracking over her cheeks. She remembered the soft feel of the ruined leather, the glint from the tiny crystal that hung from the rearview mirror. She remembered the night she gave it to him.

It was September, but summer still hung on the stillness of the night air, the long days being slowly chased away by tiny wisps of fall on the breeze.

"I got you something," Sawyer said, a smile playing at the edges of her pink, glossed lips.

Kevin's head lolled against the gray leather headrest and he grinned at her, eyebrows raised sexily. "Oh yeah? What's that?"

She pulled the little charm from her pocket—a cut glass football that she had picked up at the Boardwalk—and dangled it between forefinger and thumb. The orb caught the yellow glow from the streetlight and broke it into a thousand tiny shards of rainbow-colored light.

Kevin's fingers brushed against hers as he took the charm. Electricity, like the lights of the prism, broke through Sawyer in a thousand tiny, twittering vessels.

"Do you like it?" she breathed.

"It's from you, isn't it?" He hung it over his rearview mirror. "That means I love it."

Sawyer felt a cold shiver of delight.

"Here," Kevin said, shrugging out of his hoodie. "I don't want my girl to get cold." He slipped the well-worn sweat-shirt over Sawyer's bare shoulders and pulled her to him; she softened, fitting her curves against his angles.

"This is perfect," she said, breathing deeply, letting the familiar cut-grass cologne scent of Kevin's hoodie envelope her. "So, so perfect."

She closed her eyes and could still smell Kevin, the fading scent of cologne on his hoodie. She pushed away the photographs and held her head in her hands, breathing deeply. The edge of a photo caught her eye.

Beer bottles. Crushed brown glass on the floor of Kevin's car.

She thought of that night, the way the slick shards of moonlight glinted off his eyes, even though his face was mostly obscured by his hood. Sawyer remembered the way he pulled it up so only a few licks of his dark hair showed; she remembered the way the too-long sleeves curled over his knuckles. She remembered that he was wearing that black hoodie as she jogged away from him, the beer bottle sailing past her left ear.

And now that black hoodie was in the back of her car. Sawyer squinted, trying to remember. How had Kevin's hoodie ended up in her car? It was lying in a crumpled heap half under one of the seats and she had dismissed it at the time, but now the thought nagged at her.

She flipped through the rest of the documents in the file, pausing briefly on her interview with Detective Biggs, her breath hitching in her throat when she saw the next interview form enclosed—*Haas, Logan.*

It was dated a full month before Kevin's death, and Sawyer

squinted at the handwritten page, the photocopy imperfect, ink fading.

"Kevin bullied Logan," she mumbled to herself, laying the paper down flat. "That wasn't news." Sawyer turned the paper over, noting that the attending officer was Stephen Haas.

She pushed Kevin's file aside. It caught the corner of the stack, and the whole group flopped off the table, pages scattering and falling gracefully to the slate flooring. Sawyer leaned over to pick them up, snatching up first a handwritten incident report from Maggie's file.

...ATTEMPTED BREAK-IN THE NIGHT BEFORE; AUTHORITIES WERE CALLED BUT NO INTRUDER WAS FOUND ON THE PREMISES...

...SUBJECT REPORTED A RUN-IN WITH A STUDENT AT HAWTHORNE HIGH SCHOOL [JUNIOR SAWYER DODD] EARLIER THAT DAY. NO FOLLOW UP REPORTED...

Another page floated down, landing delicately on the floor. Sawyer's stomach lurched as she read the typewritten header:

SUBJ: Amendment to M. Gaines' Autopsy Report and Statement.

Sawyer continued to read:

J. Hugh, M.E. Crescent County

It is my professional opinion that subject M. Gaines was asphyxiated with a belt (approximate 1" width) cinched around her neck. Assailant assaulted Gaines from behind; pre-mortem bruising indicates assailant aimed the cinched area downward either deliberately or due to a height discrepancy. Once subject was subdued, assailant pushed fabric "gag" down her throat (also pre-mortem). Bruising around the trachea is consistent with these findings.

Sawyer shuddered and pushed the page aside with her foot, just enough to expose one line from the paper underneath:

First on the scene: Officer S. Haas.

Stephen was the responding officer every time.
Could he...?
Sawyer's mind started to race. She thought about Logan, slight, shy. His hands trembled when he asked her out. Was he her admirer? Was Stephen covering up for his little brother?

Sawyer shuddered, dumping the files in a hasty stack on the table, and jumped when the phone rang. She grabbed the receiver.

"Hello?"

"Sawyer, oh, thank God."

Heat raced through her. "Oh, uh, hi, Dad."

"I have been calling you for a half hour. Have you been home all this time? Do you know the police are looking for you?"

Sawyer considered hanging up the phone and running upstairs to her room, diving under the sweet-smelling covers on her bed. Instead, she started to shake. "I didn't do anything, Dad. You know that, right?"

Andrew blew out a long sigh. "Your mother will be calling you soon. I don't have her flight information yet."

"Mom's coming?"

"Sawyer, she's an attorney. You're in some pretty deep trouble here."

Sawyer pinched her lips. "Is Tara with you?"

"No, that's why I'm calling. She's not answering her cell phone, either. She barely made it to work before they sent her home."

Sawyer looked around the still house. "I don't think she's here. Oh, wait. I see her purse. She didn't say anything when I came in."

"She's probably asleep. Do me a favor, just check in on her—don't disturb her, she needs her rest—but have her call me when she wakes up."

A sob lodged in Sawyer's throat. "Aren't you coming home now?"

"I can't, Sawyer, not right now. I'm sorry. I'll be home as soon as I can."

"You know that I didn't do this, right, Dad?"

But the only answer that came was a dial tone.

Sawyer ran up to her stepmother's room and held her breath, knocking gently. "Tara?" she whispered.

There was no answer, so Sawyer pushed the door open cautiously, poking her head in. "Tara?" she asked again.

The bedroom was pristine, and Sawyer cocked her head when she heard the rush of the shower. The door to the bathroom was shut and locked, and Sawyer knocked hard. "Tara? I'm home. Dad wants you to call him when you're done, okay?"

The house was darkening. The gray of the sky was being edged out by an inky, all-encompassing blackness that seemed to weigh on Sawyer's chest. She crossed the hall to her own room and flopped down onto her bed, feeling the weight of the day—the days, actually—pulling on her limbs. Everything ached. She pressed her palms against her eyes then blinked up at the ceiling, letting the tears roll over her cheeks, drip onto the bedspread. She squinted then, seeing the tinge of red.

When she rolled over onto her stomach, every aching muscle in her body prickled with a primal fear. Her heart hammered against her rib cage, and she launched herself from the bed, backing up so rapidly that she thunked against her desk, sending a shower of jewelry and pens clattering to the ground.

She couldn't tear her eyes away from the wall above her bed, from the gashes of red paint she had grown to despise—from the words *I see everything* scrawled above her headboard.

FIFTEEN

Bile rose in Sawyer's throat.

She dashed across the hall and kicked at the bathroom door, yanking on the knob and using the heel of her hand. "Tara, Tara, get out here! We have to get out of here right now!"

Sawyer was sobbing openly now, looking back toward her room as if the words would come to life and follow her.

"Tara!" She kicked at the door again and finally pressed her ear against it, praying to hear the sound of the water softening, the tap turning off, Tara coming to her rescue. But the shower remained a thunderous rain. Sawyer stepped back to kick open the door and stopped, astonished, when her feet sunk into the carpet.

It was soaked.

"Oh my God. Tara!"

Sawyer shouldered the door, hard. She heard the splinter of the wood frame and hit it once more, sending the thing vaulting open and her tumbling into the bathroom. She slid on the tile floor, a sheen of water making the entire room slick.

The first thing Sawyer saw was Tara's bare feet, resting one on top of the other. They were kicked against the glass shower door, a rivulet of shower water pouring out underneath them.

"Oh no." Sawyer gripped the sink and made her way to the shower, where Tara was slumped. Her naked body was crumpled on the tile floor, her blond hair floating on a quarter inch of water. Her cheeks were pink and flushed, her shoulder and pregnant belly a deep red where the water was pelting her.

Sawyer's tears were steady now and she felt herself gasp—and smile—when she saw the light rise and fall of Tara's chest.

"Oh, thank God!"

She really did feel relief, her tears turning to joy, when she turned off the tap and snatched a towel from the rack. She laid it gently over Tara's body, covering her. She tapped her cheeks lightly, then harder. "Tara? Tara!"

Tara's head lolled listlessly, her mouth hanging slack. "Oh please, Tara, wake up!"

Sawyer sloshed through the water and snatched the phone from the nightstand next to her father's bed. She dialed 911 and took huge, gasping breaths of air, then stopped when she realized the line was completely dead.

"No, no, no!"

She was going for her cell phone when she detected motion out of the corner of her eye. A car was coming down the street toward the house, coasting along the slick blacktop. As it got closer, Sawyer's heart began to pound.

It was a police car.

She began to back away from the window when she realized that Stephen Haas was driving it. It was only then that Sawyer noticed the car pulled up tight against the house.

"Oh God, Chloe."

She ran downstairs and snatched the door open, throwing her arms around Chloe as she stood on the porch. "Get inside."

"Sawyer, the police—"

Sawyer slammed the door hard. "Where's your cell phone? We have to call 911."

"But the police are right—"

"No!" Again tears stung Sawyer's eyes. "I don't trust him! He's coming for me. Call 911 and get an ambulance."

Chloe gripped Sawyer's shoulders. "What is going on?"

Sawyer wagged her head, her breath caught in a plastic bubble that refused to burst. Her skin felt tight; her forehead seemed to shrink against her brain. She doubled over, rubbing her eyes with her fists.

"I think it's Stephen. He's Logan's brother. I think he's

after me—I think he killed Kevin and Maggie or he's covering up for Logan."

"But why?"

Snot and tears rolled down Sawyer's chin. "I don't know."

Chloe's eyes were wide when Sawyer straightened up again. Her mouth dropped into a little o of surprise; there was warm concern in her eyes. Her grip on Sawyer's shoulders tightened, and Chloe stepped around her, nudging Sawyer back into the house, shutting the door solidly behind her. Sawyer heard the lock tumble into place.

"Sawyer, you're about to hyperventilate."

"You don't understand, Chloe. We have to get out of here! Logan—Stephen—he knows where I live! He'll be back, and we have to save Tara—"

Sawyer was crying hard, big hiccupping sobs that wracked her shoulders and made the ache in her chest that much greater.

Chloe pulled her phone from her pocket and dialed, pressing it to her ear. Sawyer listened to Chloe give her address, speaking slowly, asking Sawyer if Tara was still breathing.

Sawyer nodded frantically, and Chloe hung up the phone. "They're on their way."

Sawyer physically crumpled, and Chloe snaked her arms around her. "Shh," she said, "it's going to be fine. Everything is going to be okay." Chloe brushed a soft, comforting kiss on Sawyer's forehead.

There was a heavy knock at the door, and Sawyer

stiffened. Her heart lurched. She felt her eyes widen, the fear coursing through her veins and making her limbs leaden. "That's him."

Chloe lowered her arms and stepped around Sawyer, the picture of calm. She rolled up on her tiptoes and pressed her eye to the peephole. "It's a cop."

Sawyer straightened. "He can't know I'm here."

The knock sounded again, hard, insistent. "Sawyer? Ms. Dodd? It's Officer Haas."

Chloe blinked back at her. "Officer Haas?" she hissed.

Sawyer swallowed heavily, her saliva sour. "He—he—that's Logan's brother."

Stephen shook the doorknob, and Sawyer's eyes were riveted to the door.

"We need to answer that," Chloe said. "He knows I'm here. My car is right outside."

Sawyer swallowed heavily, images of the past few weeks flashing in front of her eyes. "No. He wants to arrest me. Or"—she sucked in a shaky breath—"worse."

Chloe sighed. "He's not going to go away."

Sawyer stumbled backward, head wagging. "I can't answer it. I can't."

Chloe bit her bottom lip. "Just"—she snatched open the closet door and shoved Sawyer in it—"be quiet."

Sawyer held her breath, listening to Chloe pull open her front door. "Can I help you?" Chloe's voice sounded even, calm.

"I'm looking for Sawyer Dodd. Is she here?"

Sawyer's heart hammered against her rib cage. She was certain the closet's acoustics were only highlighting and broadcasting the sound.

"No," Chloe answered. "Actually, I came over here looking for her—she left school early. But no one was here."

Sawyer's teeth bored into her bottom lip. Her hands were fisted, palms sweaty.

"How did you get in the house?" she heard Stephen ask.

"Sawyer's my best friend. I have her key."

Sawyer thought she heard the tinkle of a key ring being displayed. She gritted her teeth against a maniacal grin that started to play on her lips. Chloe was putting on a great act—Sawyer had never given her the key to the house.

"Look…" Stephen's voice drew out.

"Chloe."

"Chloe, look, it's really important that I find Sawyer. She could be in some real danger."

Sawyer's heart continued its wild thump, and she pressed her palms to her chest, hoping to muffle the sound.

"Absolutely," Chloe said. "The second I find Sawyer, I'll be sure to let her know you're looking for her."

There was an awkward pause and Sawyer waited, muscles stiff, eyes wide and slowly adjusting to the dim coat closet.

"Okay. Please, have her contact me right away."

"Will do."

Sawyer listened to the front door slam and waited until

she heard Stephen's engine roar to life before she opened the closet door a half inch. "Is he gone?" she mouthed.

Chloe nodded, opening the door wide.

Sawyer stepped out tentatively, then slunk to the front window. She held her breath until she spotted Stephen's taillights sailing through the iron gates.

"Thank God."

Chloe licked her lips, smiling. "See?"

"See what?"

She turned on her heel, blond ponytail swaying. "Didn't I tell you'd I'd always take care of you?"

Someone sucked all the air out of the room, and Sawyer's stocking feet were rooted to the carpet. "What did you say?"

Chloe stopped abruptly but didn't turn around. "What?"

"Just then." Sawyer reached out, tentatively touching Chloe on the shoulder. To her surprise, Chloe shrugged away. She turned to face Sawyer, her pink lips pressed in a hard, thin line. "I said I'd always take care of you. I'd do anything for you, Sawyer."

White-hot heat seared Sawyer's spine. "Chloe?"

"Come on, sweetie." Chloe offered Sawyer a hand and Sawyer stared at it, dumbfounded.

"I said, come on!"

Chloe wrapped her hand around Sawyer's wrist and gave it a hard tug. She stopped immediately, her face contorted into apologetic sympathy. "I'm sorry." She smiled sweetly. "I wouldn't want you to think I'm anything like him."

Sawyer stopped and snapped her wrist from Chloe's hand. "What the hell is going on here, Chloe?"

Both girls stopped cold when a muffled groan and a loud thump came from above them. "Tara." Sawyer went to the window and peered out. "Where is the ambulance? You have to wait for the ambulance. I'm going to go check on Tara."

But Chloe didn't move.

"Chloe!"

"Tara is going to be fine. It's all going to be fine."

Sawyer turned to run, but Chloe grabbed her, hard, jabbing something cold against Sawyer's rib cage. It was the glint of the blade that caught Sawyer's attention first.

"Chloe, what is that?"

The knife was unlike anything she'd ever seen before. The blade was curved and looked menacing, the edge sharpened razor-thin. Chloe's eyes followed Sawyer's to the knife. Chloe rolled the tip against Sawyer's body. The move was gentle but sent shock waves of fear radiating through Sawyer.

"It's all going to be fine."

Sawyer went stone still. "Put the knife down, Chloe. My God, where did you get that thing, anyway?"

Chloe shrugged but didn't relinquish her grip on the knife, the tip still a hair's breadth from Sawyer's flesh. "You'd be surprised at the things my parents have lying around the house."

"Chloe, this isn't funny. The police are going to be here any minute."

Chloe cocked her head, a hazy serenity in her eyes. Her lips curved up at the corners just the slightest bit. "No one's coming, Sawyer."

She held up her phone, then dropped it. Sawyer watched in horror as the phone fell, the screen shattering at her feet, plastic pieces skittering across the marble floor.

"What are you talking about?"

"Don't you get it, silly?" Chloe blinked and reached out for Sawyer's hand again, this time finding it and lacing her fingers through Sawyer's gently. Chloe took a slight, tentative step forward, and Sawyer could smell the faint trace of Chloe's perfume as her lips touched Sawyer's ear.

"I've always admired you."

Blood began to pulse through Sawyer. Her eyes stung. "You?" Her voice was a hoarse whisper, almost unrecognizable in the dimming air of twilight. "You did this?"

Sawyer could feel Chloe's moist breath against her ear, her neck. Sawyer watched in dead silence as Chloe took the knife from where it rested on her rib cage and pressed it against Sawyer's neck. "I'd do anything for you."

A violent tremble started at Sawyer's head and worked its way down. "What?"

Chloe didn't answer. Though she kept the knife firm, her lips were soft and her eyes dreamy. She used her other hand to gently brush a strand of hair from Sawyer's cheek. "Anything at all."

Sawyer shook her head, images tearing through her mind:

Kevin in his coffin, Mr. Hanson's hands against her skin, Maggie... "No. No, you couldn't have."

Chloe tapped the thin steel blade against her lips, a slight smile on her face. "I couldn't have fed Kevin beers until he was falling-down drunk, then handed him his car keys? Or I couldn't have mixed a big glop of peanut oil into Señor Hanson's guacamole?"

"No." Sawyer paused, then gaped when the fabric of the bracelet brushed against her cheek. The embroidered words *Best Friends Forever* just at her peripheral. "Where did you get that?"

Chloe smiled. "We both have them again. You found Maggie's, didn't you? I know you were over there."

Sawyer felt sick and she closed her eyes tight. "You've been watching me."

"Always."

Sawyer's tongue brushed across her lips. "You killed Kevin."

Chloe rolled the strand of hair between her forefinger and thumb, her eyes fixed on it, admiring it.

"Why Kevin? Why now? How long—how long have you felt this way?"

The question seemed to make Chloe seethe, the cold steel of the knife vibrating against Sawyer's carotid artery. "Forever." She clipped the word.

"Forever?"

"God, Sawyer!" Chloe threw up her hands. "I couldn't

take it anymore! I loved you, I love you so much and I couldn't watch it anymore. He was—he was ruining you, and you were *letting* him."

Tears blurred Sawyer's vision. "No," she whispered.

Chloe's eyes glowed like the last ashen embers of a dying fire. She almost looked sad. "Don't you see?" She smacked the knife hard with her other hand, and the thwack made Sawyer jump. "He didn't care about you! He didn't love you. I wasn't the only one, either, Sawyer." She dropped her eyes for a brief second, looked at Sawyer through lowered lashes. "But you were the only one he hurt."

Sawyer's stomach dropped and an inappropriate rush of shame washed over her. "You knew about that?" Her voice was a choked whisper against Chloe's ragged sigh.

Chloe shrugged. "You let him."

"I didn't let him hit me." It was Sawyer's turn to be angry now. "I didn't just let it happen."

"Well, you sure as hell didn't stop it, now did you?"

"It wasn't like that. I couldn't—"

"Couldn't let him go?" Chloe mocked. "Couldn't ask for help? Couldn't see past your own stupid nose is more like it. You're a victim, Sawyer. Look at everything bad that happens to poor, poor Sawyer. You didn't need him. So when I saw an opportunity, I took it."

"What are you—"

"That night. You finally—finally—broke up with him. But I knew it wouldn't stick. You'd go crawling back to him.

He'd tell you how much he loved you, and you would turn into a big, sobbing bowl of jelly. So I stepped in. You know what happens when guys drink, Sawyer? They get horny. And a guy like Kevin Anderson doesn't really care where he gets it from."

"You..." Sawyer couldn't push the words past her teeth.

"Oh, don't act so surprised. You weren't the only one. And neither was I." Chloe shrugged again, the knife bobbing in her hand. The sharp blade caught the light, and Sawyer sucked in a breath.

"It was the perfect storm that night," Chloe went on. A grin spread across her face and the calm serenity in it was chilling. "One, two, three...Kevin Anderson, done in by me." She seemed proud of her macabre rhyme and laughed, the tinkling sound catching in the charged air.

"So, your brake lines? The gash on your head? That was all you?"

Chloe rolled her eyes. "Oh, come *on*, Sawyer! I had to play the game!"

"This is a game to you?"

She shrugged again, looking suddenly, chillingly, nonchalant. "Let's say I was killing two birds with one stone. Everyone thinks someone's out to get me." Chloe's eyes suddenly went hard. "Maybe paying me some kind of attention for once."

Sawyer swallowed. "And?"

"And my crap excuse for a mom gets the ride of her life on her way to work." Chloe held out her hands like a scale.

"Win, win." She licked her lips and a grin spread across her face. It was maniacal, totally gleeful, and it gave Sawyer terrified chills.

"But you said the car was fixed."

"Yeah." Chloe nodded, still grinning. "It was."

Sawyer's breath hitched on a sob as the weight of Chloe's confessions pressed against her. "You murdered my boyfriend. You were there that night. The shoe—my shoes—and the sweatshirt. You took Kevin's sweatshirt."

Chloe's lower lip popped out. "I was cold."

Sawyer worked to form the words. "You killed my boyfriend."

Chloe abruptly dropped the strand of hair and narrowed her eyes. "Some boyfriend," she spat.

Sawyer shook her head, incredulous. "You framed me, Chloe. You put all that stuff in my locker."

A ripple of fury washed over Chloe's face. Her nostrils flared, her lip curled slightly. "You weren't listening, Sawyer. I had to make you listen."

"By getting me thrown in jail?"

"It wouldn't have gone that far. I would have saved you. I needed to get your attention, to force you to listen. You can be a little hardheaded, Sawyer."

"I can't believe—I can't believe..." Sawyer's lower lip started to tremble. Chloe frowned, her eyes mirroring Sawyer's sadness.

"That's okay. You don't have to apologize."

"I'm not apologizing!"

Chloe stepped toward Sawyer so that their faces were mere inches apart. Chloe cocked her head, and Sawyer watched the blade come up. Chloe pushed a heavy lock of Sawyer's hair away with it and Sawyer tried to hold still, tried to stay herself against the rippling shiver that went through her body as a few strands of her hair, severed by the knife, fell against her bare arm.

"Do you see why I had to do it? Why I had to take care of you? I'm always taking care of you. But that's fine." A weird, slow smile spread across Chloe's face. "I like taking care of you."

"You need help, Chloe. You need serious help."

Chloe cocked an annoyed eyebrow and crossed her arms in front of her chest. "Excuse me?"

"You're crazy."

Chloe's eyes widened. "I'm crazy?" she sputtered. "I'm crazy? I try and protect my best friend, and what does she do? She goes and plays human punching bag with some cock-sucking jock. And for what? So you can be 'popular'?" Chloe made air quotes around the word, but her eyes were wild and deadly serious. "So you can sit in the cool section at the big game with all the other silicone-stuffed lemmings?" She scratched her head at the part. "Come on, Sawyer. You're pretty and all, but not pretty enough to be that dumb."

Sawyer stared at Chloe, dumbfounded, and Chloe stomped a foot. "Are you kidding me? You still think he loved you." Chloe got up in Sawyer's face again, bits of spit sticking to Sawyer's cheek as Chloe bit off her words. "He didn't care about you. But you wouldn't know love if it hit you in the face." Chloe used both her hands to smack Sawyer's cheeks. "You never even paid attention to me when Kevin came around." Her voice was a low whisper.

Sawyer wiped her eyes with her sleeve. "What? I don't understand. I mean, why—why now? Why are you doing this to me?"

"Why?" Chloe gaped, looking wildly astonished. She stumbled backward and sank into an armchair, her fingers absently running over the knife. "I really, really can't believe you'd ask me that. I mean really, Sawyer, you're making me look bad."

"But—"

"But, but, but," she mocked, "of course. Why would I do this *to you*? The answer is in the question." She laughed mirthlessly. "People are dead all around you, and you ask why I did this to you. It's not what I did *to you*, it's what I did *for you*. What I always do for you." She jabbed an index finger toward her chest. "I protect you. But do you see it? No," she dragged out the word. "Of course not. You never see it because it's all about Sawyer. Sawyer's boyfriend. Sawyer's teacher making a pass at her. Sawyer's new family. Sawyer, Sawyer, Sawyer." Chloe stood. "But what about Chloe?" she pointed the knife at herself. "What about me?" Her eyes flashed back to a fresh, clear blue, and when she blinked, a single tear rolled down her cheek.

Sawyer sucked in a shaky breath and thought about Tara lying nearly unconscious upstairs, thought about her baby sister. There was no way past Chloe and her knife. No cell phone, no help on the way. She licked her lips.

"I love you, Chloe," Sawyer said, her voice a breathy whisper.

Chloe sniffed and shook her head. "Don't you say that. You don't love me."

"I do." Sawyer took a step forward.

"Stop!" she gripped the knife and shoved it in front of her. Sawyer's eyes went to it, and she felt herself start to shake. She steeled herself, forced herself to look away.

"You don't really care about me," she murmured.

"What did you say?"

Sawyer swung her head to face Chloe and kept her words flat and matter-of-fact. "I said, you don't really care about me. You don't really love me." She chuckled. "I guess you were right. I don't know anything about love."

Chloe gaped. "Are you kidding me? All this. I did all of this for you."

"I think you did it for you. I think you like to hurt people and you wanted an excuse to do it. You don't love me, Chloe, you don't even like me half the time."

"Shut up!"

The smack across Sawyer's face was hard. It stung, and she reeled. She tried her best to stay calm, unaffected, as she wiped her hand across her throbbing nose. She looked at the blood in her palm, tasted it gushing from the front of her mouth. "That just proves it."

"No." Chloe's eyes were big, the tears falling immediately. She raked her fingers through her hair, still clutching the knife in front of her. "I'm sorry, Sawyer, I didn't mean to do that. But you—you don't understand. I love you. I love you so, so much. Can't you see? Everything I do. Are you listening to me?"

But Sawyer was nonchalantly looking around the house, kicking at the carpet with her foot, as if Chloe was trying to sell her Girl Scout cookies, the knife in her hand nothing but a box of Thin Mints.

"You're impossible!" Chloe shrieked, whirling around to pace. When she stepped back again, Sawyer was gone.

She cut through the entry hall and kicked the front door open, letting it smack loudly against the wall. She knew it would get Chloe's attention, knew that if she took off, Chloe would follow. Sawyer snatched Tara's bag from the peg by the door as she ran, her socks smacking against the damp concrete of the driveway.

It seemed like only seconds that Sawyer had been home, but the storm-dark sky was already bleeding into an inky black. The temperature had dropped at least ten degrees, and the icy cold froze Sawyer's lungs and made her legs feel tight and heavy. She heard Chloe cross the threshold and bound after her, just seconds behind.

Sawyer pushed herself harder, vaguely wishing she had her windbreaker to cut through the biting wind.

"Oh God."

She remembered the photo of herself running pinned to Chloe's wall. She was wearing the windbreaker she wished she had now—the one she was wearing the morning she ran in the neighborhood.

Her best friend had been stalking her.

Terrorizing her.

She tore down the street, looking for somewhere to go. The houses that had been so cheery and homey just hours ago seemed to scream out their emptiness. The blank, black windows reflected Sawyer's image back to her, a bitter reminder that she was all alone.

"Sawyer!" Chloe was closing in on her, and suddenly Sawyer cut left, running up her neighbor's driveway. The wind whipped her hair in her face, but her pace was steady. Rain had just started to fall, heavy drops turning the dirt into mud and pounding over the abandoned two-by-fours and other construction debris as Sawyer cleared through the unlandscaped front yard and tore around the side of the house. The fresh redwood fence and cheery neighborhood facade ended at the back of the model, and Sawyer paused, heart thundering, as she looked out at the muddy expanse in front of her.

Chloe hadn't come around the house yet, and Sawyer took the second to stop, digging through Tara's bag until she found her cell phone. She mashed all the buttons and the screen lit up, letting Sawyer know that she had only one bar of service.

"Get back here, Sawyer!"

Chloe's voice reverberated through the fresh construction, and Sawyer pitched forward, running toward the lone cell tower at the back of the development. She was at the base of the small dirt hill as Chloe burst into the backyard.

Sawyer mashed the phone again, the screen still flashing that single bar. The rain was starting to fall steadily in icy sheets and she shivered, turning back toward the hill, her socks sinking into the mud.

"Sawyer!"

Chloe was at her ankles now, her clawed fingers grabbing at Sawyer.

"Let me go!" Sawyer kicked at Chloe's hands.

The rainwater washed down the muddy hill in gales, and Sawyer slid down toward Chloe. Chloe grabbed at her, her fingers digging into the soft flesh of Sawyer's forearms.

"Come on, Sawyer, we can leave. We can go away from here."

"No." Sawyer shook her head, her tears mixing with the rainwater that pelted her face. "You're sick, Chloe. This isn't love. You don't love me, you need help."

"Stop saying that!"

"It's true."

"You are so ungrateful." Chloe's teeth were gritted and rainwater dripped from her chin. "I can't believe I loved you. I've done everything for you! You didn't even ask, and I did it." She slammed her fist against the mud just to the side of

Sawyer's ear. "You don't even care! You don't even care!" Chloe was crying now, great, racking sobs. "I did everything for you, Sawyer. Everyone wanted to hurt you, and I didn't. I didn't."

Sawyer flipped, her fingers and toes digging into the mud as she tried to wriggle away.

"Where are you going? Stop it!" Chloe's words broke on the whipping wind as she lunged with both hands toward Sawyer. When the knife plunged deep into the back of Sawyer's calf, her scream was sucked up by the wind.

Sawyer looked back, astounded. There was nothing but the urgent sense of cold at first, but then the pain was searing hot and heavy, starting from the blade and shattering through Sawyer's body. But she knew she couldn't stop.

"Sawyer!"

She couldn't help but look over her shoulder. Chloe was on her knees, her hair sopping wet and plastered to her forehead. Her clothes were streaked with mud and Sawyer's blood, and Sawyer's stomach ached but she wasn't sure if it was from the blood or for the fact that Chloe was kneeling there with the bloody knife pressed against her own throat.

Terror rained down on Sawyer.

"Chloe, put the knife down. Please."

Chloe shook her head as tears rolled over her pink lips. Her hand started to tremble, and tiny rivulets of black-red blood bubbled up at her neck. "You don't care about me. No one does! No one does!"

"That's not true. I care about you. I want to get you help. We'll get you help. Please." Her voice was little more than a whisper and almost lost on the wind and rain. "Please don't do this."

Chloe's knuckles were white. The night dropped into an impossible silence, a muscle-aching slow motion.

Sawyer picked her way down the hill, favoring her aching leg. She was within arm's length of Chloe when Chloe clamped her eyes shut, the blade pressing deeper into her skin. Sawyer reached out to touch Chloe's arm, but before she could, she felt the dizzying smack of her head against the slick mud, flashes dancing in front of her eyes. Chloe was on top of her, looking down on her, her eyes caged-animal wild.

"You don't care about anyone! I loved you and you don't care!"

"Don't hurt her!" Cooper's voice sliced through the night, and Chloe's head snapped up. He was standing in the backyard, hands splayed. Dried blood, so dark it was almost black, was smeared across his forehead, across the sucking wound at his hairline.

"I killed you!" Chloe yelled, hysteria making her voice high and frantic. "I killed you!"

"No, you didn't," Cooper said calmly. He took a tentative step forward. "And you're not going to hurt Sawyer, either."

"Don't tell me what I'm going to do!"

Sawyer was vaguely aware of what was going on. Her head was still spinning from hitting the ground, and the throb in her leg went up to her teeth. "Cooper?" She knew it was a mere whisper, but she wanted to feel his name on her tongue if only one last time. Chloe looked down at her and wagged her head.

"Don't listen to him. He's going to turn out just like Kevin did. He's only going to hurt you."

Sawyer saw Cooper moving from the corner of her eye.

"That's not true," Cooper said from the foot of the dirt hill. "And I know that you're not going to hurt Sawyer, either, Chloe."

Chloe pushed the blade of the knife against Sawyer's neck again. "How do you know that?" she spat.

Cooper took another step forward, his voice dropping to a normal level. "Because I know." His eyes went to Sawyer's, locked on hers. "You never hurt the person you love."

A warmth pulsed through Sawyer, and she wanted to smile, wanted Cooper's words—the way he said them, with his eyes staring into hers—to be the last thing she ever heard. Chloe's hand was shaking hard again, the action causing little pricks against Sawyer's throat.

"No," Chloe said, teeth gritted.

Sawyer clamped her eyes shut, waiting for the searing pain of knife through flesh.

"No," Chloe said again. This time it was softer, and Sawyer felt the knife back away from her throat, heard something slap into the mud. "I do love you, Sawyer."

Chloe's words were strained and muffled, and when

Sawyer opened her eyes, Chloe's hands were in front of her face, her shoulders shaking.

"We're going to get you help, Chloe, I promise," Sawyer said. "We're going to get you help."

"I just wanted to make you happy," Chloe sobbed. "I just wanted you to care about me."

Sawyer swallowed hard, looking away from Chloe, glancing quickly at Cooper. "It's going to be okay."

She wasn't sure who she was talking to.

SIXTEEN

A paramedic slid an itchy wool blanket over Sawyer's shoulders and clamped a blood pressure monitor on her arm. Cooper sat next to her on the tailgate of the ambulance while another paramedic dabbed Mercurochrome-soaked gauze against the gash on his head.

"Is my stepmother going to be okay? Is the baby going to be okay?"

The paramedic nodded. "She's on her way to the hospital right now, but her vitals looked good and the baby's heartbeat was steady."

Tears sprang to Sawyer's eyes, and this time she welcomed them, welcomed the whoosh of air she sucked in. She looked at Cooper, who smiled at her, wincing with the next dab of the gauze.

"I'm so sorry," she said. "What happened?"

Cooper shook his head. "It had nothing to do with you."

Sawyer cocked an eyebrow and Cooper blushed.

"Okay, I guess it did. I left school to see if you were all right. Chloe kind of T-boned my car once I got into the tract. I was dazed. Then she hit me with something and I was more dazed. Or unconscious."

Sawyer had never felt more glad to hear a survivor story.

"Oh, Sawyer!"

"Dad!" Sawyer leapt up from the tailgate of the ambulance and threw her arms around her father. Stephen Haas and Detective Biggs were with him but hung back.

"I was so worried about you."

Sawyer broke the embrace, gesturing toward the ambulance, the paramedic who was tending to her. "I'm fine, really. You should go—the other ambulance took Tara. You should go be with her."

Andrew touched Sawyer's cheek. "I need to be here with you."

Sawyer shook her head. "No, no." She swallowed. "You should be there for my new baby sister." She paused, licking her lips. "And my stepmom."

Andrew nodded, his eyes glossy.

Detective Biggs and Stephen stepped toward Sawyer next. Biggs clapped her on the back in a motion that Sawyer assumed was meant to be gentle and fatherly, but was awkward and made her smile.

"I'm glad you're okay, Sawyer."

Sawyer looked behind her at the bandage wrapped around her calf. "Mostly okay." She paused and sucked in a shaky breath. "What's going to happen to Chloe?"

"Chloe's awfully sick," Biggs said.

"Is she going to go to jail?"

Both of the officers were silent for a beat that was smothering.

"We're going to get her some help."

Sawyer glanced over Stephen's shoulder to his squad car, where Chloe sat in the back seat, head bent. Her blond hair, filthy with rainwater and mud, fell in a sheet over her cheek. Chloe looked up as if she knew Sawyer was staring at her, and they locked eyes. Chloe's were blank, wide, and blue.

"I hope so," Sawyer whispered.

The squad cars and ambulance started to peel away. Detective Biggs got into his car last, the unmarked sedan that had been parked in Sawyer's driveway what seemed like months ago. "Can I drive you to the hospital, Sawyer?"

"No, thanks, Detective. I'm going to head over there a little later."

Biggs pulled away, and Cooper, fully bandaged, came up on her shoulder. Sawyer felt the edges of her lips push up.

"I'm really glad you're okay," he said shyly.

"I may not have been if you didn't show up."

Cooper looked away, an arm's length from Sawyer. He

touched his bandage. "Does this make me look stupid?" he said with a slight smile.

Sawyer nodded, grinning. "Stupid." She fell into him, feeling him hesitate for a beat before wrapping his arms tightly around her. "And sexy."

Cooper squeezed Sawyer tighter, his heartbeat thumping against hers. She pressed her face into the crook of his neck, breathing in his fresh scent. He still smelled like detergent and soap, and despite the events of the evening, Sawyer was instantly at ease. "I'm glad you're here," she whispered to him.

"How about I drive you to the hospital to see your stepmother?"

Sawyer nodded. "I'd like that, thanks."

She fell into step beside him. Their fingers brushed and then laced, and then they were holding hands.

"Should we stop and get her some flowers or a card?" Cooper asked.

"No." Sawyer shook her head, emphatic. "Definitely not."

ACKNOWLEDGMENTS

Special thanks to Leah Hultenschmidt and the entire Sourcebooks Fire staff, including their authors, who have all been so welcoming and so great to me. Here's hoping we can be together again on the Awesome Bus sometime soon. To my agent, Vickie Motter—thanks for putting up with me. A very special thanks and overall debt of gratitude to the incredible women in my life—Grandma Schwartz for always telling it like it is, Auntie Carolyn for being my first inspiration, Amberly Finarelli for giving me a chance, Joan Svoboda for being Joan Svoboda, and Marina Chappie and Britt Parmeter for understanding my fear of the phone, my penchant for smelly markers, and my love for Disney Channel Original Programming, and loving me anyway.

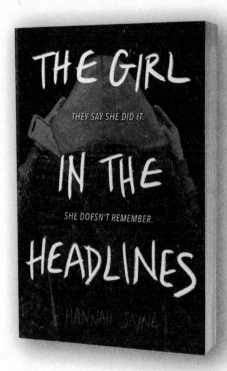

ABOUT THE AUTHOR

Hannah Jayne lives in the San Francisco Bay Area, where she rents three square inches of bed space from two enormous cats. In addition to her young adult thrillers, Jayne is also the author of the Underworld Detection Agency Chronicles. You can reach her at hannah-jayne.com or on Twitter @hannah_jayne1.

FIREreads

#getbooklit

Your hub for the hottest young adult books!

Visit us online and sign up for our
newsletter at FIREreads.com

 @sourcebooksfire

 sourcebooksfire

t firereads.tumblr.com